DEATH BY
ASSOCIATION

A SAMANTHA HARRIS NOVEL

DEATH BY ASSOCIATION

DANI CLIFTON

Dark Rose Press

Death by Association
Dark Rose Press

Line editing, proofreading, cover design, and interior book design provided by Indigo: Editing, Design, and More:

- Line editor: Kristen Hall-Geisler
- Proofreaders: Jennifer Kepler and Sarah Currin
- Cover designer: Olivia Croom Hammerman
- Interior book designer: Vinnie Kinsella

www.indigoediting.com

ISBN: 978-1-7343796-0-0
eISBN: 978-1-7343796-1-7

To my husband, Todd.
Here's to another twenty-six years of adventures!

PROLOGUE

"I'm bored, Sammy," Cindy declared. "Wanna walk down to the corner store?"

"I thought your parents didn't want you being outside once it gets dark, especially after what happened last summer."

Cindy sighed dramatically. "We're going into middle school, Sammy. We're practically teenagers! Besides, my mom's gone out, and we'll be back before she gets home. Dad's watching a baseball game; he won't even know we left. Come *on*, Sammy!" Cindy tugged on my arm and stomped her foot. "Don't be a spoilsport! If we keep acting like little kids, people will keep treating us like little kids."

"Fine," I yielded with a roll of my eyes. It was apparent Cindy wasn't going to be put off; she was going to go with or without me. Of course I'd go—as boy crazy as Cindy had become, someone needed to watch her back, and I was her best friend. Thoughts of the previous summer sent a shiver down my spine. Most parents—mine and Cindy's included—were still wary of strangers after a transient traveling the rails had terrorized the local communities with the kidnapping and rapes of two high school students. We still kept the doors and windows locked at night, even on the warmest of evenings, and my parents had insisted on dropping me off in front of school every morning for the entire school year.

After pulling five dollars from Cindy's piggy bank, we slipped out the back door and made our escape through the side yard. Once we cleared Cindy's block, we linked elbows as a united front against the world and made our way along the deserted sidewalk, talking about the past school year and the one to come next fall. Our footsteps synchronized and took us in and out of shadows cast by streetlamps. We thought nothing of the van parked at the curb until the side door slid open.

"Good evening, ladies," purred a man sitting just inside the open door. By the sound of his voice, I could tell he wasn't old, but he wasn't a kid either. We couldn't get a good look at his face because he was tucked into the shadows of his ride, but when he extended his arm, I noticed an ominous tattoo of an angel devouring a bloody skull.

"Hi!" Cindy greeted him with too much bounce. "I'm Cindy. This is my best friend, Sam."

The hair on the back of my neck stood up as if I'd plugged my finger into a socket. "Seriously," I said sternly but quietly, "come on, the store—*remember*?" I tugged on Cindy's arm, her elbow still linked with mine.

Seated on the van's floorboards, the man dropped his feet onto the sidewalk but kept his face concealed under the hood of his sweatshirt. "I was wondering if you girls might be able to help me," the man explained in a voice that was somehow too gentle. "Have you seen my puppy? He's just a little guy, and I'm very worried." The man let a quiver of emotion slip into his voice as he wiped at his eyes with the back of his hand. "I just opened the door a little bit when I went to throw away a piece of garbage, and little Roscoe jumped out. I didn't know he'd escaped until he was already gone. He isn't well and needs his medicine. Can you girls help me? I have a picture here if you want to see." The man held out a small square of paper too tiny to make out in the dim lighting.

"Oh, poor puppy," Cindy cooed and stepped forward to better see the photograph. Every synapse in my body screamed to run, but Cindy was determined to help find the man's puppy. "What are you doing, Sammy?" she chided when I pulled her back by the elbow. "It's just a little sick puppy, and he's lost. We can help!"

"No, we can't." I shot a suspicious look at the shadows inside the open van door. "Besides, your *dad* is going to be expecting us—"

"No, he's not, Sammy," Cindy gushed and socked me in the shoulder as she unintentionally sealed our fate. "He doesn't even know we left."

I didn't see the man's fist hook around until it was connecting with the side of my head. The man had his hand over Cindy's mouth before she could even think to scream, and he dragged us both into the van. Cindy whimpered beside me. The last thing I heard before I lost consciousness was her begging for my help.

{* * *}

When I finally came to, I was lying on the forest floor, my feet and hands bound together behind my back. Darkness pushed at me from all around. I rolled over, trying to gain some perspective. The van rocked rhythmically on its four wheels, and understanding raised the bile to the back of my throat. Survival instinct took over in a wave of surprising calm. I needed to get away, but I couldn't leave Cindy behind; she needed me. Fight or flee—I'd decide once I got my hands free.

A rock that was stabbing me in the side became my tool of escape. Its sharp edge made quick work of my thin rope restraints. Once my wrists were free, I used my fingers to liberate my ankles from the rope. I worked circulation back into my shaky limbs before I tried to stand. As quietly as I could, I snuck to the van and peeked through the opening of the cracked side door. Cindy's soft whimpers were muffled by the rag stuffed in her mouth. Her eyes were round and wild, darting back and forth in panic. She saw the knife before I did.

Her fate a foregone conclusion, I didn't stay long enough to witness her final breath, a decision that would haunt me for the rest of my days. The next thing I knew, my feet were catapulting me through the forest, branches whipping and tearing at my face and legs as I ran blindly. A set of headlights ahead: a road! The land dropped from beneath my feet, and I began to fall, rolling head over feet. I landed with a splat on the asphalt in front of the oncoming vehicle. The door opened, and I recognized the woman's face as a clerk from the local grocery store, probably on her way home from working the late shift.

Then, for the second time that night, everything went black...

CHAPTER ONE

THE ANNOYING BLARE OF MY ALARM CLOCK SHATTERED THE DREAM to pieces, but it would never erase the memory. I rolled over and slapped it into submission, hoping to get another ten minutes before having to face the world. I threw an arm over my eyes and took a deep breath. We experience few defining moments in our lives; witnessing my best friend's murder and being unable to stop it was mine. I had vowed I would find the man who kidnapped us and killed Cindy.

I was eventually diagnosed with survivor's syndrome, so I spent the rest of my youth in and out of therapy, trying to get a handle on the rage that boiled just below the surface. What I learned was to transmute my fury into ambition and to use that drive as fuel for pursuing and obtaining a career with the Federal Bureau of Investigation. My need for justice began at an early age, my fate written even before Cindy's.

I never was an exemplary child, but my formative years seemed to be the hardest on my parents, especially my mother, who so desperately wanted me to grow into a fine, upstanding young woman. Her biggest hope was that one day I would marry above my station, have babies, and become an extension of my parents' American dream. My sister, Frankie, willingly fit into that mold, so why couldn't I? I had refused to attend piano class, I "accidentally" ruined all of my dresses when it was my turn to do the laundry, I was always nauseous or had a headache when it was time for church, and I burned everything I tried to cook. Domesticity didn't suit me. Then there was my rebellious attitude, the occasional fights at school, and my nonchalant approach to hygiene.

When I was eight years old, my family moved from New York back to my father's hometown of Bel Air—Bel Air, Maryland, that is—a quaint historical suburb of Baltimore. My father was an electrician by trade and had decided to strike out on his own as an independent contractor. So he packed up his family, removed us from all that was familiar, and planted us where his own roots had begun. He rented a run-down shop on Main Street and hung his shingle—Electrician: Licensed, Bonded, and Ready for Hire.

Mother saw the move as a fresh start, a new beginning for us all, and none of us had any way of knowing what would befall me. Mother would attest to the fact that I had always been a difficult child, stubborn and headstrong. I truly believed she thought that if she took me away from the habits I knew, away from the neighborhood where we lived, it would somehow lead to my discovering my softer, gentler side and the joys of being girly. It was her intention that I forget about climbing trees, that I drop my ruffian ways for something more suitable and proper. That wasn't in the cards, and her dream died long before Cindy.

{∗ ∗ ∗}

It'd been an early spring morning. The birds chirped their happy little birdie songs as they sat up in the beech trees, and the air was filled with the clean smell only a recent washing of rain could bring. This was the kind of day that promised new beginnings: the first day of third grade at a new school with new teachers, new friends, and new adventures.

I walked the sidewalk's edge, eyeing the numerous puddles of water gathered along the roadside, fighting the temptations to plant my feet into them with a giant leap and splash. My bookbag, empty except for my metal Scooby-Doo lunch box, was slung over my shoulder as I precariously balanced along the curb, trying to keep my stiff new Mary Janes clean and out of the water. I was walking the fine line between good and evil. I was wearing the new dress Mother had made me. It was Pepto-Bismol pink with tiny cherries on it; a lace collar; short, puffy sleeves; and dainty eyelet lace stitched along the hem. I hated it. I thought it made me look ridiculously frilly, like a little princess, which is exactly what Father called me when I arrived at the breakfast table.

Up ahead and across the street lay the fortress of my destiny: Red Pump Elementary, where the principal and my parents were not yet on a first-name basis (short-lived), I didn't know the color of the detention hall (also short-lived), and nobody yet knew I was the one to pick for dodgeball if you wanted to win.

I walked through the chain-link fence and straight into trouble.

I saw two boys behind the bleachers next to the baseball diamond. I thought I would try to strike up a conversation, maybe gain an ally who could show me the ropes. One of the boys, a puny kid in high-water pants and a striped shirt, shifted from foot to foot with a panicked expression painted across his face. The other boy, who was almost twice the puny kid's size, towered above him with a look full of malice and intimidation. I had inadvertently walked into the middle of a frisking by the playground bully. In the bully's hand was a stack of baseball cards held together with a rubber band.

"I know you have a Walkman. Hand it over!"

"No, I s-s-swear, I left it at home." The frightened kid nervously pushed his glasses back up onto the bridge of his nose. "But I can get it. I'll bring it tomorrow, and you can borrow it for the day."

The bully, whose name I later found out was Eli, was not satisfied with this suggested arrangement. Like any pirate, he wanted some coins for his troubles.

"Gimme your lunch money too, or I'll sock you in the gut."

The poor, frightened kid began digging frantically into the pockets of his pants, looking for something to appease the bandit. Impulsively I decided to step in on behalf of oppressed playground victims everywhere. It was nothing for me to approach this self-appointed badass and tap him on the shoulder. Everyone has to listen to reason at some point, right?

Eli spun on his heel. "What do you want?" he spat.

"Can't you see you're much bigger than this kid? It's not right that you want him to give his things over to you when you clearly have no interest in making a fair trade."

"Yeah, what's it to you? Shut up and mind your own beeswax."

"I don't shut up, I grow up," I taunted as any proper eight-year-old would, speaking this jerk's language. "And when I see your face, I throw up."

Eli didn't find me nearly has humorous as I did. He forgot about Walkmans, closed the gap between us, and looked down on me with little piggy eyes that were engulfed by his doughy face. I marveled at how much larger he looked up close than he had from across the field.

"Fine. I won't ask for this freak's lunch money—I'll take yours instead. Hand it over, princess." Eli presented the palm of his ham hand.

"How about I make it so you never bother anyone ever again?" I was no longer smiling. Even back then, before the tragedy that would befall Cindy, I had an overdeveloped sense of empathy for those who couldn't stand up for themselves.

"What are you going to do, tell on me?" Eli laughed so hard his entire body quaked like Jell-O. "Tattletale! Tattletale!" he sing-songed. He must have really thought I was just a stupid, helpless girl not worth worrying about. He turned his attention back to the quivering kid who'd forfeited his baseball cards and, for whatever reason, hadn't had the sense to make a run for it while he could.

"H-h-here's my—I mean your—money," the kid said, dropping a handful of coins into Eli's sweaty hand. The kid was so skinny that he couldn't afford to miss a meal lest he blow away in the next wind. Something came over me; all I knew was that Eli was not going to get away with this. No way. Not that day, and not ever again.

I ran toward Eli with both arms out and shoved him hard in the back. "Give it back!" I screamed.

Eli didn't stop or turn around, only swatted at me as if I were a bothersome gnat.

"You're really a big jerk. I bet even your mother thinks you're a big jerk!"

The mother comment got more of a reaction than I'd anticipated. Without any warning, Eli wheeled on me and planted a balled fist in the center of my chest. It knocked the wind out of me and sent me crashing to the ground on my butt. Eli erupted in laughter at my expense.

There I was—stunned—trying to stay calm and get air back into my lungs at the same time. It wasn't easy. I looked down at my queasily pink dress. I had tried so hard to keep myself clean, but I was now covered in playground mud and smudged with grass. Mother was going to be disappointed. All I was trying to do was the right thing. Anger overwhelmed me; who was Eli to think he could steal from the other kids and ruin my dress? I picked myself up off the ground and smoothed the skirt of my dress down. "I bet your mother is so fat, when she sits around the house, she sits around the house."

Eli's belly chuckles stopped instantly as a deep-crimson rage rose into his cheeks. He started toward me, violence in his eyes. Before he could act on that ferocity, I kicked out one well-aimed foot and landed it squarely in his crotch. Eli went down, cradling his family jewels in protective hands. I waited for him to get up. He didn't.

A crowd had formed by then, all of them cheering the new girl and their newfound freedom from their playground overlord. Of course, whenever a crowd of children gathers on a playground, adults are sure to show up. I was hauled into the principal's office (first name Gil), whose secretary phoned Mother. I was grounded for a month. In my defense, I had an extraordinary sense of right and wrong. Those of us who are stronger are obliged to stand up for those who can't—or don't know how to—stand up for themselves.

My alarm began to blare again, so I moved to silence it. It was just as well. No good ever came from strolling down memory lane, especially when it led to places better left in the past. But my past was damn stubborn, like the rest of me.

CHAPTER TWO

WHEN I QUIT THE BUREAU SIX YEARS AGO AND DECIDED TO START life over again, I relocated as far away from my life in DC as I could—to Portland, Oregon. I obtained my private investigator's license as soon as I got settled but found the profession to be a feast-or-famine industry—famine at that particular point in the economy. So I got creative and decided to use what I knew, and Harris Securities was born. As sole proprietor, I was a security tester hired by high-tech, high-profile companies to find their security weaknesses, whether they be via their systems or their employees. I didn't personally do the computer aspect. That bit got contracted out to my computer hacker neighbor, Mole. What I performed were the deep background checks, personal profiles, and individual interviews where I asked fierce questions and judged the employees' body language as to whether they were telling the truth. It wasn't overly exciting work, not like being on the street, but it paid the bills quite nicely.

That afternoon was blocked out for a new client, so I grudgingly threw the covers off and rolled out of bed. The sun, already high in the sky, played a field of horizontal rays through the blinds across the hardwood floor, warming my legs as I passed.

I'd found that life is about the little pleasures. I wished I lived in one of those coffee commercials where everyone wakes up to the robust aroma of freshly brewed coffee and someone hunky and fit is waiting at the bottom of the stairs with a steaming mug in his hand. I didn't have stairs, but I made my way to the living room nonetheless. Not only was nobody there to greet me, but all I smelled was the remnants of last night's garlic pizza.

"Ack." My mouth tasted like a staler version of those same remnants.

I shuffled into the bathroom and took a gander at myself in the mirror. There were matching dark circles beneath my eyes, and I suffered from a serious case of bedhead. I needed a shower and I needed coffee—not necessarily in that order. A good, long soak would have been a nice, languid treat. But a shower would be quicker, and that meant it would be quicker to get where coffee happens. Thus I opted for speed over indulgence and turned on the water to let it heat up.

I caught myself staring into the mirror again and took the moment for a personal assessment. My raven hair was due for another cut; I hated when it got near my collar. I wore it in what I called an angry pixie—clipped short over my ears, longer up top. I either pomaded it up in loose, choppy spikes or combed it back and let it air-dry. My mother said I wore my hair too much like a boy. There were lines around my dirt-brown eyes that hadn't been there a couple of years ago. I fingered the scar across my upper lip left there by a large, skull-shaped silver ring I met in a drunken brawl a few years back; it had faded as much as it was going to. Someone once pointed out that, with the right plastic surgeon, I could get rid of it, but I kind of liked the impression it gave. The sparkle in my eyes that had gotten me into a lot of trouble in my youth had disappeared, but I found I could still hold my own gaze, and that said a lot. I stepped into the shower and let the hot water sluice down my back. My thoughts were still roiling. How did I go from troubled child to golden child and back again?

My intentions with the FBI had been honorable, but in the end, I was just another square peg. I must confess that, in hindsight, I knew my days with the bureau were numbered from the very beginning; the final confrontation with my superiors was inevitable. At the end, I lost my balance and fell from grace. After seven successful years of playing nice in the male-dominated FBI sandbox, my lack of patience and inability to swallow the force-fed bullshit undid me.

My superiors respected my work from the time I took my oath and became an agent. *Motivated* was a word frequently applied to me. By my fifth year as a special agent in the violent crimes division, I had applied for entrance into the National Center for the Analysis of Violent Crime, or NCAVC, part of the FBI's Critical Incident Response Group. I was the youngest agent at that point to be accepted into the program. At that time, I still held favor with Director Davies because I had the ability to see what others could not. An unsolved case only meant the answer was out there, and "no" wasn't it. I was driven by my curiosity and tenacity to find those answers. Nevertheless, despite all the training and everything that I'd seen and experienced, the thing I couldn't wrap my head around was that getting the bad guys and taking them down in a way that would hold up in court are two entirely different subjects.

I say I flamed out, but the truth was I lost control of myself. The FBI's first principle is pretty straightforward: "Rigorous obedience to the Constitution of the United States." As one who doesn't necessarily play well with others, I knew I was going to need a lot of personal restraint when I signed up for the job. I understood that without laws, rules, protocols, and structure, anarchy and chaos would reign. Our country works as a democracy because of those rules, and everyone here is innocent until proven guilty by a court of law. It's a wonderful concept. In theory.

At the end when I was summoned to a meeting of my superiors, I knew I wasn't being called up to the director's office for a pat on the back and a promotion. In fact, I was surprised I wasn't pushing a pencil and filing dead cases down in archives. The day was still young.

A sense of foreboding gave me momentary pause as I pushed through the door. Margaret, the director's personal secretary, looked up from her keyboard, her graying hair pulled back into a severe bun at the back of her head. She offered me a small smile devoid of welcome.

I stepped inside the director's inner sanctum and was greeted by three sets of glaring eyes, lending credence to my earlier sense of foreboding. Director Davies sat at the head of the table, as was customary for his position. To his immediate left sat Agent Bridges. At Davies's right sat Assistant Director Gouldman. I took in each solemn face in turn. The chill in the air wasn't solely due to the thermostat.

"Special Agent Harris," Director Davies addressed me, using my full title. "I'm glad you could join us. Please." He motioned to a vacant chair at the opposite end of the table. I would rather have sat beside Bridges, but I took the proffered seat without saying a word.

Once I was settled, the director started in. He looked at me from over the top of his eyeglasses and rubbed at the side of his clean-shaven chin. If his complexion weren't the color of brownie batter, I probably would have seen the red-faced irritation his words barely concealed. "Harris, you graduated from the academy near the top of your class, and you're the youngest agent to enter the behavioral science program. But ever since you worked on the Morrison case, you've gone off the rails. What's happened to your focus?"

It wasn't like I hadn't asked myself that same question. How the hell had I gotten here? I'd begun this career path with the best intentions and had followed the rules, even though it meant biting my tongue and swallowing my pride on so many occasions. What had gone wrong? One word swam to mind and out my mouth.

"Disillusionment."

The whites of Davies's eyes grew comically large. "The Federal Bureau of Investigation is an *illusion* to you, Agent Harris?"

"The bureau isn't an illusion. The illusion is that we can be the good guys without running the risk of having the carpet yanked out from under us by politics and red tape. Criminals get smarter, defense and litigation attorneys get richer, and our restrictions get tighter and tighter. Haven't you ever stopped to wonder if we're fighting an unwinnable battle under these current conditions?"

"So it would be correct for me to surmise you're still holding a grudge against Agents Dalton and Rodriguez for their handling of the Morrison case?"

"With all due respect, sir, I do not hold grudges. I take action." My voice had an edge that made even me uncomfortable. Everyone shifted awkwardly in their seats. Agent Bridges refused to lift his eyes from the table's shiny top.

"Harris, you were given a direct order to stay away from the senator's son, an order that you blatantly ignored. You not only violated protocol, you exhibited rogue behavior." Davies's words held contentious fire. He sat up a little straighter in his seat, assuring us all of his ultimate authority. "Agent Harris, your service record is a mess. Your consistent indifference to protocol obviously speaks of some other systemic dysfunction, a psychological need to challenge authority."

My voice froze over. "Need I remind you that, had you listened to me, we'd have saved Rachel Newcastle's family from having to bury their daughter—"

"That is enough, Agent Harris," Davies cut me off curtly.

"I told you Junior was a flight risk!" I pushed.

"Agent Harris, please! This isn't a time to be pointing fingers," Gouldman interjected.

"I know that you're personal friends with the senator, sir, but I can't help feeling it's because of that relationship that you chose to overlook my observations regarding his son. I told you that the moment he discovered we were getting close that he'd take another girl, but you insisted on his innocence when in fact, sir, you were upholding your own flawed judgment of character." I knew I'd overstepped my bounds with that. But you can't un-ring a bell.

Davies took a deep breath and exhaled through his nose in an effort to calm himself and remain professionally objective. We all knew he was going to fail and things were going to hit the fan. An ultimatum hung in the air like a foul stench.

"Even for you, Agent Harris, the level of arrogance and sub-ordinance you've displayed here today is appalling. If this had been a singular incident, perhaps a warning would suffice. I'm recommending to the board that you be stripped of field classi-fication and assigned to the dispatch office in New York."

"You're transferring me to the mail room?" I asked, unbelieving.

Davies picked up his pen and began to scribble on a note-pad in front of him. "You are to report to Agent Muenz at eight o'clock Tuesday morning."

"Wait a minute—are you demoting me?" I really shouldn't have been surprised.

"This is not up for discussion, Agent Harris. In New York, Tuesday morning."

I stood up with danger in my eyes. "If this is your decision," I said tersely, "then I will no longer burden the FBI with my participation."

The room looked at me in disbelief. "Are you opting to ter-minate your association with the FBI?"

"I will put it in plain English: *I fucking quit.*"

Was I bitter? I still couldn't answer that question, mostly because I didn't want to live a rancorous life. I had trusted that I worked for the good guys, and I assumed they would always win. Like anyone, I was sorely disappointed when I met my heroes.

They weren't always the good guys, and we didn't always win. In the end, the rules and regulations pushed my boundaries too far, and when they snapped back, the mess went everywhere.

With a heavy sigh, I came back to the present, stepped out, and wrapped a terrycloth towel around me. *That was then, this was now*, I told myself. *Leave the past back there where it belongs*. Sure, I'd been on the fast track for higher ground, but unlike Bridges, my motivation had nothing to do with reaching for the golden ring at the top of an organizational ladder and everything to do with silencing Cindy's final whimpers, which still echoed in my head. *Don't go there, Harris. Slippery slope*. What I really needed was a good, strong caffeine fix. With a last look at myself in the mirror, I grabbed my laptop, bundled in its nylon carrying case, and set it beside the door. Then I went to the closet.

Some women get giddy and weird over shoes or the perfect shade of nail polish. I must have missed that gene. A visual inventory of my closet always excited me, but not for the usual girly reasons. Standing vertically in their brackets were a few of my favorite things: a standard-issue Remington 870 pump-action shotgun, my Italian-made Benelli M1 Super 90 12-gauge semiautomatic shotgun with leather pistol grip and shoulder stock, and an illegal sawed-off shotgun I relieved a gangbanger of several months ago. On the shelf above them were my Beretta 93R 9mm that was fit with a suppressor; my .22 Walther; and a Glock 23, .40 caliber, with a Crimson Trace integrated laser. One of the scariest things on earth is to have a red dot suddenly appear in the middle of your chest. It'll make the stoutest mobster piss himself. Aside from the Heckler & Koch that I usually carried, there was an additional HK USP, the only difference between them being that the one in the closet had an extended barrel with a suppressor. Heckler, Koch, and I had been a threesome for a long, long time. Tools of the trade and all, God bless my Second Amendment.

Then there was my collection of blades, all of them useful, each with its own story. My favorite by far was a short, four-and-a-half-inch, T-handled, double-edged, serrated knife I could wear like a necklace beneath my shirt, which had come in handy on more than one occasion. And there was my Ka-Bar, which also held special meaning to me, as it was a gift from my uncle Chuck when he returned from the Gulf. The knife reportedly "has history."

Another shelf was filled with boxes of ammunition, cleaning supplies, a Taser baton, a bag of heavy-gauged zip ties, and two sets of steel handcuffs. No, I'd never been tempted to use the cuffs for extracurricular activities. They had ringed the wrists of some pretty sick individuals.

I considered my collection but still went with my usual—a nickel-plated HK USP Tactical .45 caliber with night sights and an MkII tactical light mounted beneath the barrel. I stuck it into the waistband of my jeans at the small of my back. It didn't fit there as well as the Walther, but I could deal. After several minutes of searching, I found my shoes under the couch, tied them on, and threw on my leather jacket, making sure it covered the goods in back. I locked up, slung the computer case over my shoulder, and headed for the elevator.

CHAPTER THREE

PANDEMONIUM WITH A DRIVING BASELINE ISSUED FORTH FROM beneath my neighbor's door. Mole would never be dubbed a morning person. Hell, he wasn't even a *late*-morning person, so this much noise at a quarter till nine meant he'd pulled another all-nighter. So for my own sake, I decided against knocking to wish him a merry good morning. I'd learned that Mole operated deep from the heart of Dickville when he was sleep deprived.

Formerly occupying the number one spot on the federal Most Wanted List for cybercrimes, Mole was aptly named. His tenacity and skills were both impressive and frightening. He wielded his keyboard and processors like the military wields bombs, and his results could be just as explosive and damaging. I'd never tried to persuade myself that everything he did on his own time was wholly on the up-and-up, but I didn't really have a problem with that. He was a handy guy to have around—if not a little eccentric. Still, there existed an unspoken pact between Mole and me: what I didn't know wouldn't hurt me. So far, that had held true. However, if something he was working on ever did backfire and came back on me, he and I would have problems, and his problems would be a lot bigger than mine.

The elevator seemed overly slow that morning, so I pushed through the door at the top of the stairs and took them down to the lobby. Out on the street, I was welcomed by the weak warmth of an unusually sunny spring morning. One thing I had learned about Portland weather since I'd been here was that it was always a crapshoot. If you didn't like what it was doing outside, just give it a half hour.

Portland's east and west sides were divided by the Willamette River, north and south by Burnside Street. Tucked into the north district of the west side was an area known to locals as the Pearl, where I lived. In the nineteenth century, the Pearl District was populated by light industry and railroad yards. The warehouses of old had gone through major urban renewal to be reborn as art galleries, upscale businesses, and lofts. Turn-of-the-century masonry was intermixed with sleek, contemporary lines, the old integrated with the new. Portland in general was a mecca for artists and musicians, but the Pearl was full of galleries, coffeehouses, and the nation's largest bookstore. I wasn't an artist by any stretch; I lived here solely for its close proximity to downtown. It also didn't hurt that there were two microbreweries and eight coffeehouses within walking distance of my front door. Location, location, location.

My mornings varied from day to day, but usually included, in some order, clients, paperwork, and getting paid. Business in corporate security was good, and it paid obscenely well, but I longed for a stakeout. I missed the thrill of the hunt, the exhilaration of the chase, and the satisfaction of the takedown. Civilians, for the most part, were pretty boring.

I stepped into my coffeehouse of choice, Steam, and caught the barista's eye. This part of my morning never varied. As usual, Seth gave his chin a quick lift and made eye contact with what was as close to a smile as he got. Seth's hipster hair was coiffed and oiled, his lean face adorned with a well-groomed beard and a moustache waxed into stiff peaks at the ends. Arm-length tattoos presented themselves to the world from the short sleeves of his red-and-gray flannel. Welcome to Portland; that was how they rolled.

Seth was a self-professed starving artist that used his day gig at the coffeehouse to fund a growing acrylic habit. He and

I had the perfect relationship, and if I couldn't have the coffee commercial fantasy, then this ran a fine second. It went like this: every morning I walked through the door, laid four dollars plus tip on the counter, and without having to say a word, I got my quad Americano exactly how I liked it—hot and strong.

Fix in hand, I hung a left out of the door and walked the two blocks to my office in less than two minutes. I rented four hundred square feet of revamped, hundred-year-old textile mill-turned-office space. My company, Harris Securities, was on the second floor at the top of the stairs. My door was something you'd see in an old gumshoe flick, with the bottom half constructed of solid oak and the top half fitted with smoked glass with my name etched in it. The interior was all refurbished wood floors and brick walls. I never had it this nice in the Hoover Building.

I'd barely gotten inside and set my coffee down when I sensed someone standing in the hall just outside my door. The shadow cast across the glass was small, either a short-statured man or a woman. I opened the door and found that it wasn't Tom Cruise, but the latter—and a petite one at that. A little girl with dark curls and piercing green eyes peeked out from behind the woman's legs, and I deduced by their matching features that she was the woman's daughter. Mom's damp hair was pulled back into a hasty ponytail. Her eyes were slightly puffy and red-rimmed from a recent bout of tears. Despite her emotionally fragile state, the woman stood straight-backed, shoulders squared, head held defiantly high.

"I'm looking for Samantha Harris," the woman announced in a strong, clear voice that contradicted her frail appearance.

"You found me," I quipped and held the door open invitingly.

The woman turned to the little girl clinging to her pant leg. "Katie, sweetheart," she said, easing the girl off of her, "I need you to wait in the hall while I talk to Miss Harris, okay? This is very important." The woman handed the little girl a small sketchbook and a sparkly pink pencil, freshly sharpened. "Can you draw a picture of a horse for Mommy while you wait?"

Katie's gaze didn't move from her feet. She silently took the proffered art supplies, pulled up a patch of carpet immediately outside my office door, and set to work, her long dark curls hanging in her face.

I kept my door cracked so that Katie wouldn't feel abandoned and escorted the woman into my office. "I'm sorry, I didn't catch your name?"

The woman extended a hand with a slight tremor. "Pamela Phillips, but please, call me Pam." She paused as if I was supposed to recognize the name, which I didn't. It would have been unprofessional to shrug.

Pam turned away to face the window so that I was looking at her left profile. "It's been in the paper and on the news for the last couple of weeks. Now the police won't even talk to me about it."

"What was in the news?"

Pam's composure cracked. She tried to answer, but a sharp sob came out instead. She took a deep breath. "My husband's death."

"I'm sorry, Pam. I don't watch much television, too much war and dea—" *Good save*, I thought. "I'm sorry, but I'm not familiar with the event. How do I fit in?"

Pam spun a quarter turn on her heel. "I want to hire you to find his killer."

Whoa there. Back up. I'd never worked in that capacity for a private civilian and wasn't really sure I wanted to open that can of worms. The FBI had a department that dealt with victims' families. "I'm sorry for your loss," I said with gentle firmness. "I'm sure the police are doing everything they can—"

Pam cut me off with a frustrated huff then turned and eased her weary body into the chair across the desk from me. "The police have officially closed Ronny's case. They've ruled his death *accidental*." Pam balled her fists in her lap. "They think he tripped while running, that his falling from the top of the ravine was—as Captain Burnell put it—an 'act of gravity.' They refuse to listen to me when I try to explain that he was a trail marathon runner and that was his training ground. He would never have just tripped and fallen. Safety was paramount to Ronny. If there had been a trip hazard, he would have dealt with it long ago." Pam's voice pitched several octaves higher as she tried to convince me she'd been wronged by the system. She reached into her purse and came out with a cell phone, which she scrolled through then turned to show me a recent photo of her husband. "He sent me this picture from the top of the mountain where there's a spot of reception from a nearby tower. He was on his way home, but he never made it off that mountain." Pam broke into fresh sobs.

Terrains shifted and landscapes changed. Pam had no way of knowing if a rock had dislodged above the trail somewhere and tumbled onto the path. I felt pretty confident at that point that she wasn't going to hear me if I offered up that possible scenario. I needed to change tactics.

"Aside from his trail prowess, what leads you to believe foul play was involved in your husband's death?"

"He seemed agitated by something, though he tried very hard to disguise it by calling it stress. I could tell something was bothering him."

"How?"

"He always checked the locks on the doors before bed, but for a couple of weeks before he died, he'd check them the moment he walked in the door. Living in the city, I always lock the doors, but he seemed extra intent on making sure."

"It is a crazy world out there. Better safe than sorry." The only way I was going to help Pam was by being up front and straightforward, not by coddling her. "So far, that's not enough to make me suspicious. Walk me through a typical day in your husband's world."

Pam's eyes brightened at my interest. She swiped at the tears wetting her cheeks and sat up straighter in the chair. "Ronny was up by six o'clock every morning. He'd go downstairs and make coffee before doing a quick five-mile run around the neighborhood. Then it was home, shower, drop Katie off at school, and on to work. He was always home by dinnertime."

"Where did he work?"

"Ronny was a biochemist for Cascade Biotech."

I wasn't familiar with Cascade Biotech. "What did he do for them?"

"He was a scientist. I'm not really sure exactly what he did. He had to sign a nondisclosure document to work there. He didn't bring his work home, and he couldn't really share much of his day with me. If he talked about work at all, it was only in generalities. I know they were involved in some sort of DNA research."

"So what did Mr. Phillips say about his workplace, in general?"

Pam shrugged. "He seemed happy. Work was just something Ronny did, like changing the oil or mowing the lawn. He didn't complain about anybody at Cascade, if that's what you mean. There was a certain culture at Cascade; it was like a family. They made themselves a desirable company to work for. Their benefits and salaries are set well above what most provide. They recruited their employees and made sure they kept them."

"Better for business, I suppose," I said, speaking as a security specialist. "What about outside of work? Did Mr. Phillips have a regular after-hours hangout?"

"Doctor," Pam corrected. "Ronny has his PhD."

"Did Dr. Phillips have a regular haunt?"

"Not outside of the usual gatherings and potlucks at the church."

"Is there anyone at church who may had a grudge against Dr. Phillips?"

"Enough to kill, Miss Harris?"

"Religion has started a lot of wars." *Just sayin'.* "If I were to call Cascade and ask a few questions, who would I ask for?"

"Elliott Robbins. Everyone liked Ronny. He was everyone's friend." A fresh wash of tears came, so I let her have her moment, mostly because I didn't know what to say. I'd never been good with feelings. When Pam composed herself once more, she continued.

"Ronny would never have gotten himself involved with anything illicit or dangerous. He was a deeply religious man, dedicated to his family, his church, and our community. What I do know, Miss Harris, is that Ronny seemed nervous in the days before his death, like he was afraid of someone. He never said who it was, and I have no idea who it could have been. Will you help me find out who killed my husband?" Pam leaned forward and engulfed my folded hands in hers. "Will you help me find who killed Katie's daddy?"

"Someone killed Daddy?" asked a small voice from the doorway. Pam and I turned at the same time to see little Katie, her eyes already welling with tears. I hated it when kids cried; it made me feel bad. And I hated it when I felt bad.

Katie ran to her mother and broke down in a mess of tears and wails on her lap. I looked around my office for a tissue to offer the poor kid, but it wasn't often I needed to console a client. I ignored the sobbing child (sorry, kid) and kept digging. "Did Dr. Phillips work from home much?"

Pam gave a snuffling nod. "Sometimes in the evenings, he'd do some work in his office, but only after Katie had gone to bed. He didn't like to take away from family time."

"Did he do this from a home computer or a laptop?"

"Both, I believe."

"Would it be possible for you to bring me the laptop and your home computer? I've got someone who can look inside them."

Pam dug through her purse and came up with a fluorescent plastic keychain in the shape of a cross. "I want to take Katie away from all of this. My parents have been staying with us since the funeral. They live in California and are returning home in the morning. Katie and I are going with them." Pam handed the keychain to me. "We'll be staying down there for a few weeks, so the house will be empty. Help yourself. When the police brought his car back home, they parked it in the garage. He never left his laptop at the office, so it's either in the trunk of his car if he took it to work with him or in his office upstairs at the end of the hall if he didn't."

"You're going to find the bad man that killed my daddy?" Katie's small voice interjected.

For a split, existential second, it was Cindy asking me for help. Maybe I was being handed an opportunity for myself. Either way, I knew I wasn't going to turn the kid down, no matter how much I thought I wanted to. I did a mental eye roll for being such a patsy and heard myself tell the two of them, "I've got a couple of contacts inside the department. Let me ask around and see what I can find out. In the meantime, I'll let myself into your place and poke around inside his computers. If I find there's any reason to believe Dr. Phillips's death was anything but an accident, we'll talk further." I whipped a fresh sheet of paper from the copier and scribbled a quick disclaimer that stated I had the homeowner's permission to enter the premises, which I had Pam sign and date. Long ago I learned the art of CYOA: cover your own ass.

"Thank you, Samantha," Pam gushed. She took my hand and gave it a squeeze, making me feel like Mother freaking Teresa. She jotted down a phone number on a piece of paper. "This is my parents' number in Sacramento. Call day or night, anytime you need to. I give you full permission to search the house if it'll help you find the person responsible." Pam then gathered her snuffling daughter and left as abruptly as she'd arrived.

I took a quick survey of my schedule. I had an appointment with the CEO of a local electronic engineering design firm who wanted to hire Harris Securities, but he wasn't due until after lunch. I decided there was enough time before then to see what I might get out of the Portland Police Bureau regarding Dr. Ronald Phillips.

CHAPTER FOUR

My contact on the inside of the Portland PB was homicide detective Stan Wickowski, whom I had met not long after I came to Portland. The bond between us owed more to our mutual outlook on life. Like me, Wickowski was a fellow nonconformist. He didn't deal with the rules and regulations of law enforcement bureaucracy any better than I did; he just lacked the balls to do anything about it. I got it, though. The fear of sacrificing his pension kept him from misbehaving too much.

Ours was a casual give-and-take relationship and strictly platonic. I did the occasional, work-related favor for Wickowski, things he couldn't do under the restraints of the department and his badge. In return, he gave me tidbits of information when I asked him for it.

I speed-dialed Wickowski's number and waited through the series of pickups and reroutes to the automatic system that asked for Wickowski's extension. He picked up on the second ring.

"Wickowski!" I exclaimed with too much energy. "How are you, my friend?"

"No," he said flatly.

"Excuse me?"

"I said no. Whatever it is Harris, the answer is no."

"Wickowski," I said with feigned disappointment, "I'm crushed. It's been what, a week or two since we've talked? I was just wondering what my drinking buddy is up to. Hey, I have an idea—let's do lunch! You pick, I'll buy."

"What do you want, Harris? I'm a busy man here. I've lost half of my team due to these damn budget cuts. I don't have time."

"Busy? I hear you've been giving murder cases the brush-off, calling them 'accidental deaths.' Doesn't sound like you're too busy to me."

I heard him curse under his breath. "What the hell are you talking about?"

"Dr. Ronald Phillips," I said, far less jovial than before. Remember, Wickowski and I are tight. "His wife came to see me this morning. She's convinced someone wanted him dead. She's calling foul play on your part."

Another bout of quiet cursing. "Dammit, Harris, don't you go singing that song too. That broad's been calling the station every day since we found her husband's body, sometimes four or five times a day. I told switchboard not to put her calls through to my desk anymore, so now she calls the night shift. Burnell presented the case to the district attorney, who ruled—without any room for misinterpretation—that Phillips's death was accidental. Which, by the way, had the coroner's report backing up the decision. I mean, seriously, Harris, this Phillips guy goes jogging along a steep, muddy trail when it was raining cats and dogs—you know what the weather is like here in early spring—and he slipped or tripped or whatever, and took a header down a two-hundred-foot ravine. Period. I was there when they brought the body up, and I tell you, nobody has any business on a trail like that in that kind of weather. We nearly lost a deputy over the edge when we were hauling the body up. I took ten years off my life just getting up the damn mountainside. Besides, what stake do you have in something like this?"

"I got a visit this morning from Pam Phillips. I tried to explain that she had the wrong person for the job, but she was pretty adamant. Then an unforeseen event occurred."

"Let me guess—she brought the daughter with her, and the kid turned on the waterworks, begging you to 'find the bad man who killed my daddy.'" Wickowski added the last bit in a little kid's whiny voice.

I sat in dumbfounded silence while Wickowski guffawed it up pretty good on the other end of the line. Damn—I'd been suckered by a kid and played by Pam. Was there no integrity left in the world?

"Look, Wickowski," I said in an effort to quiet his chortles, "let's make a deal. I'll take the heat off you and get the calls to the station to stop, and in return you let me see everything you've got on this case. I promise you'll never hear from Pam Phillips ever again. What do you say?"

"I knew there was no such thing as a free lunch with you, Harris. Fine, I'll play. The reports have yet to be digitally filed. The paper copies can get 'misplaced' for twenty-four hours. That's the best I can do."

"I'll take it, Wickowski. You're a prince among men."

"Hey, you're still buying lunch. Meet me at the tamale stand in the parking lot of Oak and Fifth at noon."

With that, the line went dead.

I hung up the phone and formulated a mental game plan. I'd start by getting the jacket on Phillips from Wickowski, which would include photos, interviews, and an autopsy report. I definitely wanted to take a look at the scene in person, and I wanted to see inside Dr. Phillips's computer and gain access to his cloud server, since the cloud is where most of us store our secrets these days. In fact, I wondered if I could get Pam to let me in this evening after I had a chance to peruse the file. *Oh! Mental head slap!* I totally forgot that I had promised Vin I'd attend his gallery opening! How did *that* slip my mind?

Vin is short for Vinardo, but it was nearly impossible for me to call him that with a straight face, and I took it as a personal insult from those who could. Thankfully he preferred not to go by his legal name. I'd never say it aloud, but *Vinardo* made me think of a fat, sleezy pit boss. Vin was what people called my boyfriend, though I did hate that term. It was so…bubblegum. It would be better to say that Vin was the guy I slept with. He was an artist and a poet and completely not my type. That said, he also possessed a peaceful, Zen-like quality that was a comfortable balance to my fire. On a scale from one to ten for roguishly handsome, he was somewhere around a twelve. And he was incredibly talented between the sheets, which absolutely *was* my type.

I picked up the landline and dialed his cell. I wasn't surprised in the least when the call rolled to voicemail. I left a message about the evening's gala. Sometimes I called Vin's phone when I knew he wouldn't answer just to hear his low, silky voice. So I had a soft underbelly—sue me. As long as you don't tell anybody.

Anybody who had ever dealt with real cops would agree with me when I claimed Wickowski was a quintessential homicide detective. I hadn't the privilege of hearing his entire story, and I doubted I ever would, but I knew it wasn't all puppies and sunshine. Cops play their personal lives close to the vest. He wasn't the touchy-feely type and was not prone to opening up and sharing, but I saw in his eyes those things left unsaid. Wickowski had spent too much time protecting and serving the city. He came off as abrasive, but the fact that he'd burned through two loving ex-wives and was regretful about the proceedings with his soon-to-be third told me Wickowski had a heart beneath that tough exterior. We were more alike than I had initially thought.

I sensed his approach before I got a visual. That was the way it was with Wickowski; his aura showed up before the rest of him. I'd learned to use this trait to my advantage, especially when he was fired up about something. It gave me the opportunity to vacate the area before the fireworks began. No one was in real danger until they pissed him off, which I'd never done. Yet.

The area around the food carts was getting thick with hungry lunch seekers. At six-foot-four and 220 pounds of Latino (on his mother's side) muscle, it was hard for Wickowski to blend in anywhere. I spied him eeling his way through a crowd gathered on the opposite corner waiting to cross the street, a thick manila folder tucked beneath his left arm.

"Harris," Wickowski said, taking me in from head to toe and back again. "Why won't you marry me?" This seemed to be a ritual we'd been going through lately. He wasn't serious, of course. I think it was how he dealt with loss.

"What would your wife say?"

"She's soon to be my ex, so technically I'm a free agent," Wickowski taunted.

"That probably shouldn't be your pickup line."

"Too needy?"

"It's a touch much."

Wickowski might make jokes, but I understood his internal frustration over being driven by the job but also needing a meaningful relationship to escape into at the end of the day. I didn't know if it made it harder for his wives knowing their husband's mistress wasn't a beautiful young woman but a small, shiny badge.

The tamale cart—all I'd ever known it to be called—served up Veracruz-style tamales, sopes, and burritos from a raised platform window. I hadn't realized how hungry I was until I caught a waft of garlic, cumin, and annatto mingling with the scent of roasted meats. My stomach demanded nourishment with a loud growl. Wickowski ordered a round of tamales for us both then stepped aside while I paid with a ten and some change. When our order was up, we each came away with a foil-wrapped paper plate. A condiments tray stood at the end of the counter, where we loaded up on napkins and filled small paper cups with salsa, sliced jalapeños, and chopped cilantro. Wickowski slopped refried beans onto his plate, along with onions, ensuring his personal space for the rest of the afternoon. I plucked two bottles of water from an ice-filled bucket, followed Wickowski to an empty bench beside the cart, and took a seat at the other end.

Wickowski slapped the envelope on the seat between us. "Twenty-four hours, then I've got to get this back." He took a healthy pull from his bottle of water and swiped his mouth with a napkin. "I'll assume I don't need to tell you not to let anybody know you have these. If this gets back to Burnell, he'll have my balls in a little jar on his desk."

Captain George Burnell was the head of Portland's homicide division. He'd swooped in from Chicago and grabbed his promotion over Wickowski, who preferred to stay active on the streets rather than be stuck behind a desk anyway. And let's face it—Wickowski lacked the tact and talent it took to deal with the brass further up the food chain, something Burnell had mastered. I'd first met the captain around the same time I met Wickowski, but Burnell's reputation as a hard-ass with slight misogynistic overtones preceded him. He didn't seem to have a beef with me until I pulled rank as a former agent with the mayor and made him look bad. Suffice it to say, Burnell wasn't one of my biggest fans.

I sat and chewed a mouthful of tamale while nodding my understanding of Wickowski's situation. If this was the only rule I had to play by, I didn't have a problem complying.

"You planning on climbing that thing today?" Wickowski was referring to the mountain trail Dr. Phillips allegedly fell from.

I shook my head and swallowed my mouthful. "No, tonight I'm going to Vin's opening at the Blackwell Gallery."

I caught Wickowski's brow raise in my peripheral. "You're still seeing Mr. Sensitive?"

"Vin isn't 'Mr. Sensitive.'"

"The guy writes poetry that doesn't rhyme or begin with 'roses are red,'" Wickowski countered.

"That's not a prerequisite for being overly sensitive."

"And he never wears shoes. I don't trust anybody who doesn't like footwear."

"Vin is a nice guy. And he's good for me," I said after taking a pull off my water bottle. "He keeps me grounded."

Wickowski gave a sarcastic chuckle. "He has a tranquilizing effect on you. *That's* hot." He took a too-large bite from his tamale.

"What are you getting at, Wick?"

Wickowski moved the food in his mouth so he could speak around it. "I've seen you bust a guy's nose with your head. I know you've got to be a wildcat in the sack! I just never figured you'd go for the fluffy, Renaissance type."

It was my turn to roll my eyes. Okay, sure—Wickowski's assessment of my personal prowess wasn't too far off the mark. I knew my way around in bed. But I knew something about artists that Wickowski didn't. Artists were a very passionate breed, and those soft-spoken types knew how to express themselves without words. Boy howdy, did they.

I pushed the last bite of tamale into my mouth then wiped my face with a napkin from the stack. "Thanks," I said when I stood to leave and tucked the file under my elbow.

"Anytime I can get you to owe me, Harris. Just remember—twenty-four hours."

"Got it." I gave Wickowski a wave and strolled back toward my office.

CHAPTER FIVE

I WAS STILL A COUPLE OF BLOCKS AWAY WHEN MY PHONE CHIRPED in my jacket pocket. I fished it out and answered, "Harris Securities."

"Babe." It was Vin, the man of few words.

"I missed you last night," I purred seductively, glad Wickowski wasn't around to give me any grief. He never tired of badgering me with jokes about going soft.

"Sorry, I had a lot of last-minute changes to make for tonight. I know it's not your crowd or scene, but you will be at the opening tonight, right?"

"Of course I'll be there. I'm even dressing up."

"Feel free to leave the guns at home," Vin teased. "The doors open at six o'clock. I'll see you when you get there."

We said good-bye and disconnected.

The Blackwell Gallery was owned and operated by Trisha Blackwell. As the metro section of the *Oregonian* had reported when they did a puff piece on the then-newly opened gallery, Trisha Blackwell had transplanted to Portland from Palm Beach after she'd divorced her successful plastic surgeon husband. The piece led the reader to believe it had been a nasty divorce. Blackwell Gallery brought with it Trisha's status in the art world and had immediately become the gallery to be accepted into, where careers were launched and dreams were made. She and I had absolutely nothing in common other than our interest in Vin.

I'd only met Trisha once, a few weeks ago at another artsy-fartsy function that I'd accompanied Vin to. Our short introduction had told me all I needed to know about the woman: she was a devious shrew. And she was plastic on several levels. It wasn't a snap judgment. I didn't have to be a super-sleuth to see that Trisha's interest in Vin had little to do with his paintings. But I wasn't a jealous person. Live and let live, right? Okay, maybe I had a small thread of possessiveness running through me, but not enough to be called a character flaw.

Vin didn't play an active part in the highfalutin aspect of the gallery scene. He was a true artist, and he had been extremely flattered to have been invited to open a show at the Blackwell. He understood the invitation would most assuredly be his coming-out engagement. The city, if not the entire West Coast, would soon know his name and work.

Sensing Trisha's true intentions, however, I battled with myself. I had to believe Vin wasn't thick and he'd seen what I'd seen. Why wouldn't he take advantage of the situation and push his art out into the community? This showing would open doors for Vin that weren't previously accessible, and he deserved the opportunity. But Vin was also a compassionate, old soul who saw the best in everyone and everything. I wouldn't say he was naïve; he just trusted that everyone was as good-hearted as he was. I wasn't sure if I should say something or just let things roll as they would. I hated moral dilemmas.

But my workday wasn't yet over, and there was plenty of time to stew over my personal impasse. Back in my office, I reviewed my notes and the information Mole had compiled on Mr. Alan Martin, owner of Quantum Electronic Design, my next appointment. Some would've called Mole's procedures unethical or highly illegal, but I kept my distance from those opinions. Mole never divulged his sources to me, and to keep myself clean, I never asked.

But let's face it, there was the world we wished we lived in—full of kept promises and people running all over doing the right thing—and then there was reality. In order to get things done, sometimes you had to look at the law as more of a suggestion than an absolute. There. I said it. As a former federal agent, I condoned breaking the law for my personal gain. I'd take it up with my conscience at another time. I knew a thing or two about the Feds versus John Q. Public and the illusion of personal privacy. I used to believe those employed by the federal government were the untarnished good guys. Then I started paying attention to how the game was being played. Now I lived by my own rules.

Alan Martin hired me to do a security check on his company, and I wouldn't be doing my job to the best of my ability if I didn't turn Mole loose on it. Quantum Electronic Design bloomed nearly overnight, moving from its humble beginnings in an outbuilding on Martin's family farm to a ten-million-dollar-a-year-and-growing company. Quantum was a leader in the cutting-edge and fiercely competitive industry of thermal profiling. Martin's company had recently come under contract with NASA to develop a temperature monitoring system for projectiles sent into orbit. Of course, Quantum was ISO 9000 compliant, which meant they'd met all criteria under the International Organization for Standardization to do business with the federal government. That said, when I read *projectiles sent into orbit* in Mole's initial report and took Quantum's recent contract with the Feds into account, my mind had made the immediate leap to weapons. Now, I was no hippie. I'd never marched against blood for oil, and it was pretty much my opinion that the leaders of the world needed to sit down, set their personal beliefs aside as they relate to invisible men in the sky, and have a good, long discussion on what it means to be human.

The clock on my desk showed there was still twenty minutes before Mr. Martin's expected arrival. I pulled the blinds and quickly changed into a navy designer business suit that I kept dry-cleaned and in the closet for interviews. Why did I change at the office? Because the less time I had to wear the monkey suit, the better. I checked myself out in the mirror mounted on the inside of the closet door and perked a few strands of hair. I swiped my lashes with mascara, added a smear of lip gloss, and decided that was as good as I was going to get.

Fifteen minutes, I decided, was long enough to grab a quick look at the Phillips file. I picked up the package and turned it over in my hands. Wickowski had gone to some effort to ensure nobody saw what he'd smuggled out of the precinct. A long strip of clear packing tape was wrapped around the folded end of the envelope that contained the file. It took me several attempts, along with few colorful expletives, to get through. I made a mental note to relocate a few of my blades to the office or buy a pair of freaking scissors. I finally opened it and tipped the envelope to spill the contents out onto my desktop.

I sifted through a bundle of papers, all neatly stapled together, and a slew of eight-by-ten glossy photographs inside individual sheet protectors labeled either "Scene" or "ME" for medical examiner. I chose the one labeled "Scene" and slid out the glossies. The first photo was of the trail itself where Dr. Phillips had allegedly fallen. The next two were of the same stretch of trail, but the photographer had changed perspectives, shooting up and down the trail. Wickowski hadn't been exaggerating in his description of the area—rocky, muddy, and steep.

The next several shots were taken from the trail and looked down into the bottom of the deep ravine. It was hard to judge distances from two-dimensional photographs. I flipped through the police report and found that Dr. Phillips had plummeted 250 feet, knocking against boulders on the way down. That'd take the life out of anyone. The next photo was of Dr. Phillips's crumpled body splayed out on the rocks at the bottom of the ravine, his head turned at an unnatural angle, his lifeless eyes staring into the sky.

The rest of the photos were taken at the morgue, where Dr. Phillips's broken body was laid out on the ME's sterile steel table. Quickly I thumbed through the graphic photo record of Dr. Phillips's autopsy and decided to take a closer look at a later time, preferably not right after a Mexican lunch.

Using the computer scanner on the small table beside me, I scanned each of the photos for my own file. Then I unassembled the paper report and copied it as well. Burnell would have kittens if he knew I was copying official police files. I couldn't help a small smile of satisfaction. With the copies made, I reassembled the report and slid the whole thing back into the envelope, not taking the time to even look through the reports, lest I got sidetracked before Martin arrived.

Promptly at two o'clock—which made me wonder if he hadn't been standing in the hall, counting the seconds on his wristwatch—Alan Martin made his timely appearance. My immediate impression was that he was shorter than I expected, which he made up for with arrogance. His graying, dark hair was as impeccably cut as his cashmere Armani suit.

I came around from behind my desk and met the man halfway. "Mr. Martin," I said, extending my hand in welcome.

"Ms. Harris," he responded, clipped but pleasant, quite blatantly resting his gaze on my boobs.

I fought the urge to bend my knees so he would look me in the face rather than the chest. "Please," I said, gesturing toward the chair on that side of the desk.

Martin made no move to sit. His gaze was no longer fixed on my breasts, but on the wall behind my desk where all the accolades and certifications I'd received while with the bureau hung. It wasn't that I liked to brag, but I'd done my job well, and clients seemed to be impressed by them, which was good for business. I must have passed Martin's scrutiny, because he unfastened the button of his suit jacket and took the proffered seat, crossed his right leg over his left knee, propped both elbows on the chair's armrests, and steepled his fingers together in front of his chest. His demeanor and piercing gray eyes were probably quite intimidating to most people. Fortunately I wasn't most people.

I flashed one of my best smiles, making sure it reached my eyes, and cleared my throat to begin. "Mr. Martin, I want to first thank you for trusting the security of your investments to Harris—"

"Let's skip the niceties and get directly to the meat of it," Martin said. He was obviously used to running the show. "Quantum's recent contract with NASA is a major coup for our company. The people I have under my employ are brilliant and hardworking, but that does not mean they're immune to temptation."

"Everyone has their price," I interjected.

"Yes, well. Each of my employees signed a nondisclosure contract that binds them to confidentiality. However, as you've pointed out, everyone has a price. I want to assure both my board of directors and my investors that our company is secure. Is that something Harris Securities would be able to provide me with?"

Martin was a man used to getting precisely what he wanted from whom he wanted it. Self-confidence was good and all, but his domineering and pompous approach wasn't going to last long with me. However, my consummate professionalism, plus the fact that I needed to make a living, helped me keep my snarky comments to myself. My services didn't come cheap. I'd have no qualms about taking Martin's money.

I shot him another reassuring smile, carefully shuffled a random stack of papers on my desk, and tapped them into a neat, even pile. There was no need for me to do this other than to make the point that this was my office and he had sought me out. We locked eyes. I gave him my best interrogation stare and held it there for a second longer than needed.

"In the last twelve months," I began citing from memory, "Quantum's profit margin has jumped forty-two percent. As owner and CEO, your personal take-home salary would have been much larger than your last income tax return reflected. This information prompted me to do some further digging, and it wasn't long before I was able to find your name attached to a handful of offshore companies."

Martin's eyes remained steely, never flinching. Damn, I bet he was one hell of a poker player.

I continued, "I won't waste time by rattling off your home address or the location of your vacation homes in Bend, Colorado, or Saint Thomas. Those were easy to find. I did, however, discover a condominium here in Portland, up in the West Hills, leased by a company called Avistar LTD, which is based in the Caymans." I paused. Still no reaction. *Wait for it...* "You are, as a matter of fact, sleeping with the blonde living in that condo, and she isn't your wife." *She shoots, she scores!*

Martin's body language gave away his surprise with raised eyebrows and wide eyes. He cleared his throat. "You are, um, very thorough, Ms. Harris. I'd believed my personal affairs"—Martin smiled slyly at his choice of words—"were more...discreet. However, now that you know some of my little secrets, I must ask you what you mean to do with the information?"

I was taken aback and then insulted by his insinuation. "Mr. Martin, I believe wholeheartedly in client confidentiality, even though we've yet to sign a contract. That's just how I do business."

"Your methods obviously go very deep and are quite exhaustive. I must ask, what gave her away?"

In that moment, I knew I had him hook, line, and sinker. "Honestly? The mistress part was only a guess. Your tan is very dark, as if you've been to your vacation home in the Caribbean recently, but you've been fiddling with your wedding ring and there isn't much of a tan line beneath it. Also I drove past the condo and saw a blonde in a Jaguar pulling out of the garage. I thought she could have been a visiting representative of Avistar's, until I observed the blonde hairs on your suit jacket. There is one on your left shoulder and one at the bottom, near the pocket. They're a brilliant contrast against the dark fabric." I smiled like a Cheshire cat. "Shall we go over the contract?"

For the first time, Martin smiled in earnest. "I believe that's a brilliant idea."

"Great." I opened my desk drawer and brought out the already-prepared contract outlining my terms and what Quantum could expect from Harris Securities. "I will need a list of the employees who you'd like to be included in this check. Please read this carefully and sign at the bottom."

"I'll email this over to my attorney and have him give it a read-through."

"That's fine. You can have him email me the signed copy and courier the original to me tomorrow, if that gives you enough time?"

"That should be sufficient."

"Have you given any further thought to what we discussed earlier, having your information systems people set up a file we might try to retrieve?"

"Yes, I spoke to my IT department. They're preparing the target." Martin stood to leave. "I will have my assistant send the contract over in the morning, along with a thumb drive loaded with all our employee information. They agreed to security checks when they were hired, so no one can come back on me with an invasion of privacy suit."

"That will be fine."

Martin buttoned his suit jacket and plucked the blonde hairs from it. We shook hands to seal the deal, but I wouldn't start working until I had his signature on the contract. He tipped a finger to his forehead and disappeared out the door.

{∗ ∗ ∗}

The mailman was just leaving the curb when I arrived back home. My box was filled with the usual adverts and junk mail. I made my customary contribution to the blue recycle bin at the end of the row of mailboxes and took the stairs two at a time up to the third floor. I could still hear the repetitious rhythm of a drum and bass mix coming from Mole's place. It was different from what had been playing when I left, so at least I knew he wasn't dead.

My loft looked and smelled like a dorm room rather than an adult's home. Housekeeping had never been my forte. I threw open the windows and addressed the collection of empty take-out containers and pizza boxes that had collected in the kitchen. Who knew where Vin and I would end up after his shindig? There was a real possibility that it would be here, and he didn't need to know what kind of slob lay under my fabulous exterior.

Once the dirty clothes and dishes had been stashed in their respective appliances and I felt the loft was fit to be seen, I moved on to making myself presentable. I was just stepping from the shower when I heard Crosby, Stills, Nash, and Young serenading me from my cell phone, the ringtone I'd assigned to my aunt Zelda.

The earliest memory I carried of my aunt was her attendance at my sixth birthday party. She'd worn a dress made from an old American flag. My father, staunch and patriotic Republican that he was, just about died on the spot. Her bright orange hair, passed down to her from a distant maternal ancestor—a gene I fortunately dodged—was a wild mass that sprang forth from her head as if it were alive and on fire. Aunt Zel's tales from the Farm Aid concert in '85 are some of her more colorful and mysterious. I'll probably never know what really went on with her and Willie Nelson that year in Champaign.

When I was older and well into my teens, my aunt shared with me more detailed and flamboyant tales of her life: hitchhiking across the country with a rock band she met in New York; her summer-long affair back in '81 with a Frenchman named Jacques that inspired volumes of sappy poetry; epic psilocybin-fueled discussions about consciousness with Terence McKenna. I never tired of Zelda's mind-expanding perspectives.

Present-day Zelda wasn't all that much different than she had been in her youth, though her flaming hair was worn in a shorter version of out of control and new wrinkles lined her face. She'd also mellowed with time, having found the path of presence and the power of now. I understood loosely what she was talking about, but so far I had been unable to put all that love and light stuff into practice.

"Sammy," Aunt Zel said, her usual upbeat tone holding an edge of anxiety, "I got a vibe this afternoon, so I read your tarot cards, and they're rife with conflict."

A derision-tinged laugh escaped. "You don't have to be a seer to know that one, Zel. Sort of the story of my life."

"Negative encounters are no joking matter, Samantha," Zelda scolded. "This feels close."

The smile slid from my face. Once upon a time I'd doubted my aunt's insights, writing her gift off as just good guesses. Then she saved my life. Now I listened. "I'm going to a gallery opening tonight. What sort of conflict are we talking here?"

I could practically hear Zelda squinting in her effort to better tune in to her prediction. "Squalling cats; that's all I'm getting."

Squalling cats? I was going to be seeing Trisha that evening. Oh boy. "Thanks for the heads-up, Aunt Zel. Anything else?"

Zelda was silent so long that I thought she'd hung up. When she did finally speak, my aunt's voice was distant, and I wasn't sure if she was talking about that evening or something else entirely. "Things aren't as they seem." I heard the telltale shuffle of tarot cards and the sharp snap as they were turned over one by one, revealing their messages. "Change is in the air, but the source remains hidden. Someone holds a secret close. Tensions are high around this, yet it remains veiled to you—to me as well." Zelda sighed with frustration. "I'll meditate for peace tonight, darling. Just try to enjoy yourself and stay out of trouble."

My aunt telling me to stay out of trouble was like telling a swimming fish to stay dry. I promised to be good, though both of us knew the words were simply lip service. I hung up and returned to the bedroom to dress. The open closet doors revealed my options. Looking past the leather and tactical gear, I found a simple, black, A-line dress with cap sleeves. I matched the dress with a pair of sheer, black thigh-highs and black heels. My attire was more fitting for a funeral than a party, but *damn*, I looked good.

As a finishing touch, I dabbed on a bit of essential oil, a fusion of amber and sandalwood that Vin had given me as a gift after we'd begun dating. Feeling particularly spirited, I dabbed the oil onto some very strategic points of my anatomy.

At a quarter till, I phoned for a cab. Even though the gallery was less than six blocks away, I knew my limits, and I wasn't willing to make that kind of urban hike in heels. My house key and ID went into a small handbag no bigger than a wallet that was suspended from a leather cord. I spent a full two minutes trying to figure out a comfortable and tactical way to carry a firearm, even though I'd told Vin I'd leave them home, but I decided it just wasn't in the cards. Which reminded me of Aunt Zelda's warning—it would probably be better if I didn't have a weapon on me.

Before leaving, I grabbed the smelly trash bag from beneath the kitchen sink and deposited it in front of Mole's door, payback for the same offense he'd pulled on me a week ago. His lair had quieted, but it wasn't silent. Gregorian monks chanted softly within, a sign that Mole had finally burnt out and found sleep. Seventy-two hours without sleeping. How does he do it? Better living through chemistry.

My cab arrived just as I stepped out the front door. I climbed into the back seat, which smelled suspiciously of unwashed dog, and gave the driver the gallery address. We arrived moments later, the driver pulling curbside just outside the front door. I dropped a few bills onto the front seat and got out. I straightened my dress and started for the entrance, wondering how Aunt Zel did with her peaceful meditation. We'd all know soon enough.

CHAPTER SIX

THE BLACKWELL GALLERY WAS A NEW CONSTRUCTION BUILT INSIDE the solid bones of a former gristmill. The front façade had a contemporary design, all angular glass and chrome surrounded by century-old masonry. Through the front wall of north-facing windows that spanned from floor to ceiling and were tinted to protect against sun damage, passersby had unobstructed views of the art installments mounted on the gallery walls. The window-panes were made of four-inch-thick, bulletproof polycarbonate, the same material used in armored vehicles. If a thief wanted any of these pieces, he'd need to find another point of entry—no smash and grab available here.

Other guests arriving by cab were gathering outside the gallery's main entrance. The art world was a small and intimate one. All the key players knew each other and swapped European-style cheek-to-cheek kisses, each of them comparing their dresses and baubles like it was Sunday morning on the church steps, their insincerities at political levels.

Obligatory greetings made, the art patrons began filing in with their invitations at the ready. Opening night of a new show at the Blackwell was a sought-after, by-invitation-only event. It wasn't uncommon to open the local paper and see a visiting dignitary, celebrity, or famous sports figure standing arm in arm with Trisha inside the Blackwell, so security was tight. No invitation, no entry.

Even though I knew this small, trivial fact ahead of time, it never occurred to me that I would need the embossed paper to get in. I mean, I was with Vin. My assumptions had never been so wrong.

"Your invitation, please?" asked the doorman, a small, thin person who was less than threatening. His bald head gleamed in the late-evening sun that poured through the open door. His pinched features made me think that an invisible turd was being held just under his nose.

"Oh, I'm sorry," I said, using my nice voice as I held the fingers of one hand lightly over my mouth in mock surprise. "I didn't bring an invitation, but my name is Samantha Harris. I'm with the artist." I needed to tone it down; I sounded nauseatingly sweet even to my own ears. Mr. Doorman made no reply, so I pushed on. "I'm sure Vin put my name on the guest list, if you'd just check it quick." Another award-winning smile, which I was sure was going to seal the deal. I began to move forward, only to be halted by the doorman's hand on my shoulder. I challenged his grasp by continuing forward, and he in turn applied enough pressure not only to stop me but also to make his point.

"This is not a concert hall, ma'am," the doorman sneered. "We do not keep a list. Our staff mails out invitations weeks in advance to those whom Ms. Blackwell and her artist specifically select. If you do not have an invitation, then I am sorry, but I must ask you to leave."

One thing I really wasn't a fan of was people inside my personal bubble without my permission. It didn't make me cranky; it made me volatile. *Take a deep breath, Sam.* I only meant to calm myself, but when I leveled my eyes on the doorman's, it felt more like intimidation. Slowly I dropped my eyes to his hand on my shoulder and let my gaze rest there for the span of a heartbeat or two before I looked back up to his face. I must have had *the look*, because his grip momentarily faltered and I saw the blood drain from his face.

Seeking aid, the doorman looked past me and summoned backup. The man who joined us could have been his bookend. Then I had not one but two twiggy bald men on either side of me. I looked at bald guy number two, back to bald guy number one, back to number one's hand on my shoulder, and said, "I bet you do most things with your right hand."

Now I had *the voice* to go with *the look*, and at that moment I felt like Dirty Harry in drag. Luckily we were all saved from any sort of awkward altercation when Vin appeared before us. He apologized to the Baldy Twins for the confusion, trying to suppress a smile while doing so.

"Well, that went smoothly," I quipped as we stepped away from the seething doormen.

Vin gave a small chuckle, as if he were half expecting such a confrontation. *God, please don't let me become predictable.* In the center of the room, Vin turned me around and held me at arm's length. "You look incredible."

"You look pretty good yourself." *Delectable is more like it*, I thought with more than just my mind. Vin cleaned up very well. He'd dressed in a dark, forest-green jacket cut to mid-thigh over rust-colored pants and an off-white linen shirt. As he was known to do, Vin had gone barefoot. His shoulder-length sandy hair was still in need of a cut, but he'd subdued it with a comb, so it was less unruly than normal. He smelled of spices and wood, and his green eyes gleamed with excitement. He had a small dimple in his chin that wasn't as evident when he had a few days' worth of stubble, but it added a nice touch to his slightly rugged features. Overall Vin had a weathered look about him, as if he'd spent long stretches of time wandering in the elements. Even with his classic male looks, nobody would ever consider Vin overly pretty. Uniquely handsome, yes, but he would never model for the cover of a romance novel.

Vin took my hand and led me deeper into the bowels of the gallery, which was even more impressive from the inside. The ancient oak floors had been refinished, lacquered, and buffed to the endless sheen of a second life. The lighting, suspended from the high ceiling in a series of small, can-like fixtures, had been perfected and angled to show off each painting where it hung and gave the entire room a warm glow, as if consideration to one's complexion had been figured into the interior design.

Vin hailed down a roving cocktail attendant and obtained two flutes of bubbly. With spirits in hand, he walked me around the room, offering me a personal tour of the show and giving me small explanations for the inspiration of each. I wasn't really into art, but I was into the artist, and I loved listening to the passion behind his words.

Vin saved his biggest canvas for last, the piece that the rest of the show revolved around. I found myself standing in awe before a monstrous six-by-ten-foot abstract in the most vibrant colors, the strokes fluid yet delicate, strong yet bold. The sheer size of the painting alone made quite an impression. A small bit of paper with a handwritten message was affixed to the center of the painting. I took a step closer and read it.

"Attempting to cage her is akin to ensnaring the sun: futile."

I didn't quite get it, but then I wasn't part of the abstract art scene either. It wasn't until I caught the painting's title etched on a small brass plaque mounted to the wall that I began to understand. The painting's title was *Samantha*.

"Surprise," Vin cooed, wrapping his arms around my waist from behind.

Wow. I didn't know what to say, so I stayed silent until I began to sense Vin's uneasiness as he interpreted my silence as disapproval.

"Vin, this is incredible. It's larger than life. Breathtaking. Almost overwhelming." I turned in his arms.

When Vin threw his head back with a heartfelt chuckle, his cheeks crinkled all the way up to his eyes. "Sam, *you* are larger than life," he said as he cupped the back of my head and locked my lips with his own.

Our display of affection was long and publicly awkward, but I rolled with it even though I could feel eyes watching us. Being the center of attention, for me, was akin to being in the crosshairs. I could have broken our embrace off, but a pleasant flutter that tickled that space between my chest and my navel kept me from doing so. Electricity flooded my synapses in a current that ran directly to my private pink bits.

The noise in the bustling room amplified when a new wave of patrons arrived. They honed in on Vin like hornets to a picnic, eager to meet the evening's superstar. He was quickly swept away by the incoming tide of enthusiasts spearing him with eager hands and drowning him in praise. When an art dealer approached, I stepped away to give Vin a private moment.

I snagged a passing flute of champagne from another wandering waiter and watched the crowd admire my namesake. You bet your ass I was feeling smug. A tray full of garnished crackers passed at eye level, and I snatched one up, popping it into my mouth before I realized too late that the garnish was fish eggs and I hated caviar. Discreetly I deposited the mouthful into a cocktail napkin and located a trash receptacle.

My anxiety about the evening was unfounded at that point, which made me wonder where Trisha Blackwell was. Probably waiting to make a grand, fashionably late entrance. *Calm down. Where's the canvas titled* Trisha? I laughed out loud at my little voice then remembered it was the same voice I always heard just before I did something stupid, like bringing a knife to a gunfight. *Just be your fabulous self. And have another drink.* My little voice was right. Aside from the dress, I was rocking the heels. And I had inspired a painting, after all. In addition, I was going to sleep with the artist after the show, so Trisha had nothing on me.

My catty opinion of the woman wasn't even an echo in my mind when Trisha Blackwell appeared across the room as if conjured. She'd pulled her platinum hair up into a twist, the better to show off the diamond-and-ruby choker at her throat. She was the ex-wife of a plastic surgeon, and Trisha's gown clung to her every enhanced curve. When my little voice reminded me that Trisha was the kind of woman that other women wanted to be and every man wanted to be with, I snared a passing snifter of brandy meant for someone else and changed the subject.

Vin caught my eye and smiled at me from across the room, making my heart flutter, which in turn made me panic. I was all for a good time, but long-term relationships in general weren't my thing. Clichés aside, our attraction was an anomaly. No two people could be any less alike than Vin and I. At first we were just in it for the hot, sweaty sex, but now...now it was different. There was a deeper connection. We were much slower and more deliberate. I knew in the end he and I were going to have to end things. The world I knew was a dangerous and unpredictable place where lovers could become liabilities.

The sound of my name being called from the most unexpected mouth broke my reverie. Trisha had me in her sights and was quickly approaching. A fly on the wall would have thought that the two of us were friends when she came to stand at my side and engaged me with smiles and chitchat.

"I can give you the number to my ex-husband's clinic again if you've misplaced it," she said, gesturing to the left side of her mouth, the same side as my scar.

I responded by not responding.

Trisha altered the conversation. "He's going to be a star someday, you know." She swooned admiringly toward Vin.

"Someday?" I questioned.

Trisha sensed I wasn't in the bait-taking mood and switched tactics. "Vinardo tells me you were once a security officer or something like that?"

"Yes, a special agent with the FBI. I still have all my firearms." Then I added, "You know he prefers not to be called Vinardo, right?"

Trisha smiled and waved across the room to someone who eagerly waved back. "How much would it cost me to make you go away?" she asked, still smiling at the room.

A calm settled over me, the same calm that settled over me on the firing range, when only me and the paper target at the end of my scope existed. It was my brain shifting modes. Not a good sign.

"Miss Harris, let me be perfectly frank. Artists like Vinardo come along very rarely. I have the ways and means to take him to the top of the international scene, but it won't happen if he's tethered to a girlfriend back home. You know these artist types—everything is about emotions and feelings. And let me be blunt, you're not really that sort of woman. Don't destroy Vinardo just as he's emerging into greatness. Let him go while he has his pursuit to distract him."

I turned to face Trisha and lifted myself off my heels onto my tiptoes. When Trisha puzzled at my actions, I apologized. "I was just wondering if *Samantha* is going to fit in my loft; it's terribly large." *Good one.* My little voice wanted to high-five someone. Then I got sincere. "I can fully understand your crush, Trisha, believe me. But if I look like someone you should mess with, you've not been paying attention." I tossed back the contents of the snifter in my hand in one long, burning gulp. A lengthy trail of fire flamed its way down my esophagus to my stomach, where it heated me from the inside, but I never let the searing surprise show. My eyes remained on Trisha's, my features never flinching.

Trisha's steely grin and wicked eyes faltered momentarily, like a taunting feline who'd realized the pit bull was no longer chained. She recovered quickly and stiffened her spine. "Do not think you can threaten me on my own turf, Samantha. Rest assured that I have never not gotten what I've set my sights on."

Trisha had no idea how she stoked my inner fire, and it was my own determination not to fall victim to my Scorpio predisposition that kept her from harm. I swallowed the nasty rebuttal that sat on my tongue, forcing it down in a bitter lump. I hated the higher road. As if by divine intervention, we were interrupted by a small throng of oblivious guests who unknowingly gave me an out. I used the opportunity to turn the other cheek and walk away, leaving Trisha to her sycophants.

By nine o'clock, the crowd began to thin and fade back into the night full of champagne and false flattery. The leftover revelers, well-disposed admirers who had spent the evening clinging to Trisha's every word like a bunch of political groupies, finally dispersed, and Vin was able to call it a night.

The evening was clear and chilly, and I wished I'd thought of bringing a shoulder wrap. The spicy aroma of East Indian cuisine from a late-night restaurant down the street wafted in sumptuous drafts on the light breeze. My feet—as officially broken in as my heels themselves—had me pulling off my shoes, sacrificing my stockings, and hoping not to tread through anything disgusting on the sidewalk.

"Your place or mine?" I asked playfully.

"Which one is closer?" Vin asked coyly as we strolled hand in hand.

"Six blocks either direction from here, but I have clean sheets."

"I have a coffee pot," Vin tempted.

"I have a shower and a tub."

After a half-second consideration, Vin nodded. "Okay, you win."

We arrived at my building less than eight minutes later. Vin did his best to keep his hands to himself as I punched in the security code at the front gate. The elevator seemed especially slow. Once we'd fumbled our way through the front door, all bets were off. We freed ourselves from our clothes like butterflies escaping the confines of their cocoons. A trail of fabric led from the front door to the bedroom, with a brief stop at the kitchen table. The next several hours were spent in erotic bliss as Vin and I proved why it was so important to lease a home that had both a shower and a tub.

We ended up in a heap on the bed, satiated and exhausted, smelling like sandalwood oil, vanilla, and sweat. I lay beside Vin, my body abuzz with warm, postcoital fuzzies. Sleep gently slipped its shadowy arms around my consciousness and softly cradled me in its comfortable embrace. I had just slipped beneath the veil that separates the sleeping world from the waking when I heard Vin's soft, passive voice from far away.

"I love you, Sam."

{* * *}

It was only a few hours later when I woke up on my stomach with the morning sun blinding me through the window. That was when I realized I'd forgotten to lower the blinds the night before, distracted by the heat of passion. My neighbors could have sold tickets to the show Vin and I must have put on, especially when he did that thing with his—

My cell phone chirped from somewhere in the vicinity of the living room. I pulled back the covers and eased out of bed. I followed the third and fourth rings out into the living room, where my handbag lay on the floor under Vin's jacket and shirt. I was surprised to learn it was nearly one in the afternoon.

"Samantha," chimed a familiar voice before I had a chance to say hello. "It's been a month since I've spoken to you on the phone. Even though you've not kept in touch, I trust you are well?" My mother's passive-aggressive tone could still make me wince, even from the other side of the continent.

"I'm fine, Mother." I yawned and rolled my eyes.

"I can call back later if you're too busy to visit with me." She sighed. "It's just that my doctor said my lipids are high, and he's concerned. You know your grandmother passed from a heart attack when she was just about my age. The doctor said I'm fine, but I know I haven't got long. I can just feel it."

"Mother, you've felt that way since I can remember. You're not dying."

"But if you're busy, I completely understand, now that you have a whole new life. Frankie and I were talking about visiting you with the girls, but I told her you were probably too busy." *Wait for it…* She sighed wearily before continuing. "If I had a magic wand, I'd arrange it so you could make some room in your busy schedule for your family, and the girls could spend some quality time with their aunty Samantha for a couple of weeks to give you an opportunity to reconnect with them now that you live so far away from us all."

This was a classic tactic my mother used to get what she wanted: lead with a doctor-certified health anxiety and follow up with a guilt-laced statement that was really a desire wrapped in a question. The point was, my mother wanted to come for a visit but couldn't come out and say it. Instead she dropped strong hints that the other person was meant to pick up. She believed it bad form to outright invite herself. She wanted me to extend an invitation, one that she would initially turn down (on my behalf of course) until I found myself all but begging her to come out west. But I wasn't going to play that game. "Yeah, Mother, I'd need that wand to get some time off right now, but," I said with a *tsk*, "it's too bad there's no such thing as magic."

Derailed, she changed the subject to Father, who was reportedly doing well and, with retirement looming in the next few years, had been trying on different hobbies, from model trains in the basement to woodworking in the garage. Thus far nothing had stuck. Mother said he might try restoring an old car, like a Studebaker, though I didn't know him to be mechanical at all. By the time I hung up, I felt mentally drained.

Even though my body was still tired, I was wide awake with no hope of going back to sleep. I crawled back into bed, buried my face into the pillow, and stifled a frustrated scream. Vin rustled beside me but never fully woke up, dammit. I could always wake him up. I slid my hand down his leg then back up the inside of his thigh. Nothing, not even a physical response. Fine. I wanted coffee then.

I opened the closet door and threw on the first things I saw, a pair of jeans and a sweatshirt from my academy days, neither of them freshly laundered. My bare feet slipped into a pair of leather slippers, and I closed the front door silently behind me.

Vin was up and dressed when I returned from Steam with two paper cups in my hands. I offered him one of the coffees, but he turned it down. "I'm abstaining from caffeine for a while."

"Why would you do that?" I asked, honestly flummoxed.

Vin shrugged and leaned his hip against the counter. "I'm interested to see if my focus changes." He hooked his index fingers through the two belt loops nearest my zipper and pulled me to him. "What are your plans for the day?"

"I have a house call to make. What about you?"

Vin shot me a queer look with one brow arched, trying to decide if I was being metaphorical. "I've an appointment to meet Jacob from Café Urban about a mural."

We said our long good-bye at the door, sharing a kiss that most assuredly would have delayed us another hour or two had he not broken away. I watched him walk down the hall toward the elevator. I loved watching Vin walk away.

I shut the door behind him with a long sigh. I had things to do myself. Wickowski's envelope was on the sideboard. I carried it, and Vin's untouched coffee, into the bedroom and made myself comfortable in the center of my bed. With a cup of coffee carefully balanced on the comforter between my crossed legs and the other waiting in the wings on the nightstand, I spread the photos and report out around me in a wide arc.

Dr. Phillips's autopsy report was on top, so that was my first read. Phillips died from a head trauma. Not surprising, considering the height from which he had fallen. The medical examiner reported no other major wounds save for cuts and abrasions, all consistent with that type of accident. Toxicology reports found nothing incriminating, not even caffeine. The bottom line according to the report was that there had been no suspicious cause of death found. Dr. Phillips simply took a nosedive and bought the farm.

I perused the rest of the report, still finding nothing that even remotely suggested foul play. I had to agree with the ME; it was tragic, but Dr. Ronald "Ronny" Phillips had died an accidental death. Surely anything worth discovering would have already been located, and any other evidence lying out there undiscovered would have been destroyed by time and the elements. I wasn't making any final decisions, however, until I got a look inside his computers.

CHAPTER SEVEN

The Phillipses' home on Chestnut Lane was easy enough to locate using Google Maps on my phone. Theirs was a quiet neighborhood made up of Victorians resurrected from ruin. Their refurbished towers, turrets, and roof finials gave the feeling of oversized dollhouses. The yards were a decent size, and the streets offered curbside parking, but two cars couldn't pass abreast without one pulling aside to make room for the other. Maple trees as old as the homes themselves formed a living canopy, shading the street and its inhabitants.

I pulled over behind a green pickup truck parked at the curb to let an oncoming red Prius pass before I pulled into the Phillipses' cobbled driveway.

"They're not home," announced a detached voice from the yard next door when I stepped out of my car. "Katie went to her grandma's. She lives in California."

The kid, no more than seven or eight, dropped down from the tree in a flurry of leaves knocked loose by the unexpected windfall and hung by his hands so that he was at eye level with me. A shock of tousled red hair and dimpled cheeks leant to the mischievous twinkle in his blue eyes. "Mom says I'm not supposed to talk to strangers."

"Is your mom home?" I asked, keeping a nonthreatening distance from the fence.

"She's putting my baby sister down for a nap." The kid tilted his head to the side like an inquisitive cat. "What's your name?"

"I thought you weren't supposed to talk to strangers."

The kid shrugged. "Everyone says I'm precocious, but Mom thinks I'm insolent."

Imagine that. "My name is Samantha, but you can call me Sam."

The kid's impish baby blues widened like saucers. "My name is Samuel, but everyone calls me Sam, too!"

"Of course they do," I said with a wink. "Don't you know all the cool kids are named Sam?"

This earned me a terrestrial face-to-face. Little Sam dropped to the ground and came to stand at the fence. "Is that really true?" he asked in all seriousness.

"If I'm lyin' I'm dyin'."

Sam screwed up his brows. "Huh?"

"Never mind. From one Sam to another, have you happened to see anybody odd or out of place hanging around the neighborhood at all?"

With all the seriousness of an amateur sleuth, his thin lips set in a firm line, Sam shook his red mop fervently, blowing back a stray lock with puffed cheeks.

"Samuel James Oswald! There you are." The wailing toddler perched on her jutted hip coupled with the fact that her belly was again round with child let me know the woman coming at us like a bear from hibernation was Mom. She hurried across the well-maintained lawn the best she could in her condition. The child on her hip ramped up her wails to an ear-shattering pitch. Mom had to yell over the din to scold her son. "What was my answer, mister, when you asked if you could go outside and play after missing school for two days because of a cold?"

"You said I should use my common sense. Studies show fresh air and physical exercise are key to health, and in fact some Scandinavian children nap outside starting at fourteen days old, even in the winter," he answered, then offered a shrug.

Exasperated, momma bear turned to me. Her face and tone both softened. "Sorry if he was bothering you." Her apology, though sincere, was said automatically, like an oft-used phrase.

"No problem," I said, but she was already steering Samuel back inside. He turned back at the top of the stairs for one last wave.

A path of stepping stones meandered toward the front door. Both sides of the path were bordered with blue primroses and pansies that accented the house's sky-blue and lavender trim. The boards of the wide porch were weathered beneath a coat of fresh white paint and creaked in loud protest when I stepped onto them. From my pocket, I pulled the key Pam had given me and slid it into the door, unlocking it. It swung open on well-oiled hinges and closed again just as silently. Standing in the foyer, I debated taking off my shoes—it seemed like that kind of house—and decided not to.

An arched doorway to my immediate left opened into a spacious living room that would have been the sitting room or parlor back in the day. The room reflected Ronald and Pam's keen eye with keeping to the house's history. A green wingback sofa faced a bricked fireplace. A mantel made from a single slab of wood was laden with old, leather-bound books. Even though a fine layer of dust covered everything, the air carried the scent of lemon furniture polish and pine cleaner. An old phonograph was displayed on a side table next to a grouping of framed, sepia-toned photographs filled with sullen-faced men and women in uncomfortable clothes. A tall floor lamp with stained glass dragonflies stood beside the table. The hardwood floors were properly distressed with time but still shone. Nothing appeared disturbed.

The parlor cleared, I returned to the foyer with the intent of following the hall to the back of the house when a small sound from above caught my attention. I froze and listened. A creak and groan of floorboards confirmed my suspicion. Someone was upstairs.

Walking on the balls of my feet to lessen the surface area of my steps and thus lessen the chances of my steps being heard, I crept to the foot of the wide wooden stairway. The scent of furniture polish was strong, yet it was overridden by a more intrusive odor—the stench of stale cigarettes. Not the smell of a freshly lit ciggy, but that invasive reek a chain-smoker carries around with them and leaves in the wake of their passing.

Pam's flight had left hours ago. She wouldn't have forgotten to tell me that someone would be at her home, and I didn't think that a concerned relative would just let themselves in. That was two too many negatives for my comfort.

I pulled my gun, switched off the safety, and started up the stairs, keeping it and my eyes trained on the landing above me. I rolled my foot onto each step, keeping to the right of center where I was least likely to trigger a loose board. Finally I reached the landing with the element of surprise still in my favor.

A partially opened door at the opposite end of the hall cast a pie-shaped wedge of muted light onto the carpet. Someone was in Dr. Phillips's office. There came a squeal of metal being forced followed by a crash and a chorus of colorful curses along with a hoot of victory. The intruder must have gotten what he came for, because he stepped into the hallway and found me standing there.

He was bigger than I would've hoped, with linebacker shoulders and a deformed nose resulting from too many brawls. Sweat glistened on his shaved head. Arms the size of tree trunks strained the fabric of his short sleeves. He ran his eyes over the length of me, starting at my knees. Not knowing what else to do, I flashed a cheeky smile and said, "Hi."

The nostrils of his ruined nose flared like a bull ready to charge, and the surprise in his eyes quickly turned to rage. He brought up a meaty hand. It was wrapped around the hilt of a ballistic knife, a weapon with a spring-loaded, self-propelled blade that could be ejected and travel several meters by pressing a trigger on the handle. One flick of his finger and eight inches of stainless steel would embed itself into the center of my chest. Shit just got real.

He was jumpy, but I stood my ground. If he'd wanted me dead, I already would be. Tucked under his left arm was something small and metallic, about the size of a paperback book. It looked like the hard drive out of Dr. Phillips's computer. I could tell by the way he started taking deep breaths and forcing the air out of his lungs that he was trying to psych himself up to attack.

The intruder's bulk belied his speed. He careened toward me. My attempt to get out of his way was a heartbeat too slow. He clipped me with a shoulder, sending me bouncing backward like a pinball and knocking the gun from my hand and out of reach. At the last second, I snaked my hand out, caught him around his ankle, and held on. Inertia pitched him forward, and he crashed down in a twisted pile of arms and legs. He didn't stay down long. We each fought to be the first one standing. He won.

The blade in the intruder's hand glinted as it viciously sliced the air above me. I turned my head and scrambled backward, in the same direction my gun had skittered, in an awkward crabwalk. I was unable to avoid catching the tip of the knife across my brow in a long, clean slice. He made sure I stayed down by driving a fist into my jaw. My head spun atop my neck, and I collapsed to the carpet. Critical alarms went off inside my skull as the taste of blood filled my mouth.

Then everything went black.

{∗ ∗ ∗}

There was no way of knowing how long I was out. When I opened my eyes, the light outside hadn't changed much. My cheek was sticky on the hall carpet, and my blood that soaked it had gone cold. The cut on my forehead stung. I worked my jaw open and closed and from side to side. Nothing but my ego was broken.

All around me, the house was silent. I lay unmoving in the hallway for a long time, trying to assess where I was hurt. I wriggled my fingers and toes, then used my hands to push up from the floor.

Still a touch unsteady from the wallop to my head, I followed the wall to the hall bathroom. Inside the medicine chest, I found a bottle of over-the-counter pain meds, so I popped three of them into my mouth and chased them down with a pull off the faucet. I wetted the clean washrag that hung from the towel rack and wiped the blood from my face. The cut over my eye was lightly crusted, so I left it alone lest it open and start bleeding again.

Retracing my steps back down to the first floor, I followed the hallway to the rear of the house and into the kitchen. The back door that the intruder had kicked in stood off-kilter on its ruined hinges. My eyes caught something in the bush off the side of the porch: a cigarette burned down to the filter. A concrete path led around to the front of the house.

Back upstairs, I stood just inside the door of Dr. Phillips's office. It was evident the intruder had been quite thorough in his search. I knew he'd made off with Dr. Phillips's hard drive, which stored all his vital information, but I sat down behind his desk anyway. His cell phone had been listed in the police reports as being found on his body, but there was no sign of it in the house. The intruder must have made off with that as well.

The desk drawers had been pulled out and dumped on the floor, their contents scattered across the carpet. I rummaged through the mess, finding nothing more exciting than tax returns, pay stubs, old movie tickets, kids' drawings, and various other papers that a family collects over the years. None of it was significant.

Because I had the time to observe and wasn't in a rush to grab and go like the room's previous visitor, I took my time looking around. People with secrets love hiding places, and I had an inkling Dr. Phillips was the same. *Slow down to move faster* was what one of my instructors at the academy used to say. His words paid off. Just below the desktop surface, I spied a thin drawer flush with the desk front yet lacking a handle or any other means of opening. It was nearly invisible, and I would have missed it if I'd been distracted with trying to steal a hard drive. The drawer was easy enough to open using the business end of a letter opener. Tucked into the back of the drawer was a mailing envelope date-stamped three months prior and addressed to Dr. Phillips. Inside was a single photograph of a much younger Dr. Phillips with his arms over the shoulders of two comrades. All three were wearing bright-blue t-shirts with Phi Mu Delta printed across the chest in bold yellow font. The date stamped in the lower right-hand corner was July 1984. *We'll always have Skynyrd* was written on the back. One of the men in the photo looked familiar, but I couldn't quite place him.

I decided to hang on to the photo for no other reason than that I wanted to know who the man was. What I needed was Dr. Phillips's class photos from college. I found them beneath an overturned box labeled "Ronny's College Stuff." They were in a white, leather-bound book with the University of Massachusetts logo on it. Ronald Phillips's name was printed across the cover in embossed gold letters. I flipped through and found Phi Mu Delta toward the back of the book. There was Ronald along with the two guys in the mailed photograph. Putting names to the faces, I read the names in the caption: William "Willy" McPherson and Steven Talbert, who turned out to be the familiar face I couldn't place. Steven Talbert was now a senior-level attorney at S.T. Finance, a financial company that helped small businesses. Of course, in this grad picture Talbert was much younger, his hair darker, and his overall features leaner, but there was no mistaking it. This was the man who'd hired me less than a year ago. It wasn't that big of coincidence; local big business was a small world.

I pulled another photo of McPherson on skis with a rifle over his shoulder: *Captain of the Frozen Bullets biathlon team.* There was another of Talbert hamming it up for the camera with a broad smile, each arm encircling a cheerleader: *Future ex-wives.* A single shot of Ronald before he'd become Dr. Phillips posing with a certificate that read *Recipient of the Isaac Newton Medal in Physics.*

Blood dripped onto the open album, splattering on the opaque plastic sheeting. I held a tissue to my brow, leaving me only one hand with which to paw through the wreckage. Dr. Phillips's laptop wasn't there, and the intruder hadn't had it when he tackled me. The photos were all I was going to walk away with.

As a courtesy to Pam, I jury-rigged the back door so that it would at least stay shut, though it wouldn't keep out anyone who was determined to get in. On my way out, I noted that the green truck I'd seen parked at the curb out front was gone and wondered if it belonged to my attacker. I encountered no one on my way home.

{* * *}

Back at my loft in the Pearl, I nursed another caffeine fix from Steam while holding an ice pack to my head. My phone was turned off, my way of dodging Vin and Wickowski, at least until morning. I wasn't in the mood for condolences, explanations, or lectures. I wanted to nurse my ego alone—just me and my barely legal, twenty-one-year-old Scottish friend, Glenlivet.

I was refilling my tumbler again when I heard a knock at my door. I wasn't up for visitors and hoped whoever it was went away, until I heard Vin's voice.

"Sam, you in there?"

I froze and entertained staying stone silent in hopes that Vin would go away then laughed at my own foolishness. I downed what I'd already poured and opened the door. I kept my brow averted from his line of sight until he got inside and I swung the door shut.

"Sam, what happened?" Vin asked when I turned and he caught sight of the goose egg on my brow.

"Oh, this?" I touched the wound then pulled my fingers back with a wince. The skin above my eye was swollen and probably could have done with a few stitches. "It's just a scrape."

"That's more than a scrape, babe." Vin pulled me close to get a better look. "Self-medicating?" he asked, eyeing the bottle of whisky beside the couch.

"Today sucked. I went to the house of the guy who died, but someone else beat me to it. Then this happened." I pointed to my head and reached for the whisky bottle again.

"I think this is just going to make your head hurt even worse," Vin said as he took the bottle back out of my hand and recorked it. "Why don't I carry you to bed?"

"I appreciate the gesture, but I can make it on my—"

Vin lifted me off my feet, disregarding my protest. It was more the whisky than his chivalry that had me melting into his shoulder. He laid me gently in the middle of the bed and pulled the comforter up to my shoulders.

"Give me a few minutes to rally," I mumbled. The whisky, the day, and my bed had me suddenly feeling extraordinarily tired.

"No rallying tonight. I'm just going to lie here, hold your ice pack, and make sure you keep breathing."

I have no idea what else Vin said. That dark chasm that comes with overindulgence claimed me before he had finished his sentence.

CHAPTER EIGHT

"BUT WHAT IF I RUN INTO A RABID BEAR, OR A METHED-OUT REDNECK?"
I asked the next morning as I tried to coerce Vin into joining
me on my journey to the crime scene. He did a lot of volunteer
work with local environmental groups. He'd once climbed a
mountain at night in the middle of winter for the inspiration of
a sunrise. He'd also been known to disappear into the Table Rock
Wilderness for a week at a time with nothing but a knife and his
camera, foraging on the abundance of edibles the forest provides,
simply to get in touch with his muse. No matter how hard I tried,
I couldn't relate. I'd grown up in a place where the only patches
of nature available were the well-tended, chemically enhanced
yards of the neighborhoods. And people who live in East Coast
cities don't typically sleep outside unless they're homeless.

"If you happen upon a bear, it'll be more afraid of you than you
are of it and will run away. Same for the redneck—if he's smart."

"Aw, you say the sweetest things—ouch," I grabbed my head
with both hands and took a deep breath. It was a slow-going
morning. I shook two pain relievers from the bottle on the bedside table and chased them with a gulp of day-old coffee.

"You sure you know where you're going?" Vin asked.

I looked at Vin incredulously. "I think I can handle it."

"Are you going armed?"

Another dubious look. "Of course," I said, as if he had asked
if I planned on breathing.

A pink box from Voodoo Doughnut lay open on the end of
the bed. Vin had made an early morning run, convinced sweet

grease was the best way to tame a hangover. I was down with that. Fritters cure everything.

When the pain relievers and doughnut had kicked in, I said good-bye to Vin. He was getting started on the café mural and was under a deadline. Neither of us knew what the day would bring, so we made no plans for later but did keep it open for possibilities.

On the bottom shelf of the linen closet I located a small backpack, into which I tossed a chocolate bar from a kitchen drawer and a water bottle from the fridge. Never knowing what the weather would be like, I dressed in layers like the local outdoor enthusiasts advised. All I had were blue jeans, so that was what I pulled on, along with a short-sleeved t-shirt and a hooded sweatshirt. I also added a nylon windbreaker to my pack in case the weather turned sour.

Rifling through a box in the bathroom closet, I came up with a pair of latex gloves for evidence collecting. They joined the jacket and chocolate bar in the pack. A drawer in the kitchen produced a box of zippered plastic bags. Three of the baggies and Dr. Phillips's file went into the pack too, and I zipped it shut. My shoulder holster went under my sweatshirt.

I was topping off the magazine of my HK when I was interrupted by a knock at my door. I rarely had visitors; therefore I assumed it was Mole, either lonely or needing to borrow something random, like an apple peeler or a sponge. The HK was still in my hand when I wrenched the door open and found it wasn't Mole after all but a bicycle messenger sent by Alan Martin from Quantum. The messenger's eyes grew saucer-wide at the piece in my hand.

"It's all right," I quipped. "I promise not to shoot the messenger."

"Yeah, whatever you say, lady. Just sign here, and I'll swear I never met you."

The bike messenger handed me a sealed envelope and a clip-board with shaky hands. I took the board and scrawled my name on the appropriate line. Without another word, he turned and walked briskly down the hall, anxious to be on his way.

I closed the door with my foot and ripped into the package, discarding the wrappings onto the table beside the door. I flipped through the contract, making sure that Mr. Martin had signed and dated everything on all the appropriate lines, then tipped the envelope further, and a thumb drive slid into my hand. I was satisfied enough to put Mole to work.

The pack slung easily over my shoulder, I took the thumb drive with Mole's detailed instructions and locked my door. There was nothing but silence coming from within, which I found puzzling. I put my ear to the door and listened to the faint, rapid clacking of fingers as they raced across a keyboard. I knocked. After waiting the requisite minute with no sign of movement from within, I repeated my rap, putting a little more force behind my knuckles. No avail. Was Mole ignoring me, which he'd been known to do, or was he plugged into his headset? There was no way of knowing unless...I kicked the bottom of the door with the toe of my shoe, creating an obnoxious amount of racket.

Seconds later, there was a shift in the lighting coming from beneath Mole's door, and the security peephole darkened. Unless he was expecting the Feds, who else would be at his door but me? After a long succession of locks were disengaged and the security chain was pulled from its track, the door finally opened. I stepped inside without waiting to be invited.

Mole's loft lacked anything that could be construed as homey or cozy. It had more of a science-fiction prop-room feel to it. Thick, dark drapes permanently covered the windows—whether to keep out the sun or prying eyes, I wasn't sure. There was no way to open a window, a big factor in why the air was so thick and smelled of microwaved food. A constant hum emanated from the multiple computers, which added to the stuffiness of the room.

"Morning, Scout," Mole deadpanned when he caught sight of my backpack.

To be honest, I had never asked Mole how old he was. I guess I had always assumed he was around my age, a few years north of thirty. His pasty complexion was a stark contrast to the jet-black hair that, as usual, hung past his ears in uncombed hanks. His black-rimmed eyeglasses were vintage military issue, circa mid-1940s, and had left permanent indentations at his temples. By the length of the stubble on his cheeks and chin—and the goatish smell coming from him—I'd say Mole was in desperate need of a hygiene break.

"I'm following up on something," I explained. "In the meantime, I have a job for you."

There are two kinds of computer hackers in the world: those known as white hats and others known as black hats. White hats are usually employed by federal alphabet agencies—FBI, CIA, DOD—to protect against being infiltrated by black hats. Black hats are usually no more than brilliant and bored loners, teens using their smartphones and laptops to break into organizations, businesses, schools, or other government offices for kicks. Mole claimed the title of gray hat with a dark overtone.

"Have you ever heard of Quantum Electronic Design?" I asked.

"Quantum? Are you kidding? They're that local company who recently scored a gig with NASA with their cutting-edge temperature profiling technology."

I nodded. "I met with their CEO, Alan Martin, who wants to assure his board that the company is bulletproof. I need you to do the usual. Here's your info." I handed him the thumb drive.

"Piece of cake. I don't suppose you care if I look around while I'm in there? These exec types always have the best porn stashes."

Mole never left home and, therefore, never dated tangible people, though I had heard more than I cared to about his on-line relationships. His entire life, social included, existed on the web. There's a fine line when it comes to stuff you didn't want or need to know about your friends, and Mole crossed it often. I'd learned not to cringe at the graphic details because it only encouraged him.

"Let me know when you have something," I said, "related to the job." With Mole, clarifications were best.

Mole gave a mock sigh. "You take all the fun out of life."

"But I pay well," I countered and turned back toward the door. Mole gave me a military salute as I left.

Crosstown traffic was light as I drove east on I-84, which follows the Columbia River into the Gorge. The sun and the clouds were competing for dominance overhead, with the sun failing to yield. According to the police report, the trailhead I was looking for was at exit fifty-eight, roughly an hour's drive out of town. I set the cruise control at a legal sixty-five and watched the pristine scenery go by. Road signs directed me to pull off the highway and into a graveled parking lot beside the designated trailhead. There were no other vehicles in the lot, which was a good sign. I didn't want to run into anyone, and the fewer people slogging along the trail the better, in case any evidence had been left behind.

With my pack on my shoulders, I began my ascent on the clearly marked trail, which looked to be rarely used other than by the true die-hards. Okay, poor choice of words, given the reason for my visit. The trail was rocky, a little soft in places, and immediately sloped uphill. I wasn't that far from the city, but the air was so clean and crisp, the surrounding beauty so natural and untouched by man, it felt like I'd wandered into the last wild place on earth. The appeal that drew trail runners like Dr. Phillips was immediate. That was to say, I got the scenery bit, but not the running up and down mountains piece. I'd stick to the relative flats of Forest Park, thank you very much.

Forty-five minutes later, I was struck by the thought that Dr. Phillips had been sadistically deranged. I'd already peeled off the sweatshirt. My calves ached, my quads burned, and my lungs didn't know how to handle the unadulterated air. The climate at this altitude was much cooler than on the valley floor, and a fine sheen of sweat made my shirt stick to my body, both warming and chilling me at the same time. The pain reliever masked my headache, but my stomach was trying to stage a coup as I burped sour fritter. Sweat ran down my forehead and into the gash across my brow, stinging like a mother—

"Holy hell!" My entire train of thought derailed when a grouse erupted from the brush beside me. The sudden dump of adrenaline cleared my head, giving me pause. Something niggled at me just under the surface of my awareness, a mental itch I couldn't scratch, something I'd taken in at the time and set on the mental back burner in hopes it would disappear from memory. It was about Vin. Well, not the man personally, but something he had said the night of his gallery showing.

I love you, Sam.

A shiver ran through me that had nothing to do with exertion or altitude. Some would say I'm a commitment-phobe, but I like to think of myself as cautious. I watched my parents go through the motions of marriage, and nothing I'd witnessed there made me want to run out and join that club. Not that I didn't try on a few casual relationships over the years, the longest run having lasted an entire six months. Of course, I was a walking cliché. I tended to cut out when things started to get serious. Love makes people messy.

Vin was different from any of the others, though. He was sensitive, yet strong. He could be both gentle and rough, and he knew exactly when to be either without any cues from me. He penned poetry and painted amazing works of art, even naming one after yours truly, but he was never gushy or clingy. Just thinking of Vin brought butterflies to my belly and prompted another shiver.

Man, I needed a drink. Preferably a double whisky, a bit of the hair. Sliding the pack from my shoulder, I grabbed my water bottle and took a long, deep pull, which my body gladly received, but it was best not to drain my supply so early in the journey. Reluctantly I twisted the cap back on, dropped it back into the pack, and popped half of the chocolate bar into my mouth before returning my burden to my shoulders.

I'd committed to memory a hand-drawn diagram of the alleged crime scene, complete with an orange-highlighted X marking the spot where a deputy had tagged the trail with a shot of fluorescent orange paint. I figured it was less than a half mile farther, so I continued my uphill slog while trying to avoid any thoughts not related to the case.

Finally I arrived at the scene of Dr. Phillips's death. The sweatshirt that had been tied around my waist became a makeshift ground cover onto which I spread the contents of the police file, arranging the photographs in chronological sequence. Then I hovered, getting a bird's-eye view and hoping the perspective and environs would prompt a brainstorm.

When nothing particular stirred, I focused on the photo of Dr. Phillips's supine body at the bottom of the ravine. I shifted my weight and peered over the edge of the trail—way the hell down. Nobody could have survived a fall like that. If bouncing off the cliff wall didn't do them in, meeting the boulders below would have.

First responders were on the scene after the 911 call from a hiker had gone out. They'd rappelled down to the ravine floor and pronounced Dr. Phillips on scene due to the extent of his injuries. Another photograph showed the disfigured form of Ronald Phillips in running clothes, his legs twisted the wrong way and his head lying at an impossible angle on his shoulders. Cause of death was evident by the large, gaping, blunt-force injury to the back of his head that had speckled the stone beneath it with gray matter. Thumbing through the ME's report, I read the results of the autopsy, which were inconclusive. The massive head trauma to the back of Dr. Phillips's head was consistent with the surfaces with which he'd come into contact on his fall, but the specific cause of the trauma could not be determined.

I understood Burnell's ruling a little better, given the lack of evidence otherwise. Still, nobody breaks into a dead man's home and steals the hard drive from his computer unless he was involved in something nefarious. I was tired, I was hungry, and since I'd stopped climbing, I'd begun to get a chill. Glancing at my watch, I realized I could be back home in less than two hours if I started off the mountain right then.

Don't give up five minutes before the miracle, Sammy, I heard Cindy's young voice in my head. That happened from time to time, ever since the kidnapping and Cindy's murder. The shrink my parents took me to as a kid had said that it was delayed post-traumatic stress brought on by survivor's guilt. I didn't know if I agreed with that, but whenever Cindy "spoke" to me, she tended to be spot on.

Cindy was in good company. The late Dr. Patrick James, "Doc" to his students, had been head of forensics at Quantico. He'd believed in me before I'd believed in me. "To successfully process a crime scene, one must look through the eyes of the perpetrator. An undisturbed crime scene will always reveal its story. It is your job to be able to read it." It had been Doc's unsubstantiated belief that every event leaves an impression behind, like a psychic echo.

Doc had become my mentor, taking me under his wing when he saw my potential. When I graduated from the academy, he'd pulled me aside and said, "Harris, your drive is commendable, like no other I've seen. You remind me a lot of myself when I was a young agent. But I fear your heart will get in the way of your work if you are not diligent. That inner fire that drives you is both your strength and your weakness."

I'd sought out Doc's guidance often in those early years with the bureau, especially when things got frustrating and my heart tried to override my judgment. "Sometimes I just feel like I am the only person in this agency that sees the system as broken."

"I understand your frustrations, Harris. We have a democratic judicial system, and everyone has rights that cannot be stripped during any point of an investigation. It is our job to make sure everything is done correctly the first time."

"You make us sound like babysitters."

"No, we are the Federal Bureau of Investigation. You're one of the most astute cadets that Quantico has churned out in a very long time, but it may come to pass that you inadvertently draw a line in the sand." Dr. Patrick James, teacher and prophet.

I closed my eyes, took a deep breath to still my senses, and listened to the wind whispering its secrets to the pine boughs. Water trickled in tiny streams down the rocks from all the rain the past few days. A bug buzzed its wings nearby.

Was this what it was like as Dr. Phillips jogged down this trail, heading home to his wife and daughter? What had he seen? I turned to face up the trail toward the bend that Dr. Phillips would have rounded just before reaching the point where I stood. There were no obvious signs of altercation. But more importantly, I couldn't see any obvious newly dislodged stone or any other overt trip hazard. The path was defined at its edges due to Dr. Phillips's frequent passing and hikers who used the same trail. If Dr. Phillips had encountered another person, where would they have come from? My attention turned to the embankment on the opposite side of the trail. Would they have waited here on the trail and in plain sight? Perhaps they'd taken cover—maybe up the embankment—which would have provided an excellent view of the trail in both directions and allowed them to have heard Dr. Phillips's slapping through the mud on his approach.

Glad to have brought them, I pulled the latex gloves and a zippered bag from my pack and stuffed them in my pocket. The brush along the embankment side of the trail was weather worn, and who knew how many deputies had trampled through it. But don't give up thirty seconds before the miracle or you'll miss the fern fronds at the edge of the embankment that had been bent and bruised.

In and of itself, this meant little. It could have easily happened when the body was being recovered, or it could have been a hiker or passing wildlife. But it was what I saw when I looked closer that had me scrambling up the incline: a branch about an inch in diameter had snapped in half under the weight of something, suggesting that whatever passed through here was heavier than a deer or a coyote. Could have been a decent-sized cougar, but it could have just as easily been a human. It wouldn't hurt to follow up.

The embankment sloped upward gently before it leveled out about twelve feet up. I began my search, starting with pacing out a fifty-square-foot grid. The native vegetation made progress tough. Oregon grape, a ridged-leaf evergreen shrub that thrived on forest floors year-round, made seeing what might be on the ground challenging. Light gray moss hung thick off the trees, giving the tall guardians an ancient, wizened look. *Talk to me*, I pleaded of the forest, but it offered me nothing. I had no chance of finding footprints on the forest floor because of all the vegetation and dead fir needles.

After what seemed like the longest forty-five minutes of my life, I had nothing to show for my tenacity except frustration and hunger. A log offered a place to sit and come to grips with my field trip not being as enlightening as I had hoped, but the scene was old, and banking on any sort of discovery had been my bad. The moss was damp against the seat of my pants, but I didn't care. I rested my elbows on my knees and my head in my hands as I tried to conjure Doc for a bit of advice, but his voice in my head was as silent as the forest.

I stood up and wiped the dampness from the butt of my jeans and decided to call it a day. I stepped over the log I'd been sitting on and turned to gather my things left on the trail. That was when I saw them. I nearly slapped my own forehead. I'd been so busy looking down that I'd missed the cigarette butts—all eight of them—that had been stubbed out and crammed into the rough, crevassed bark of an old-growth fir tree.

Okay, I didn't want to jump to conclusions. These butts could have come from anyone, not necessarily a killer. However, I found that idea very unlikely, since only devoted hikers—outside of the occasional curious securities specialist doing a side job—would make this trek. It's not the sort of locale teens or nicotine addicts would come to sneak a chain smoke. Logic dictated that die-hard hikers and trail runners tended to be on the healthier side of nutty, so the chances of one of them maintaining a smoking habit was slim to no way. There was a lot to be said for human nature, and this felt like someone that had been completely out of their element. Like a hired gun—someone who knew Dr. Phillips's schedule and routine. All they had to do was settle in and wait.

I snapped the latex gloves on and set to collecting the cigarette butts, to which the scent of stale smoke still clung. Exposure to the weather would make trace DNA unlikely to run or to match to a suspect, but lo and behold, each one of the butts had been smoked down to the filter. Just like the ones I'd found at the Phillipses' back door.

The cigarettes hadn't been stubbed in the same spot. It was as if the perpetrator had made a game of it, finding fissures just the right size and angle to hold the foreign object in place. But there was something else tucked into the bark of the tree. I pulled at the dark bit of paper—a rolled-up, empty matchbook. In a perfect world where weather and time weren't an issue, this would undoubtedly have had the killer's fingerprints on it. However, in these conditions, getting a print was wishful thinking. Careful not to rip the damp paper, I gently unfurled it and found a rearing white horse printed on a black background but no text and, therefore, no way of knowing where the matchbook came from.

I stashed the matchbook in a separate plastic bag from the cigarette butts and gave the rest of the tree, and those immediately surrounding it, a closer look, but I made no further discoveries. By then, I was exhausted and outright starving. I backtracked to my stuff, scribbled some notes onto the back of a report page, drew a quick diagram of where I'd found the butts, and then zipped the lot into the backpack.

Climbing down the mountainside was considerably easier than going up it. It might have been the gravity thing, but I was like a barn-soured steed headed for food and a shower. The steep trail was treacherous and slick in spots—hell, it was a wonder I didn't take a header into the ravine. Even so, a shadow of doubt had crept into my perspective. Of course, I had nothing solid yet, but today's discoveries made me want to dig just a little bit deeper. Pam believed someone wanted her husband dead, and I needed her to expound on that idea.

CHAPTER NINE

BACK AT MY LOFT, I IMMEDIATELY MADE MYSELF A SANDWICH. Having something in my stomach improved my outlook in general, so I fished out the matchbook, which could possibly be my first lead. Or it might just be clueless garbage. It had dried a bit inside the baggie, so it was a little stiff and quite fragile to unroll. There were no identifying marks—no names or numbers—to distinguish the book of matches as having come from any specific place, aside from the depiction of a rearing white horse. Pictures saying a thousand words and all, I opened a new browser on the computer and started an online search for anything pertaining to a white pony, horse, or stallion. I came up with an album by Deftones, an alternative metal band. "White stallion" seemed to be associated with the porn industry, while "white horse" led me to the city council page for a small town in the Yukon, a pub in London, and a hole-in-the-wall tavern in a small town just south of Portland. The latter was promising.

By the looks of the bar online, it wasn't a dress-up sort of establishment. I changed out of my muddy jeans, showered, and opted for a fresh pair and a clean Rolling Stones t-shirt. Gun in the usual place, fully loaded with one in the chamber, safety on.

Getting out of Portland past rush hour proved easy. Traffic stayed moving all the way to Oregon City, where I joined a steady line of cars making the thirteen-mile trek south to the bedroom community of Sawtell. The overpowering, pungent wafts of road-killed skunk were potent reminders that I'd left the city. Green-and-white road signs directed me off the highway three miles from town. At first glance, the town didn't seem occupied. There was no foot traffic doing evening business (nothing except fast food and bars appeared to be open past five o'clock). I saw a few people tending their lawns and a couple of kids on their bikes with their baseball gloves slid over their bats and balanced on their handlebars riding home after ball practice. There were a handful of delinquents occupying the swings in the park beside the fire station in the center of town, but not a homeless person in sight.

I took a left at the four-way in the center of town, and the saloon was on my right, made obvious by the life-sized, rearing plastic horse mounted above the door. A rebel with a sense of humor had hit the stallion's molded genitals with a shot from a hot-pink paintball, which made me laugh out loud.

I pulled into a small alley on the east side of the building and found a place to squeeze in between two tall trucks whose drivers were obviously compensating for something. One had an oversized Confederate flag flying off the truck bed and a bumper sticker that defined gun control as using both hands. I shook my head and kept walking, all comments safely contained inside my head.

Big trucks meant little men with big attitudes. Or big men with little...feet. These were homegrown good ol' boys for sure, the sort that stick together in a stand of rural unification and blind allegiance. There might be more trouble inside than I wanted. Or the exact amount to get what I'd come for.

None of the trucks in the lot matched the one parked outside the Phillipses' home, but that didn't mean the man who'd done this to my face wasn't inside. I itched to return the favor. I ducked past a crowd of big-haired twentysomethings gathered on the sidewalk just outside the door having a vape or a smoke. The air inside throbbed with the bass of a live band playing covers of classic rock. The doorman, a wide individual whose belly lapped over his belt and peeked out from under a black button-down, asked me for my ID and a four-dollar cover without looking up from his phone. I laid the bills on his outstretched palm and flashed him my driver's license. Only then did he look up, and he winced when he saw my face.

"You should see the other guy," I said as I waved off his offer to stamp the back of my hand and stepped inside.

The saloon was divided into two sides by a long bar, with seating and restrooms on the left and a handful of tables around a raised dance floor on the right. A stripper pole was in the middle of the dance floor; I could only hope it was just a prop. Half of the tattered barstools were claimed by a group of grizzled, old men bent protectively over their beers. The rest of the seats were vacant. I didn't like the floor plan. There wasn't an easy way out if the front door wasn't an option. I ended up taking a table in an unobtrusive corner on the left side and waited for a waitress. As was my habit, I kept my back to the wall so I had full view of the front door and both sets of restrooms.

The band, CRUSH, according to the limp banner that hung behind the drummer, was set up near the dance floor. They'd cranked up their amps to eleven and were playing a Guns N' Roses cover tune. They weren't half bad.

The cocktail waitress came by with an empty tray and a friendly face. The name tag pinned to her overstretched t-shirt read Denise. I would've bet her cowboy boots had never seen the top side of a cow patty. "What can I get for you, hon?"

"What do you have on tap?" I asked, hoping for something other than the usual weak American swill most commonly advertised during sports events. She named a local porter that was my usual go-to, so I ordered a pint with a shot of Jameson on the side. Denise disappeared with the promise to be right back. She wasn't lying. I dropped a twenty on her tray: ten for the drinks, the rest for her.

"Do you work here every night?" I asked, hoping my generous tip made her willing to talk.

"All but Thursdays and Sundays. Why?" Denise gave me a coy smile that said, *In case you're hitting on me, I don't really go for girls.*

"I'm looking for someone—a big guy, bald, might drive a lifted green pickup, and he may be a regular."

Denise's cheeks paled slightly. She eyed the room around us and lowered her voice lest anyone possibly hear her over the band. "Sounds to me like you're talkin' 'bout Russell Tompkins. He's usually in here 'bout now. What would a decent gal like you be wantin' with Russell?"

I ignored her question. "What can you tell me about Tompkins?"

"I can tell you he's one mean son of a bitch." Denise leaned near my ear and dropped her voice. "You hear about what he did to his old lady?"

I shook my head.

"Well, the way I heard it is the cops had to keep going out to his place in the hills outside of town 'cause he kept using his wife's face as a punching bag. She finally got the guts to get a restraining order on him, and then two days later she up and disappears. Nobody's seen hide nor hair of her since. Russell says she's run off, but we all know that's a bunch of bull. Russell didn't have a wife, he had a possession. Ain't no way he'd just let her go like that. He'd hunt her down, drag her back, and beat the hell out of her, then kill her for her daring."

"Well, I'm sure the police are looking into it," I offered.

"Local cops? No way. They all grew up around here and are either friends with Russell or scared of him." Denise squared her shoulders and looked me in the eyes. "You didn't hear any of that from me, you understand?"

"Hear what?" I discreetly slipped her another twenty. "You'll let me know if you see him, won't you?"

"Sure, but what are you going to do? You're just a woman! Russell will tear you apart."

Oh, I'd like to see that attempt. "Just let me know if he comes in or you hear where he is, okay?"

Denise's next smile said, *Whatever. Your funeral.* I tossed the Jameson down my throat and chased it with the porter, finishing it off just in time for Denise to come around and ask if I wanted a refill.

Two hours, two whiskys, and two beers later, Tompkins still hadn't shown. It was time to change tactics.

It had been my experience that bartenders knew everything that happened inside their establishment, both behind the bar and in the front of the house. It was guaranteed that they knew more about their customers than they really cared to. The White Horse's bartender stayed busy pulling shots of well tequila for a twenty-one-year-old's birthday party just getting started on a long night at a table beside the dance floor.

By that hour, the old men who had been occupying the bar-stools had left and tottered back home. Two younger guys who would have blended well into a Jeff Foxworthy show took their places. They were like mismatched bookends. The taller one of the pair had a mop of dirty-blonde hair tied back into a long, messy ponytail. His shorter, stockier counterpart wore his black, wavy hair to his shoulders. They both smelled like they'd never formed a relationship with a stick of deodorant. Motor oil stained their jeans; tattooed forearms like stamped lamb shanks jutted from the rolled sleeves of their Carhartt work shirts. They were the two musketeers, each other's sidekick, Blondie and Shorty. The kind of guys you didn't want to meet in that proverbial dark alley.

I stepped up to the bar and slid onto a stool two down from Blondie. The bartender dropped a thick cardboard coaster on the marred bar in front of me and lifted his chin: *What'll it be?* His eyes showed a hard life mixed with a certain strain of meanness cultivated at a young age by the heavy hands of a parent. I didn't know whether to pity him or fear him.

I decided to charm him instead. "Good evening, sir. Wondering if I might ask you a question or two."

His steel eyes took in my every detail but gave no inkling of reply. My best poker face didn't flinch under his scrutiny. I could tell he was a man of few words, so I decided to make the ones I might muster from him count. "Russell Tompkins—where might I find him?" It's been my observation over the years that males were overtly loyal to their own kind and tended to not want to rat out another fella.

"Somewhere fuckin' your momma," he said with a sneer.

Ignorant humans like this were dangerous. Their position dictated loyalty to the establishment, yet their associations within the town couldn't be denied. They knew who was going down on who, who was dealing what to who, and all the dramas in between. They were the poor man's therapists. Sure, I could've risen to the occasion and given this redneck a verbal ball-kicking, but I still needed to find Tompkins. So I took a deep breath and pushed on. Sweetly.

"I just need three minutes of his time to answer a couple of questions." I reached into my pocket for a business card, and the bartender flinched like I was going for my gun. I slid the card wrapped in a hundred across the bar with two fingers. "If you see Tompkins, please pass him my card."

The bartender looked down at my offering but didn't make a move to take either. His mouth was a hard, thin line of indecision. Pocketing the cash was as good as saying *Sure, I'll cooperate.* Outing Tompkins might get him and his bar trashed.

As I knew they would, Blondie and Shorty had been eavesdropping on our exchange, and it had clearly piqued their interest. "What d'ya want with ol' Russell?" asked Blondie.

"You a cop?" spouted Shorty.

I turned my hard eyes on them both. "My business with Russell is my own. As far as who I am, that is of no concern of yours either." I turned my attention back to the bartender, and pointed to my card still wrapped in a Benjamin on the counter. "You give that to Russell when you see him."

Without another word, I slid from the barstool and made for the door. I could feel the three men's eyes boring into my back as I walked out.

CHAPTER TEN

A BRISK, EASTERLY WIND HAD KICKED UP WHILE I WAS INSIDE EN-joying the local culture and had scattered the clouds to expose hints of a star-filled sky. I backtracked through the pothole-ridden alley to the lot where I had left my 2010 Geländewagen, the only German SUV in the lot. I almost made it.

The two musketeers from the bar, Blondie and Shorty, appeared from out of nowhere, effectively cutting me off from my getaway.

"What business do you have with Russell?" asked Blondie insistently, obviously the mouthpiece for the two.

I turned to keep the circling pair in full view. "You know that saying about how I could tell you but then I'd have to shoot you?"

They guffawed in unison. "Bullshit," Blondie threw in, then worked a gob of phlegm from deep in his throat and lobbed it in my direction where it fell short of my foot. The thick smell of bourbon coming from the two would make their movements sluggish and awkward. Never underestimate angry drunks, how-ever, especially when there are two of them and only one of you.

Even in the unlit alley, their darkening expressions were evi-dent. I was purposefully taunting two feral dogs. My best option was to strike hard and fast and not stop until they were down.

"You've got a pretty smart mouth for a woman standing by herself in a dark parking lot," Blondie egged. "Bad things could happen in a place like this."

"Oh," I smirked, "guaranteed." I threw the first punch, a pow-erful jab that exploded the center of Shorty's face. His look of shock was to be expected. He went to the ground and stayed there.

I knew Blondie was going to be a whole different ball game. He came at me with fire in his eyes. He telegraphed his first blow weeks in advance. I deflected the punch with a sweep of my left arm while taking a step closer and accompanying the block with a counter jab to his jaw using the side of my elbow. The blonde behemoth swayed for a second, and I thought he was going to go down. I thought wrong. His rage made him quicker, and he grabbed me up in a bear hug. My hands were free, but of no use. There was no space for attack. Blondie's face was snugged up to my shoulder, so I brought the meaty part of my palms up to his cheekbones to mask his face and put my thumbs in his philtrum—that indent beneath the nose and above the lip—pushing back and up in one move until I knocked him off his center of gravity and exposed his neck. My counterattack continued with a solid punch to his esophagus followed by a knee to the groin. I didn't want to kill him, but I needed him down.

Shorty regained consciousness and picked himself up off the pavement. The moon glinted off the knife in his hand. One glance at Blondie assured me that he was going to stay where I put him for the moment, but he was rallying quickly. Whether he'd have any fight left in him when he got vertical was another story.

Shorty sneered at me as he circled. I kept one eye on Blondie and the other on the knife in Shorty's hand. We orbited the same spot on the parking lot three times before Shorty made his move. He pounced and slashed the knife out in a wide arc aimed at my belly. I deflected the attack with my arm and jutted my hips back, taking his target out of his reach. Had he connected, Shorty would have gutted me like a pig, which wasn't a good way to go.

Instead of sliding Shorty's arm away and attempting to dis-arm him with a classic defense move, I brought my body to his. From this stance, I was able to force his hand up and back so that his arm was hyperextended in the wrong position, forcing him to double over at the waist or dislocate his shoulder. A series of rapid knee blows to the stomach drove the air from his lungs. His fight gone, the knife clattered to the ground, and I kicked it under a car parked nearby. When I released Shorty's arm, he crumpled to the ground a second time, but he needed to stay there once and for all. I struck out with the side of my hand in a pseudo karate-chop and connected with the side of his neck, a strategic pressure point. He fell back, alive—but dead to the world.

Jesusmaryandjoseph! Blondie was on his feet *again*. What was in the water around here? Was he stupid or just...stupid? I didn't give him a chance to gather his gusto for another attack. I drew the HK and leveled it at the space between his eyes.

"Get down. *Now!*" I screamed when understanding didn't seem to register on his face.

Air whistled through Blondie's mangled nose when he breathed, and he spit a bloody tooth onto the ground. He knew he was beaten and lowered himself to his knees.

"I'm going over and getting into my rig. If you move, I will shoot you, understand?"

Blondie nodded. Defeated, he began to sob, which almost made me feel bad. I said *almost*. Alcohol giveth courage, HK taketh away. The parking lot was still empty except for myself and the two fools, so I jogged to the Geländewagen, jammed it into reverse, and got the hell out of there.

{ ∗ ∗ ∗ }

Vin was waiting at my building's front door when I pulled in. Only then did I remember our plans for a stay-in date night. My apologies were plentiful as I walked up to him and dug out my keys.

Vin held the door open while I squeezed past. "You were with your detective friend?"

"Nope. This wasn't police related." Okay, it was a gray area. It was more like I was cleaning up the PB's mess.

Vin pressed the button for the elevator. "Do you think that's a good idea—going out in the field without backup?"

The elevator doors slid open, and I got on first so Vin didn't get the chance to see me roll my eyes. Vin's only experience with police work, or "going out in the field," came from television and movies. He just assumed that I worked with a team who watched my back until we all high-fived at the end of a case. I'd experienced firsthand what happened to relationships after lovers had discovered that nothing scared me, and they were presented with the whole gritty truth. Guys like Vin want to see the good in everyone. I'd seen some of the worst that humanity had to offer.

The elevator doors shut on my silence. We rode up to my loft without another word. At my front door, I paused and turned toward Vin with a seriousness in my eyes that he'd never seen before. "I appreciate your concern, Vin, but this is what I do. I chase bad guys, always have. Trust me when I say I can hold my own. I'm really all right."

I fumbled my key into the lock and let us inside. Vin locked the door behind him and turned with a concerned look on his face. "The FBI," he randomly began. "You never really talk about your time with them."

"No," I said flatly, "I don't."

"But why not?" He closed the space between us and took my hands in his. "You can, you know. I find it...interesting."

Interesting? That had me cocking an eyebrow. "What part of it do you find interesting?" I was well aware of the change in my tone.

Vin sensed it as well. "I just mean, interesting in a Hardy Boys, mystery-novel sort of way. You were one of the good guys, like in films."

"Maybe film noir."

Vin angled his head and knit his brows questioningly.

"Let's just say the good guys don't always win, and the bad guys frequently go unpunished." I felt my ire begin to raise. I took a deep breath and softened my manner. I slid my arms around Vin's waist. "I've always found the past has no right infringing on my present moment, especially moments like this." Our kiss in that moment was much more enjoyable than chatting up the past.

We spent what was left of the evening on the patio off my bedroom with glasses of wine, looking out over the city and talking about everything and nothing. When the evening chill set in, we moved inside, settling back on my bed and watching my favorite movie as a kid, *The Princess Bride*, until we both found more interest in each other. That night, for the first time in a long time, I slept dreamlessly, wrapped in Vin's warm embrace.

By the time I woke up the next day, the morning was almost gone. I yawned and stretched—and found I was alone. Vin was gone. "Vin?" I called out, expecting to hear him answer from the kitchen. Only quiet.

I threw the covers aside and, wearing nothing but my own skin, padded into the empty kitchen. From behind me came the sound of the knob being turned. In all my nakedness, I turned back and made a hasty retreat toward the bedroom. I only made it as far as the door.

"You know," said Vin, surprised, "I had a fantasy that went a little something like this when I was a teenager."

I turned seductively to face him, my skin reacting to the cool breeze that followed him in through the door. Vin swung the door shut with his foot and set a white paper bag with two steaming cups on the table. "Want to know how my fantasy ends?" His arms circled my waist, and he pulled me against him. I could judge by his rigidity how this particular fantasy was going to end. Like a new bride, Vin swept me up and carried me back to bed.

{∗ ∗ ∗}

Our coffee had long gone cold. The sheets were in a tangle at our feet, and the ceiling fan turned lazy circles above us. I could have lain like that the rest of the day.

Vin lifted himself up on an elbow and looked down on me. "I didn't press you for the details last night because I thought you would tell me eventually, but what really happened the other day, Sam?"

I folded my arm under my head and cleared my throat. "I was hired to look into something and found somebody got there before I did. We scuffled, he hit me. I lived, he got away."

"But where were the police through all this?" he pressed. "I thought you worked with your cop friend on these things."

"This wasn't through the police department. This was a private client."

"Maybe it should be police business."

"Yeah," I scoffed, "funny you should say that." I really didn't want to get into that.

Vin suddenly got very serious. "Look, Samantha, I'm no fool. I know how much our lives contrast each other. You keep things close, and trust doesn't come naturally—"

"You make me sound like a wild dog."

That made Vin throw his head back and give an honest, eye-crinkling chuckle. "More like the most beautiful, spunky, dangerous cat that I hope to one day earn the trust of enough that you'll drop some of those walls."

I wasn't excited to pick up where we'd left off about my time with the FBI. I'd always been vague with everyone about my past, including the abduction. I know what you're wondering: How can I have a relationship with a man and keep the bulk of what makes me *me* out of our conversations? I knew from experience that men got instantly insecure and threatened when they found out that the woman they're sleeping with could incapacitate them six different ways with her bare hands. Their penises simply couldn't process that sort of information, which tended to put a damper on the relationship.

"That sounds like you want to tame me," I laughed.

Vin pulled me closer. I turned onto my side and wrapped myself around him.

"I love you, Sam. I want to keep you safe."

A familiar paralysis clenched my chest, reminding me that love makes people messy. I found it a gesture of love to deceive the people I cared for, and I kept them in the dark for their own good. It made all our lives easier. It helped me keep *them* safe.

We would have gone for a third roll in the sack, but Vin needed to get across town. I walked him to the door—with clothes on this time—and our parting was sweet. Vin planted a kiss atop my head and told me to watch myself. I smiled and told him to have a great day, then watched as he walked down the hall and got into the elevator, the doors closing behind him.

After Vin's departure, I showered and dressed in jeans and a clean black t-shirt that had The Ramones printed across the chest in big red letters. I was just pulling a comb through my hair when there was a series of short, swift, impatient-sounding raps on my door. It was probably Mole emerging from his lair to give me news on the Quantum job.

Turned out my assumption was way off. It was Wickowski, wearing an unusually angry shade of red in his cheeks. The minute I opened the door, he stormed in, forgoing the customary invite.

"Hey, come on in," I said, shutting the door behind him. "To what do I owe this pleasure?"

Wickowski turned with sarcasm on his tongue but stopped short when he got his first good look at the wound on my brow. "What the hell happened to you?"

"There was a misunderstanding," I said vaguely.

"Should I be worried about the other guy?" Wickowski's question lacked humor.

"Not yet."

"'Not yet'—what the hell does that mean?" Wickowski's simmering temper began to heat up. He'd walked in with an attitude, and my flippancy wasn't making it any better.

"Means I haven't found him yet. But I will, so ask me how he is after that."

The scarlet of Wickowski's cheeks deepened. I imagined he was counting to ten in his head before changing the subject. "Phillips's neighbor phoned her local precinct, concerned that your lengthy visit seemed suspicious. She found the Phillipses' back door busted. What the hell are you into, Samantha?" Wickowski was fuming. He'd never addressed me by my first name. This couldn't be good. "If you've found a lead in the Phillips case, you're bound—not only by my policy and protocol but also by professional courtesy—to keep me and the department in the loop. But that's not why I'm here. I told you twenty-four hours." Wickowski jabbed a finger at his wristwatch.

The Portland Police Bureau ruled Dr. Phillips's death an accident. If you and the department had done your jobs right, we wouldn't be having this conversation was what I wanted to say. Instead, I made the wisest choice and said nothing. Once again someone else's protocol was tripping me up, and I wasn't even employed by the Portland PB. It was petty, I knew, but I'd never responded well to scolding. Awkward silence stretched between us like an estuary. I made the first move by breaking away, retrieving the file from my bedroom, and slapping it into Wickowski's outstretched hand.

Wickowski glared at me a second longer. When he realized he wasn't going to get an apology, he turned to leave, giving the door a frame-rattling slam behind him.

CHAPTER ELEVEN

I'M NOT PRONE TO SULKING, BUT MY FIGHT WITH WICKOWSKI tainted the rest of the afternoon. Normally an hour at the boxing gym around the corner would have helped my mood, but by the end of thirty minutes, my head was pounding and sweat was running down my forehead, stinging the cut on my brow. I walked back home as disgruntled as I'd been when I left.

There was a message slid under my door when I got home: *Sammy, bring me a beer.* I smiled at the message because it was code for "I found something you should see." Mole was known to get very ornery if I arrived empty-handed. He'd once withheld information until his demands were met.

By chance, there happened to be two bottles of porter—my last two, but this was worth it. I made a mental note to restock and knocked on Mole's door.

"Christ on a crutch, Sammy! What the hell happened to your face, and what does the other guy look like?"

"Ask Wickowski." Mole looked at me, confusion written on his face. I shook my head. *Never mind.* "So what do you have?"

Mole popped the cap off his bottle against the side of his desk and took a long pull from it. "All right"—he swiped the back of his hand across his mouth—"to start with, I finished up the Quantum job. Getting to the embedded file was cake. In my opinion, if Martin wants to assure his board of the company's security, he should resign now and forgo the embarrassment." Mole snorted a laugh and shook his head as if recalling a joke. "Like most companies, Quantum's security is outdated. They're relying on over-the-counter software. By the time it hits the store shelves, someone like me"—Mole took a small bow like a ballerina—"has already figured out how to hack it. I've made several suggestions in the report. Long story short: I got inside through three different firewalls. I set some temporary patches, and I stress *temporary*, but ultimately Quantum needs to upgrade their security system across the board. He keeps his kinky porn under better protection."

"I trust you'll word your findings more professionally in your report," I suggested. "I don't have time to translate and rewrite them for the client."

"Oh, totally. And I'll omit all comments regarding his tastes for contortionist porn."

"Mole, how many times have I told you that you can't wander around while you're inside a client's computer?"

"Fuck that. These guys keep the best porn on their computers at the office where their wives can't get to it. You really need to know a person's tastes if you're going build a profile on them."

"Martin's taste runs on the blonde side," I pointed out.

"Blondes with oversized ta-tas," Mole said, holding his hands up in front of his chest.

"They do say blondes have more fun."

"And that chick on there—man, talk about flexible! She could bend herself in half and—"

I held my hand up to silence him, which saved me from the details. "Mole, please, I don't want to know. I have something else for you. See what you can find on a Russell Tompkins. T-O-M-P-K-I-N-S."

Mole took a seat in the captain's chair in front of his twin monitor screens, and I watched him hack into the Portland PB's mainframe. A dialog box opened up and asked for a ten-digit password. That was when I diverted my attention. I couldn't lie if I didn't know what he was doing. Ignorance can indeed be bliss.

A long, low whistle made me look back to the screen. "Wow, Sammy, you pick nice friends." The printer on the table beside me woke up and spat out page after page of text. When it was done, I took the bundle, tapped it into a neat stack, and began to read.

"He killed his neighbor's dog when he was nine because it was barking at him through the fence," Mole read from the screen. "It says here that he slit the dog's throat with a broken bottle. I think I saw a horror movie about this kid."

I picked up reading where Mole left off. "He broke into the hard stuff at fifteen with his first armed robbery, and he did a stint inside as a juvenile for attacking some kid in shop class with a hammer. In '94 he was arrested for rape and assault, but the woman wouldn't press charges, and they cut him loose. Two months later, he was busted on a possession charge and sentenced to ten years in the Oregon State Penitentiary. He was released after serving his entire sentence and married his prison pen pal girlfriend." I had already heard about the former Mrs. Tompkins.

Mole continued reading. "Last report on Tompkins is that he's listed as a person of interest in the disappearance of a local gal, a backup singer for a classic rock tribute band. Nice guy." Sarcasm dripped from his words. "And you know him how?"

I pointed to my head. "I ran into him yesterday."

Mole's eyes grew round. "He's the other guy? Please tell me he doesn't know where you live."

"I can't be that hard to find. My name is on the buzzer."

"Great," Mole fretted. "But you should know that I don't do interrogations well—like you and rules. If anyone comes asking, I'm going to pretend I don't know you. It isn't that I don't love you, Sammy. I just do alive much better than dead."

With Tompkins's rap sheet and Mole's Quantum report in hand, I returned to my place. The odds of Tompkins coming after me were slim. He couldn't possibly be that stupid. Regardless, I set the dead bolt. I had every intention of kicking it on the couch and watching movies for the rest of the afternoon, but I couldn't get my mind to shut off long enough to settle into anything, so I went for a walk to clear my mind.

I didn't have a destination and wasn't planning on walking past Blackwell Gallery until I found myself outside, looking in. *Samantha* had been relocated to the wall just inside the front door. A small "Property of Artist/Not for Sale" note had been affixed to the wall beside it. *Property of artist.* In my current mood, I couldn't even muster an internal dialogue for how I felt about that.

I kept walking and found myself pushing through the doors of a local brewpub-slash-hotel. I ordered a dungeon burger to go, which came loaded with grilled mushrooms and melty swiss cheese and Cajun-spiced tater tots. I downed a pint of the house stout while I waited. With bag in hand, I hurried home so I could eat while it was hot.

Nobody was waiting for me when I got home, and I didn't encounter Mole on the way in. The door secured behind me, I helped myself to a few fingers of whisky and settled onto the couch with my burger and tots. Nothing of much interest was on the television until I came across the *Magnum, P.I.* marathon on cable. Twelve hours of Tom Selleck and his red Ferrari bumbling through petty crimes in paradise. I couldn't imagine a better way to waste what was left of the night, but the moment I was horizontal, I fell asleep.

My cell phone woke me up several hours later. Daybreak was already underway.

"Harris." Wickowski sounded grumpy and irritated, which meant his attitude hadn't improved with the hours. "Patrol found a body a little while ago down at the waterfront. The ME is taking it away right now. How fast can you meet me at the station?"

"What does this have to do with me?" I asked.

"We'll chat when you get to the precinct."

"Does this mean we're cool?"

"This means I'm professional enough not to bring my personal grudges to work."

"So we're not cool?"

"Just get your ass downtown."

"That almost sounded like an ord—" The phone slammed down in my ear, cutting me off midsentence. I guess that answered my question.

{* * *}

A half hour later, I was let in through the precinct's front doors by the guard on duty. I could have arrived in half that time, but I'd delayed myself purposefully so as not to appear to be following anyone's orders. I was sort of a brat that way. The guard escorted me across the lobby floor to the security kiosk that had been set in the center of the room post-9/11.

At the security station, Richard, as his badge denoted, had me sign in and surrender in my weapon. I made sure the chamber was clear, ejected the magazine, and passed the two pieces over the counter to him. He tagged them with my name and locked them in a cubby beneath the counter before waving me through the metal detector. On the other side, he clipped a visitor's badge to the lapel of my jacket. I knew my way to the third floor from there.

Recent statewide budget cuts had affected everyone with a city or state job, but the cuts had been felt most deeply among public servants. The place was deserted.

Unfortunately the one person I least expected to see was sitting at his desk behind a closed door. Captain Burnell and I made uneasy eye contact through the glass walls of his office as I passed. His salted brown hair was worn at regulation length, high and tight. Twenty years my senior, Burnell had kept himself military fit. He wore a sour scowl on his pasty face like a trademark, but

I never took it personally. I shot him a sweet smile and gave a little four-finger wiggly wave hello. He glared at me and pulled himself up straighter in his chair.

The third-floor homicide detail had an open layout, its desks scattered in a semi-organized pattern. Wickowski's desk was in the corner, farthest from Burnell's office.

Wickowski poked his head out from a windowless conference room. By the bags he was hauling beneath his eyes, it looked like he hadn't slept between shifts and wasn't looking forward to the challenges of another day. The door closed behind me. I took a seat at the table, and Wickowski did the same opposite me. He was doing a fine job of keeping the lid on his temper.

"At 0400 this morning, a patrol car spotted a vehicle parked beneath the west side of the Marquam Bridge." The area Wickowski was referring to was popular with hookers. A lot of things went down under that bridge. "The inside of our vic's truck was redecorated with what used to be inside his head. Forensics is still working the site, but the body was just delivered to the ME downstairs."

"That's great. And you called me down here for this because...?"

"Because we found a business card in the vic's front pocket. Want to venture a guess as to whose card it was?"

"How many guesses do I get?"

"Just one."

"Mine?" I ventured, knowing damn good and well that was where this little song and dance was leading.

"Yours."

I yawned. "Do you plan on calling me in every time my business card shows up on a dead guy? If so, I might have to start charging mileage—"

Wickowski slammed a flat palm on the conference table. "Cut the shit for once, Harris, and be square with me. What's going on?"

"Did your vic have any ID on him?"

"None on his person, but the expired temporary on the truck was issued to..." Wickowski referred to a folded piece of paper in his pocket. "...a Russell Tompkins. Ring a bell?"

Judging by the color in Wickowski's cheeks, I figured getting dodgy would only exacerbate things. I came clean about the entire story, from the surprise visitor I'd found at the Phillips's house, to finding the matchbook on the mountain, and then the subsequent brawl in the parking lot of the White Horse.

"When were you going to catch me up with all this?" Wickowski asked.

"It would have come up eventually, Wick. Now seemed like a good time."

Wickowski puffed his cheeks out and exhaled long toward the ceiling. "And you wonder why the FBI and you didn't get along."

"Oh, I've never wondered that."

"Dammit, Harris, you've really put me in a spot here." Wickowski pushed away from the table and began to pace the long side of the room. "I'm going to allow you to stay with the Phillips case—but with stipulations."

A sarcastic guffaw escaped before I could catch it. "*Allow* me to stay? Wickowski, if it wasn't for me, this case would still be listed as closed and a murderer would be walking around, free and clear."

Wickowski kept talking as if I'd said nothing at all. "Stipulation number one: Any leads will be followed up through the department. And you will go in with backup—no more of this lone gunman crap." Wickowski raised a hand to silence the tirade he sensed was coming. "Stipulation number two: If and when the time comes to make an arrest, you will call me immediately. These terms are nonnegotiable. If you go rogue, I'll see to it you never work in this city again. Do I make myself clear?"

Wickowski's conditions sounded to me like he wanted to keep me on a leash while he babysat me. I could tell by the set of his mouth and the way his jaw muscles bulged that he wasn't going to budge on this one, and I didn't need any more drama. Of course, I didn't say any of that out loud but instead grudgingly nodded my consent.

"Good." Wickowski didn't have to look so smug. I think he expected more of a reaction to his new rules. There was still a chance. "So who benefits from Tompkins's death?"

"Aside from the whole of society?"

Wickowski raised his brows. "Perhaps you could be a little more specific?"

"I'm alleging that Tompkins killed Dr. Phillips then broke into his house and stole the hard drive from the doctor's computer. I couldn't find Phillips's laptop or cell phone either, so I have to assume he absconded with those as well. But Tompkins wasn't the mastermind behind the crime. I believe he was just muscle who did what he was paid to do. There's something on that hard drive that somebody's willing to kill to keep secret. We figure out what that is, we'll have whoever is behind Dr. Phillips's murder."

"What do you have so far? Did you get anything useful at the residence?"

"Not really. Maybe a couple of character witnesses—Dr. Phillips's frat brothers might know him on a different level than his wife did. Aside from that, my leads died with Tompkins." I scooted my chair away from the table and stood to leave. Wickowski made no move to stop me. "I'll keep you posted."

"You better," Wickowski shot back.

I stopped at the door with my hand on the knob. "You going to share all this with Burnell, or should I catch him up to speed?"

"I'll handle Burnell and damage control on this end. You just do what you do best and wrap this case up nice and tidy." I wasn't sure if I felt a bite of sarcasm in Wickowski's words or if I just needed coffee.

"Okay, but at some point Burnell and I are going to discuss how an accidental death suddenly becomes a homicide. Fair warning."

Wickowski shot me a cautionary look, but I only smiled back and slipped out the door. Burnell was still glued to his phone. He turned his back on me as I walked past. The elevator took me back downstairs and spit me out in the lobby, where I claimed my sidearm, returned my visitor's badge, and signed out.

The sun had crept up over the east side when I stepped out onto the sidewalk. Portland was just coming alive. A city bus lumbered away from the curb with a diesel cough. Birdsong filled the air the way it does in movies when things were looking up for the film's characters. I was lost in that daydream when I rounded the corner and ran straight into Vin, who was as surprised to see me out so early as I was to see him. When I realized he was walking elbow-twined-in-elbow with Trisha Blackwell, I did my best not to let the trigger show on my face.

"Sam, what are you doing here?" Vin dropped Trisha's arm and left her side to give me an awkward embrace. "I thought about calling and inviting you to breakfast with us, but it was so early and last minute."

Okay, he had me there—I'm not a morning person—but that didn't negate the fact that he was strolling arm in arm with Trisha Blackwell! Just beyond Vin's shoulder, Trisha caught my eye, looking like the cat that'd eaten the canary, and all I could imagine was seeing those pearly whites scattered on the sidewalk. I did what my anger management therapist taught me to do: without engaging, I turned and walked away, counting to fifty silently in my head and breathing deeply through my nose. Vin made the right choice by not chasing me down.

It was six blocks before I no longer felt like putting my fist through something. The bureau shrink said that I avoided close and meaningful relationships as a way to deal with the tragedy of losing my best friend at such a vulnerable age. Whatever. All I knew was that I hated feeling these sorts of emotions. Worse, I was angry with myself for reacting to seeing Vin in the company of another woman. I was not going to be that fragile girlfriend! My heart tripped over itself for a beat when I realized I was more attached to Vin than I'd wanted to let myself believe, and that, irrationally, pissed me off even more.

CHAPTER TWELVE

MY FIRST STOP ON THE WAY HOME WAS AT STEAM FOR MY usual—only to find it closed due to a plumbing issue. With a disappointed sigh, I turned back for home with a plan to go back to bed and start the day over fresh. I'd found my lover on the arm of another woman, my coffee shop was closed until further notice, and my only lead in the Phillips case was now a stiff in a little metal drawer downtown. Could the day possibly get any worse?

The Universe, I learned long ago, has a wicked sense of humor and shouldn't be provoked. Of course things could always get worse, and when the Universe feels challenged, you get to see just how much worse they really can get.

I was just outside my front door when my cell began to ring. Since I thought it might be Vin, I wasn't in a rush to pick up and let it roll over to voicemail, which of course I played once I was inside.

"Samantha darling, it's your mother—oh, I wish you'd pick up. I'll wait." My mother has never fully grasped technology and still thinks voicemail and answering machines operate the same way. When she realized I wasn't going to pop on—or she was tired of waiting—she returned to leaving a message. "Anyway, assuming you're still alive out there on the West Coast, I wanted you to know that your father and I sat with our attorney and made out our wills. He and I discussed it, and if, God forbid, your father should pass on before I do, or vice versa, we've listed you as our caregiver. We'll discuss our living arrangements when you call me back, which at my age, should be sooner rather than later. But

I understand if you're too busy. I'm sure they'll be able to track you down to tell you I died. And my funeral is to be on a Saturday, when your business might not be so demanding."

My mother turned her passive aggression into a ninja skill. I picked up a pillow from the couch, buried my face in it, and screamed until my throat was raw. The only way to salvage a day like the one I was having was to put my head down and lean into the propeller blades.

Pam Phillips's number for where she was staying stared at me from the table. I didn't know what I hoped to glean from the widow, but I needed to make forward movement. When a man answered (her father, I presumed), I asked for Pam and waited while he fetched her.

Pam came to the phone breathless, like she'd run to take the call. I filled her in on my visit to her home, the break-in, and the temporary fix to her back door. I let her know that the suspect was in custody, purposefully leaving out that he was in the custody of the medical examiner.

"I'm missing one giant key to this whole mystery, Pam: motive. Is there anyone you can think of that might benefit from Dr. Phillips's death?"

"Benefit?" Pam asked dubiously, the pitch of her voice rising several octaves. "How could someone benefit from my husband's death?"

"Money, lust, and power are big motivators, Pam. Think back over the past couple of months. Is there anything that struck you as odd, maybe seemed insignificant at the time—a late-night phone call or a credit card receipt that you questioned, even if only to yourself?"

"No." Pam's single-word response gave away her frustration. We'd already been through all of this. To her ears, I was rehashing the same details and questioning her late husband's integrity and motives. I got that Ronald had been the cornerstone of the Phillips family; if he wasn't who Pam believed him to be, then what else in her life wasn't as it seemed? I didn't envy her situation.

My skills with handling the emotionally fragile weren't the best. My kid gloves were clumsy. Give me an interview room, a suspect, and a couple of hours, and I'd get you what you needed. But a grieving widow had me tripping on eggshells. I decided to come at things from a different angle. "How about his friends?"

"Ronny and I had the same friends, all of them from our church, and all of them good, proper folks, Detective."

"Is it possible that Dr. Phillips had relations with people you weren't aware of?"

Pam grew weary and sighed. "I knew everything that went on in Ronny's life. He went to work, and he came home to his family at the end of each day. On rare occasions he traveled for work to conferences and such."

"Pam, I know these next questions are going to be upsetting, but please, bear with me. I have to ask them. Did Dr. Phillips ever have any problems with gambling, or did he ever get mixed up with the wrong kind of people?"

"Absolutely not! Ronny wasn't that sort of man. He coached Katie's soccer team, and he volunteered for several charities through the church. He even drove several of our senior parishioners to appointments or shopping." The memory of her late husband's good deeds brought on fresh tears. I did my best to comfort her, promising to keep her informed as things developed, then hung up.

Great. Ronald Phillips was not only a candidate for Father of the Year but was also heading toward sainthood. But even the devil looks good on paper. Who would want to eliminate an upstanding citizen such as Dr. Phillips, and what had he known that was worth killing for? It was time to start rattling some other trees to see who fell out.

The envelope of photos I'd taken from the Phillips home was on the edge of the desk. What did Talbert and McPherson know about their friend? Did they have an alternate perspective of the man?

It took a little of my own prowess to track down a working contact number for McPherson. My call was routed through an automatic directory until I got to someone who spoke English and knew how to find him. Unfortunately he was on a short sabbatical, but I was assured that he received his communications and did his best to return them as quickly as possible. The woman jotted down my message and request to speak with him regarding Ronald Phillips, and I was left with a promise to hear back from him by the end of the next business day.

I hung up feeling restless. Patience may be a virtue, but it was something I had little of. A couple of months before, Mole had installed a program on my computer that gave me backdoor access to read-only government search engines. It was frighteningly easy to tap into the US Department of State's Bureau of Consular Affairs system and download McPherson's passport activity, which read like a global guidebook to warmer climates. There were multiple stamps from exotic locals—Bali, Tibet, Malaysia, Costa Rica, Venezuela, and Colombia. The last entry stamp was into Brazil after six months of hopping back and forth between Costa Rica and Venezuela. What was he up to? Time to put Mole to work again.

It was early, but I took the chance Mole might still be up.

"Who's there?"

"Me," I chimed.

The floorboards squeaked as Mole crossed the room to the door. "Are you alone?"

"Do you see anyone with me?" I could tell he had his eyeball screwed to the security peephole.

"All right, hang on."

After several seconds of clicks and clacks as locks disengaged, dead bolts slid back, and chains dropped from their tracks, Mole opened his door just enough to verify that I was indeed alone.

"You seem a little more paranoid than usual," I commented as I eeled my way through the very narrow door opening.

Mole immediately began resetting the locks behind me. "The Feds shut down Sneaker42 earlier this morning; sanctimonious government bastards believe they're the only ones with a right to knowledge. Sneak has been my contact for years, and most of the software he uses I wrote. He's careful, though." Mole sounded more like he was trying to convince himself of this rather than me. *Couldn't have been too careful if the Feds busted him*, I wanted to say, but decided not to.

"Wouldn't it feel great to stick it to the man one last time?" I egged.

Mole eyed me suspiciously. "What do you have in mind?"

"I need information on this guy." I handed Mole a printed copy of McPherson's passport page.

"What sort of info do you want?"

"Whatever you can find. Ultimately I'm trying to track him down in-country. Check where he's staying, what his activity has been, who he's working for, who his connections are, et cetera. I'm looking for motive and opportunity for murder."

"Murder?" Mole gave a low whistle. "Do you want superficial, or do you want me to go full Hoffa?"

"Deep. I'll sift through what I don't need."

"Do you want anything to read differently when I'm done? Taint his past, revoke his legal status?"

"No, I just want hard copies of whatever you find."

"This will take me some time. Payment?" Mole had barely finished locking the last lock when he turned around to find me waiting to leave. With a sigh, he started with the locks all over again.

"I'll have to owe you for now and pay you back with interest," I told the back of his head. He disengaged the last lock and let me out.

Back at my own place, a message was waiting for me on my cell. I pressed play, hoping it might be McPherson calling me back. Instead it was Vin's awkward acknowledgment of how the morning must have looked. He ended with an "I love you" that had me hitting the delete button. *Compartmentalize.* Drama was the last thing I wanted, especially my own.

I had no leads at the present, and I was waiting for a return call from McPherson and didn't know what to do with myself. I could hoof it to my office; there was always something to do there, but if I was being honest with myself, I didn't feel like doing that. It took me fifteen minutes to find the television remote stuffed between the couch cushions. I flopped myself down and began surfing until I landed on a channel showing an *X-Files* marathon. After two hours of mind-numbing entertainment, my stomach began to growl, and I had a sudden hankering for phanaeng curry from the Thai restaurant down the road. I dialed up Lucky Dragon and ordered enough food to feed a small army.

Twenty minutes later, the downstairs door buzzer announced the arrival of chow. I met the deliveryman at the elevator and exchanged a wad of cash for a bagful of paper cartons filled with spicy Thai food. Then I knocked on Mole's door.

"Identify yourself."

"Just open the freaking door, Mole." I held up the to-go bag displaying Lucky Dragon's logo so he could see it through the security peephole.

After another succession of door locks and chains being undone, Mole opened his door to me once again.

"Payment for services rendered," I announced as I strode in.

"Why aren't you out lunching with Mr. Sensitive?" Mole asked, resetting only the chain and a dead bolt.

"I don't want to talk about it," I mumbled.

"Trouble in paradise?" Mole called from the kitchen, where he'd gone in search of utensils.

I ignored Mole and cleared off a corner of the coffee table to spread out our veritable feast. Mole came back into the room carrying forks, a roll of paper towels, and plates, which we filled with fried rice, chicken with cashew nuts, pad Thai, spicy basil stir-fry, spicy larb salad, and fresh salad rolls. Mole dropped down on the couch beside me, and we dug in.

"Sam, you ordered enough food for five people."

"I couldn't decide what I was craving, so I ordered all of them."

"No one person orders this much food unless they're feeding the emotional beast. Or eating for two. You preggers?"

I spit pad Thai halfway across the room and gave him a solid punch in the arm, which made him cry out, "What the hell?"

"You are not funny, Mole."

"Indecision means one of two things: you're sick, but you look quite healthy—except for that thing on your forehead."

"Or?"

"Or you're having relationship issues." Mole made a quick scoot to the other end of the couch, out of my reach.

I slurped up another peanut-sauce-drenched noodle and chewed it insightfully. "How is it a guy who never emerges from his house has insights about people and their relationships?"

"I catch *Dr. Phil* sometimes, and I read a lot of stuff online."

"Well, I'm not having a problem with anyone. I'm just having an off day."

"Come on, Sammy. You know Vin is crazy about you. Women like you turn guys on."

"Women like me?"

Mole's face was a sketch of seriousness. "You've broken bones; you've shot at people; you're like Lara freaking Croft. I figure you've gotta be a freak in bed."

"Let it go, Mole." I shot him a look that left no room for negotiation and reached over to flip on the flat-screen monitor that served as his television via the remote on the table. The monitor was already set to the Syfy channel, so we joined the *X-Files* marathon during a clone-themed episode titled "Eve." When Mole began a running commentary of why Scully and Mulder's personal relationship was forever doomed by the ever-present shadow conspiracy, I thought I'd have to shoot him. A commercial blessedly interrupted his ranting, and he turned sideways on the couch to face me as if he'd just had an epiphany.

"Is there anybody whose credit you want me to ruin?"

"Naw."

"How about that art gallery lady—I could issue a bench warrant for unpaid parking tickets. That'd at least ruin her day."

"No thanks."

"Create an oversight in the IRS computers?"

Now that one was tempting. "Thanks for the offers, Mole, but I'll handle things myself."

"Hey, what are friends for? But if you ever need dirt on anyone, let me know." He daringly leaned over and gave me a cautious, one-armed hug.

"Mole," I asked casually, "you've never dug up private information on me, have you?"

"As if I would tell you," Mole retorted with a snort. He must have felt my burning gaze on the side of his face because his laugh turned into a cough and then fell silent.

I'd be kidding myself if I believed Mole had never pulled up my old FBI files. Of course he knew more about me than I'd ever shared. It was his nature to know as much as possible about everyone he came into contact with. It was a security thing with him; I get it. But there are things about me and my FBI past that he would never discover. Besides, what was getting upset about anything going to do, other than cut off a valuable resource? "I'm going to go take a nap," I said, rising from his couch.

"Before you go, I've got the information you requested." Mole handed me a manila envelope with McPherson's name scrawled in Mole's familiar penmanship. "The guy appears clean."

"Yeah, that's what I was afraid of. Any clue what he was doing in Venezuela and Costa Rica?"

"I don't know, but there are major investors in both countries, so maybe his travels were business related."

"Most likely." Satiated by food, I took the envelope, bid Mole a good evening, and went home with it tucked under my arm.

CHAPTER THIRTEEN

RAIN PELTED MY OFFICE WINDOW IN WHAT PROMISED TO BE A STE-reotypical Portland day—gray and drizzly. The people born and bred in the Pacific Northwest were hardy folk. And rust resistant. One sure way to tell the tourists from the locals was by their umbrellas; out-of-towners carried them, locals didn't.

I sat behind my desk with my morning coffee and went over the McPherson file. Nothing questionable jumped off the pages at me. Mole was right—the guy was pretty straight. He'd begun a research and development pharmaceutical company cleverly named Asclepius, after the Greek god of medicine. A decade later, the company went through a major restructuring, changed their name to Novus, and, like most major pharma-ceutical companies, moved offshore. That was where Mole ran out of trail. There was no indication as to why McPherson had been MIA from Novus or why he'd been spending his time in Venezuela and Costa Rica.

The phone beside my elbow trilled loudly. As fortune and synchronicity would have it, someone was calling from South America. "Hello?"

"Señor McPherson is on the line for you, por favor," stated a woman with a heavy Latin American accent. "Hold please." Latin jazz music played in my ear while I waited.

Finally the music broke and the woman came back on the line. "Thank you for holding, Ms. Harris." She pronounced my name with a long *e* sound. "Here is Señor McPherson."

The line clicked once, followed by the twang of a southern

drawl. "Ms. Harris, William McPherson. I got your message. You wanted to speak to me about Ron? What can I do for you?"

"I appreciate your calling me back so promptly, Mr. McPherson. I—"

"Please," he interrupted, "my friends call me William."

It was a little early in the day to say we were friends, but whatever. "William, Pam tells me you and Dr. Phillips were good friends and that you both belonged to the Phi Mu Delta fraternity at the University of Massachusetts."

"Yes, ma'am, those were the days." McPherson gave a hearty chuckle, and I heard him slap his knee.

"Did Dr. Phillips confide in you after you graduated and went your separate ways?"

McPherson's party-boy tone became serious. "In what way?"

I kept it light. "Well, you know...the two of you were friends—frat brothers, as a matter of fact. Men tell their brothers things they would never mention to their wives, for whatever reasons. Maybe they think they're protecting their loved ones."

"Yeah, I suppose," McPherson said warily, not yet guessing my angle.

"One might assume you and Dr. Phillips had that sort of friendship, being fraternity brothers and all. Did he ever mention being concerned about anything that was going on? Was he ever nervous or anxious that you noticed?"

"No, not at all. I mean, sure, Ron and I talked about things, but he never mentioned that something was bothering him. The last time I saw Ron, he seemed just fine."

"When was that?"

"Excuse me?"

"You said the last time you saw Dr. Phillips. When was that?"

There was a long pause followed by a sigh as McPherson tried to recall the last time he'd seen his friend. "A couple of months ago, I guess. Why? Can I ask what this is all about?"

"There's been a few things that have come up surrounding Dr. Phillips's death. I'm just trying to answer some questions."

"Such as?"

I figured I might as well go for broke. "Why Pam might question the medical examiner's accidental death ruling?"

"Ms. Harris," McPherson rebuked, "I don't mean to come off sounding insensitive, but has it occurred to you that Pam may be desperately seeking a place to lay blame in her grieving state?"

I moved past his question without giving it an answer. "You and Dr. Phillips were both in the pharmaceutical business and such good friends. Did the two of you ever collaborate?"

McPherson paused suspiciously. "No, my father once suggested I never to do business with family. Ron was like a brother to me, so I figured he qualified."

"Can you think of anyone who'd want to hurt Dr. Phillips?"

"I've already made my opinion known."

"Yes, you said that you believe I'm chasing a dead end. What I want to know is, did someone kill Dr. Phillips?"

"I do not believe so. What I do believe is that the good Lord brought Ron home because it was simply his time. Are the police reopening the investigation?"

"Not yet. But if Dr. Phillips—your brother and friend—was murdered, then you have my word that I will find whoever did this."

"Well, the best of luck to you, Ms. Harris, for Pam's sake. And if you ever find yourself in South America, be sure to look me up. A friend of Ron's is a friend of mine. He wasn't only a good friend; he was a good man as well."

"Thank you for your time—" The line went dead before I could finish my sentence. I hung up with the opinion that McPherson wasn't being completely honest with me. I just couldn't put my finger on it what it was that made me doubt him.

With biotechnology on my mind, I dialed up Cascade Biotech and asked for Phillips's boss, Elliott Robbins. The hold music wasn't bad—much more soothing than what McPherson had to offer—and it made me want a nap. Fortunately I only had to wait through half of one of Chopin's nocturnes.

"Elliott Robbins here." He sounded much like Garrison Keillor, and I could easily imagine him to be a good-natured, middle-aged man in a sweater vest.

"Mr. Robbins, good morning. My name is Samantha Harris. I'm calling on behalf of Pam Phillips in regard to her late husband, your employee, Dr. Ronald Phillips."

"I'm sorry, but who did you say you're with? And what about Ronald is this concerning?"

"I'm with Harris Securities, formerly a special agent with the FBI." I liked to throw that in from time to time. It got people's attention. "I was hired by Pam Phillips to look into her husband's death."

"The paper said Ronald fell, that his death was an accident."

"Maybe that is all that happened, but Pam has some unanswered questions. And frankly, sir, I'm beginning to agree with her."

"I'm not sure how I can help."

"What exactly was it that Dr. Phillips did for you there at Cascade?"

"Without going into too much detail—for security reasons, you understand—Ronald was head of research and development in our DNA lab, working with the cloning of proteins for the pharmaceutical industry."

I nodded into the phone as if I had a clue as to what Robbins was talking about. "How did Dr. Phillips interact with his peers? Were there ever any tensions between him and anyone that you knew of?"

"Ronald was a highly respected employee. He had no enemies that I can bring to mind."

"Did you notice anything out of the ordinary the last few weeks of his life? Did he change any habits—arrive earlier, leave later than usual? Did he have any unusual appointments or guests?"

"Not that I can recall, though you have to understand that he was one of our senior staff, so his comings and goings weren't monitored, never questioned. We trusted and relied on Ronald one hundred percent."

"One last question. Did Dr. Phillips ever travel to South America for business with your company?"

"We do have contacts and some business in South America, but Ronald was never involved in that aspect of the company. He did travel for us, but always in-country."

I thanked Robbins for his time. "If you think of anything later on, please feel free to call me."

"It is my sincere hope that you can provide Pam with the answers she needs and this all turns out the way she wishes."

"I'm good at my job, Mr. Robbins, but I can't bring Dr. Phillips back from the grave."

"No, I suppose you can't. It was a poor choice of words on my part. I apologize. Good day, Ms. Harris."

Cascade Biotech and Robbins were strike two. Even though it was a past job, Talbert's files hadn't yet been boxed and put into storage. I located them easily enough and dialed S.T. Finance.

"I'm sorry," his receptionist informed me without sounding sorry at all, "Mr. Talbert is with a client all day and sees people by appointment only. The soonest I could fit you in is tomorrow afternoon." I made the appointment for the next day and hung up.

An overstuffed pigeon settled on the sill and stared expectantly at me when I swiveled my chair to look out the window. Soon he was joined by another and then another, like a feathered flash mob looking for handouts.

"Sorry, guys, I don't have any birdseed."

The trio cocked their heads as if questioning my honesty. Then all three turned in unison and pooped on the brick before taking flight. I looked at the green, liquidly blob and wondered what kind of omen it was.

Nothing was panning out as far as the Dr. Phillips investigation, but I still needed to make some money. The Quantum file sat on the edge of my desk.

From time to time, I used the services of a global company, Intellifacts Inc., who only worked with law enforcement above a certain clearance level. Thanks again to Mole, I had access in the form of a cloned nine-digit PIN that identified me as George Burnell. Once I'd gotten inside, I was rerouted to an internal search engine where I made my requests for criminal, Social Security, and credit reports, and I did an international warrant search of all the names in Quantum's file.

Criminal history was standard procedure these days, and most employers applied for one on all perspective employees. However, I preferred to update those reports so that I had the most current versions to work with. Truth was, human beings made thousands of decisions a day; oftentimes, they made the wrong ones.

Social Security reports would tell me if an employee had purposefully omitted any past addresses at which they may have lived. Discrepancies sparked a deeper search into why. Many substance addictions had come to light in just this manner; addicts liked to leave their pasts behind them. This might seem insignificant, but in today's cutthroat business culture, transparency was key.

A credit report would give Quantum insight to their employees' reliability and responsibilities. Employees in highly competitive fields who carried large debt outside of the normal responsibilities—vehicles, homes, that sort of thing—were tagged with a red flag. Sometimes those red flags were just a result of poor financial decisions. But poor financial decisions sometimes made desperate individuals attractive to headhunters whose clients were willing to pay for any advantage. An international warrant search was simply that—it let me know if somebody was facing charges or was wanted anywhere in the international community, which could lead to a whole slew of headaches.

When I finally finished filling in the appropriate fields, I made a quick scan for any errors. Finding none, I scrolled over the send icon and pressed enter. When Intellifacts got back to me with the results of my searches—which could be instantaneous or the next morning, depending on their workload—I'd go over each report line by line, make any appropriate calls to validate information, and then rate each individual employee on a scale from one to five. Anyone rated over three warranted advanced searches that took longer and cost more to perform. On a few occasions, I'd dialed law enforcement directly. White-collar crimes are a federal offense (ironic, I know, considering my standing with Mole). My findings and I had been subpoenaed to court a handful of times.

A typical job like Quantum ran the client around thirty grand, which might seem a little steep to a small electronic manufacturing company. But when there was cutting-edge technology on the table, it was worth the investment. Sure, I'd probably made a few enemies since entering this line of work. People tend to get a little irrational when their finances are challenged and their secrets exposed. But I didn't worry about it. Anyone who thought I was an easy target was clearly not paying attention.

My cell rang like an old-fashioned rotary phone and broke my concentration.

"Sammy, where are you?" asked Mole. "There's a guy nosing around your front door."

"What does he want?"

"How the hell should I know?"

"I don't know. Maybe open the door and ask him?"

"What? He could be with the Feds working some bad intel. I don't want him at my door."

"What would the Feds be wanting with me, Mole?"

"Exactly my point!" Mole's concern grew to a piercing level. "It might be someone much worse!"

"I'm on my way." I sighed and hung up.

I gave Intellifacts another four minutes. When the reports still hadn't come through, I closed up shop and headed home to rescue Mole from himself.

{* * *}

Expecting to see someone nefarious lurking, I was pleasantly surprised to see Vin and the largest bouquet of roses I'd ever seen, both on the sidewalk outside the security gate of my building. There was no stopping the girly beam that radiated from out of my chest.

"I know you think flowers are silly, that they just dry and fade, but..." Vin shrugged like a shy schoolboy. His eyes met mine. "I really want you to know how I feel about you, Samantha."

Feeling self-conscious, I took Vin's token into my arms. It was like holding a large baby. I wondered how many stems were in the bunch.

"Ninety-seven," Vin said, reading my mind. "One for each day we've been together."

Okay, sure—memorializing each day of our relationship with a bloom was a little cheesy, but it was romantic too. As I recalled my reaction at seeing him with Trisha yesterday morning and then not returning his calls, I felt more than a little hangdog. I pulled Vin to me by the front of his shirt and kissed him long and deep, not caring about who might have seen our public display of affection.

Vin and I and the roses took the elevator up. Mole was all but forgotten when we stepped off on my floor. However, his frantic call came rushing back when his door whooshed open and he stepped out looking anxious.

"Oh, good, it's you," he rushed and then stopped dead in his tracks when he saw I wasn't alone.

"Vin, this is my crazy neighbor. Don't make eye contact and you'll be all right," I only half joked. "Neighbor, this is Vin. He's with me. He's okay."

"Howdy, neighbor." Vin smiled and held his hand out to Mole in greeting. "Do you have a name?"

"I do." Mole said but gave no indication that he planned on sharing. Or shaking hands.

Mole's name wasn't mine to give, so to avoid the boys sizing each other up, I moved on to my front door. I'd always suspected Mole kept the place wired; he was that special sort of paranoid. I hadn't much cared, or at least not enough to make it an issue. The way I saw it, Mole kept an eye on the back door, so to speak. An early warning system is always nice. I slid my eyes toward my door and shot him a look that said, *How'd you know?*

"My spidey sense never lies," Mole whispered covertly.

After I'd handed Vin the roses and given him directions to a big jar under the sink, I unlocked the door and let him inside. "Give me a sec," I said before slipping back out to the hallway.

The door lock didn't appear to have been tampered with. "He was alone?" I asked Mole, who was pacing the carpet in front of his door like an expectant father.

"He was alone, but he was working for someone."

"How could you possibly know that?"

Mole pointed to his head and nodded slowly. "Spidey sense. Trust me, I know these things."

"Did your spidey sense happen to tell you who he was working for?"

"Negative."

"Can your spidey sense give a description?"

"He was wearing a black hoodie—hood up. Average build—six-foot, hundred and eighty pounds, give or take five.

No discernable body postures or gait. Couldn't tell if he had ink because of the hoodie. But I've got a screenshot, so why don't I just show you?"

"You captured his image?" I asked. Mole nodded enthusiastically. "Maybe lead with that next time."

I followed Mole into his apartment and watched the high-definition playback of the man Mole described. It was an accurate nondescription. The perp took care in keeping his face hidden deep within the cavernous hood.

"When did he leave?"

"Only a couple of minutes before you and your boy toy arrived. You probably passed him outside."

Mental recall. Had I passed anyone? I wasn't sure. I'd been so distracted by Vin, I wasn't able to recall anything beyond the mass of roses, the look on his face, and the swell of emotion that had hit me.

"Your spidey sense will let us know if this guy, or anyone else, returns?"

"No worries, Sammy. I've got your six."

Even with the intrusion on privacy, it was good to know Mole had my back. He was the closest thing I had to a friend, the only person I could just be myself around without expectations or complications. Mole didn't like many people, and he trusted no one. To be honest, I'm not totally sure how we connected. Maybe we were both square pegs in a round society and we'd figured out how to work the system to our advantage. Neither of us were saints, but then, we weren't the bad guys either. We just lived life better when it was by our own rules. Our hearts were in the right place.

Vin came out of the kitchen with an industrial-sized pickle-jar-turned-vase held balanced on one hip as if he were carting a toddler and a glass of pinot in his other hand. "Is everything okay?"

"He's eccentric. Let's just leave it at that." I relieved Vin of the roses and set them in the center of the coffee table where they splayed out, wide and fragrant.

Vin was suddenly behind me, taking my hand and leading me toward the bedroom. Our relationship wasn't completely physical, but the part of it that was made my body ache. Every one of my previous relationships had been nothing but physical. With Vin, there was something much deeper at play. Not much in this world frightened me, but to open myself to Vin meant opening myself to heartbreak, and that scared the pants off me. Affairs of the heart had a mind of their own and knew no logic; they answered to no one. Love was a wild card that couldn't be tamed. *What do I do with that?*

To be safe, I'd taken to leaving the blinds closed at all times, lest I get my neighbors reason to notify the landlord. Vin started off with a series of tender kisses down my neck but wasted no time getting us both naked. I preferred his zeal to his romance-movie approach of slow and deliberate. The term *making love* had always made me cringe. Love was hearts and flowers and long walks on a sunset beach. This was furious and sweaty, bordering on primal. But it wasn't just sex—it was Vin claiming me, making my body his with every thrust. Competing emotions—want and fear—battled for dominance. My body responded with as much hunger as Vin's. I cupped his face in my hands and held his green eyes with mine as he looked down on me. Our bodies fell into deep rhythm that built to an inevitable crescendo, which left us in a breathless heap of twisted sheets.

My body tingled from both exertion and pleasure. I wished relationships could be this and nothing more, no compromises or plans, just good times and fabulous sex. The events of my childhood had left me with trust issues. Having never let anybody in closer than arm's length, I wanted to throw my arms around Vin and tell him I loved him, but the words paralyzed me.

Vin rolled over to raise himself up onto his elbow and smiled down at me. There was no gushing of affection, no proposals of the future, just a simple smile. A smile that was just about perfect.

CHAPTER FOURTEEN

SIRENS SPLIT THE NIGHT AS THEY SCREAMED ACROSS THE CITY. WAS I dreaming, or was I really detecting a faint waft of fire through the open window? The implications snapped me from my unconscious state like a mainlined shot of caffeine.

Naked, I eased out of bed, tiptoed over to the French doors that led to the balcony off my bedroom, and moved the curtains aside just enough to peek out. The fire trucks were close. Their rotating lights bounced off the low, smoky atmosphere just a few blocks down the street in the direction of—*oh shit!*—my office.

My cell rang, and I swooped it up before it had a chance to ring a second time. An automated message from the security company that contracted with my office building was calling to tell me that the fire alarm had sounded and the local fire department had been notified. The message also advised me to hold on the line for a representative should I have further questions; otherwise, press the star key to return to the menu. I dropped the phone on the bed and threw on the jeans and t-shirt that Vin had pulled off me earlier.

"Sam." Vin yawned. "What's going on?"

Vin's flannel shirt was the closest thing to a jacket I saw nearby, so I pulled it on. "Apparently there's a fire at my office building. I'm going to go check it out."

Vin bolted up in bed. "I'm going with you." He threw the sheets aside.

"Stay here." In the dark, Vin didn't see the HK go into my waistband at the small of my back. "I won't be long."

"Sam—"

The door cut Vin off when I let it fall shut behind me. It was rude of me, I knew. In my defense, I didn't know what I was about to walk into. If someone meant to do me harm, what better way than to set a trap and lure me in? The last thing I needed in that case was a charge to keep track of.

The air was thick and burned my throat the closer I got to the fire. The block had been cordoned off with yellow tape, and the Portland police had officers on the scene to keep the growing crowd at bay. The curious onlookers breathed through their sleeves or pulled the necks of their shirts up over their noses.

Through the glassless windows, we watched the fire act like a hungry beast just out of hibernation as it devoured everything it touched. All the businesses that the building housed were consumed by roiling orange-and-yellow flames. Everything in my office was already gone—my antique desk, computer, printer, and all of my work files, including the ones for the Quantum job. Fortunately everything I had was backed up in the cloud. Fire was a moot effort to cover one's tracks, meaning this was personal. A message. A warning.

Keeping to the fringes of the crowd, I made my way around to the other side of the building. As my eyes moved away from the fire to take in the onlookers, I scanned for body language or other indicators that might give away the arsonist as they hung around to admire their handiwork or make sure I got the message in person.

"A code went out for crowd control." My focus pulled away from the crowd when Wickowski came up behind me with his hands resting in his pockets. "I recognized it was in your part of town, so I wondered if you were in any way involved."

"Not this time. My office, on the other hand..." I hooked a thumb over my shoulder toward the blaze.

"Who did you piss off?" Wickowski teased.

"On this coast?" I countered. I knew all I needed to about this fire, save for who struck the match, but I sat on my thoughts for the time being.

"I let the fire chief ride on a poker debt a couple of weeks ago, so he owes me a solid. I'll get his thoughts on the fire and get back to you. In the meantime, contact your insurance company."

"I was already itemizing in my head."

"Let me give you a lift home," Wickowski offered.

"Nah." I waved him off. "But thanks." It wasn't that I actually wanted to walk back. I wanted to see if anyone else broke off from the crowd to follow.

My loft was as vulnerable to an arsonist's torch as my office building. Brick buildings themselves might not burn, but everything inside of them does, and I happened to have something near and dear to me upstairs. I quietly let myself in, stripped off my clothes after placing the HK in the nightstand, and reclaimed my side of the bed beside Vin, who'd fallen back into a sound sleep. As I lay on my back and stared at the dark ceiling, I tried not to think about the fire or dealing with the insurance company, even though that was where my brain wanted to go. I turned onto my side and snuggled up to Vin so that the contours of my body fit perfectly into the contours of his. I wasn't even close to tired. The shock of the fire had begun to dissipate as reality began to solidify. I started to get pissed off. I took a deep breath and let it out slowly, willing sleep to find me again. But the moment I began to feel its drowsy tendrils, my mind circled back around to the fire.

Not worried about waking Vin, I got out of bed. Returning to sleep was my only thought as I padded into the bathroom and rummaged beneath the sink for a bottle of lavender bath salts. The bottle promised to be a soothing and relaxing experience. There must have been some truth to it; the moment I slipped into the comfortably hot water, I began to not give a crap about much of anything.

When I opened my eyes, the water had gone tepid and my skin looked like that of a raisin. Vin was up and already at it when I emerged from the bathroom in a pungent lavender cloud. As someone allergic to beestings, I realized I may have set myself up for an adventurous day.

A fetched breakfast of bagels and cream cheese with lox, alongside coffee from the bagel company three blocks away, was waiting on the counter. Vin was peeling the lids off the coffee cups. "You smell like...bee fodder." He'd settled on my worst nightmare.

"Lavender bath salts. They're supposed to calm and soothe me."

"Did they work?"

"What fire?" I asked facetiously.

Vin considered that for a second. "I walked past your office this morning. It's gutted. You seem to be taking this exceedingly well."

"Isn't the first step to stopping personal drama to accept what *is* as a fact?" Some of Aunt Zelda's enlightenment journey might have sunk in, though it was rarely put into practice.

"That was impressively Zen, babe." Vin pressed his hands together and gave me a from-the-waist bow.

"Yeah, well, don't get used to it."

"Arson?" Vin asked, circling back to the hot topic.

"Maybe." I shrugged.

"Do you think it had anything to do with you?"

Why did everyone automatically think of me when shit went sideways? "No," I lied.

Vin took a bite of his bagel and chewed it to one side so he could talk around it. "What'll you do now?"

"There's the insurance issue to deal with." *Ugh—adulting.* "Then I need to retrieve my backup files from the cloud. I'll have to work from here until I figure out other arrangements."

"You could share my studio space," Vin offered.

That sounded too much like moving in. "I'd make a heinous roomie. I can operate out of here until I find a new space to lease."

Vin looked a little disappointed with my response. After seeing him off, I dressed and began the first round of phone calls with the insurance company, retelling the events of the fire to a cheerful representative who explained fire wasn't her department and offered to forward my call. The phone clicked in my ear, and another representative came on who was equally enthusiastic as the first. She was also full of questions, to the point that I felt like I was being politely interrogated. In the end I was told to expect forms in the mail and a call from an adjuster out of their office.

No sooner had I hung up the phone when the downstairs buzzer sounded through the intercom by the front door. I could tell by the way the visitor leaned on the buzzer for longer than necessary that it was Wickowski.

He entered carrying a cup of coffee in each hand. "I thought this might soften the blow." He passed me a cup before flopping himself down onto the couch.

"Soften what blow?" I asked cautiously, downing the first coffee that Vin had brought before diving into the second. Vin must have taken up caffeine again because he'd left with his cup.

Wickowski was holding up a finger while he took a tentative sip from his own cup. "I got a call from the fire chief. Inspectors found traces of accelerant all over the second floor, but the greatest concentration was in your office. Also, on another note, the security company's internal alert system shows the front door's electronic panel was hacked. That's how the arsonist got inside and had the time to set the fire without triggering the silent alarm."

"So"—I ran a hand through my hair—"I'm dealing with someone who knows how to bypass security systems as well as sets fires."

"It's just procedure in cases like this, but they're going to want to get a statement from you."

"They think I set my own office on fire? To what end?"

"Like I said, it's just standard operating procedure whenever they find accelerant or any other traces of arson."

"This is related to Phillips. Someone is trying to clean up their trail."

Wickowski nodded in agreement. I hoped it didn't pain him too much to do so. "It's also safe to assume that whoever whacked Tompkins is connected to the person who started the fire." Wickowski sat back and sipped his coffee while waiting for me to say something. I had nothing. "Any idea what they might've been after?" he asked.

I shook my head. "Not a fucking clue, except...they took Dr. Phillips's hard drive, which contained electronic data. I'm guessing if destroying evidence was their motive, they'd have to know I'd have everything uploaded to the cloud. Either way, their message was delivered loud and clear."

"But you're not going to stop digging, are you?" Wickowski shot me a smirk.

"Oh, so you've met me!" My words dripped with sarcasm, but my smile was genuine.

Wickowski chuckled as he checked his wristwatch and stood to leave. It was in that moment I knew we were back to being friends again. He tilted his cup back and drained it before depositing it beneath the kitchen sink. "Are you packing?"

I knew he didn't mean for a trip. I nodded. "Full magazine with one in the chamber."

"Oh, Harris, I love it when you talk dirty." At the door Wickowski turned, serious once again. "I mean it—watch your back. I don't want to have to open a file on you."

I gave him a *pshaw* and a light slug in the shoulder. "I got this." The level of Wickowski's sincere concern for my safety was a bit unsettling.

I opened the door and watched him saunter down the hall to the elevator. It wasn't nearly as nice watching Wickowski walk away as it was to watch Vin. He raised his hand and gave me a final wave good-bye before the elevator door slid shut and he was gone.

At Mole's door, I heard the clacking of the keyboard, so I knocked. He answered my knock with a grunt, which was followed by the various sounds of locks being disengaged. When he finally opened the door, he looked like death warmed over.

"What time is it?" Mole grumbled as I stepped inside his lair.

"It's already tomorrow," I said, knowing he'd been up all night.

"Really?" Mole looked perplexed then scratched his head and returned to his computer. "What brings you by?"

"Yesterday you said someone was hanging outside my front door."

"Yeah, what about him? I told you I didn't really get a good look at him."

"Did you hear those sirens early this morning?"

"Not really. I've been gaming all night."

"There was a fire in my office. Someone bypassed the alarms and torched the place."

"Ouch. Who'd you piss off?"

I was seriously getting tired of that being a foregone conclusion. "Mole, I know you have the hallway bugged. Probably the elevator, stairwell, and front door too. I'm not here to bust your balls," I quickly explained when Mole's mouth began to work like a fish out of water. "I want to know if you upload the images into a file, or if the cameras are closed-circuit only."

Mole took a moment to decide whether to confess. "Okay, it's true—but only the stairwell, elevator, and hall. I switched everything to see-only when the Feds detained Sneak and I was dumping files and shoring up firewalls."

"So no video of the guy, then?"

"I switched the internal processors to record, but..." Mole rolled his chair to another monitor and brought up a grainy thirty-second video that gave me no more information than the screenshot. "The elevator and front door are on entirely separate systems, so he got out the door before I could capture anything. Sorry, Sammy."

"If you haven't already done so, set everything you've got running to download. I have a feeling this isn't over."

"Understood. But no worries. This place is wired like Fort Knox during the best of times." Realizing what he'd just said, Mole changed the subject. "I could make a phone call and get a system installed in your loft—door, windows, motion detector, voice recognition, the works."

"Seriously? How much would all that run me?"

"I've got a guy who owes me big after I worked my magic and got him out of a serious jam. System won't cost you a dime. I could get it done for you today, if you want."

Mole meant it would only cost me my silence on all the privacy violations he'd racked up. "Sounds good to me. No video inside my place, though—I mean it."

"I wouldn't dream of it," Mole said, already typing out an instant message to his contact.

"Call me if something happens, and if you can't get me, use one of your burners and call Wickowski." I scribbled Wickowski's number on a pad of paper and left it beside Mole's keyboard. "Tell him you're with me." I let myself out and returned home to get ready for my appointment with Steven Talbert.

CHAPTER FIFTEEN

S.T. FINANCE WAS LOCATED IN THE HEART OF THE BEAVERTON'S business district, a suburb west of Portland that was known for its strip malls, middle-class subdivisions, and traffic. I arrived on time, despite the gridlock, and checked in with the perfectly coiffed receptionist perched behind an expensive-looking mahogany desk. She gave me a general sweep of her hand to indicate I needed to wait. I took a seat in one of the wingback chairs that looked more comfortable than it actually was.

It wasn't long before a slim woman in a business suit with an updo appeared as if from nowhere to escort me into S.T. Finance's inner sanctum, a glass-walled conference room. In lieu of the low-backed, inexpensive chairs usually found crowded around corporate conference tables, these were high-backed, upholstered in genuine leather, and would have been at home in a personal library. The dark wood of the conference table was polished to a high gloss so that I could see my reflection in it. A matching media center sat across the room.

I wasn't left to wait long in the conference room before Steven Talbert strode in dressed in a dark gray suit with a steel-blue button-down beneath and a bloodred tie. His dark, wavy hair was cut short, and his face was void of the moustache and goatee from his reunion days. Talbert's very essence screamed power. My own ego had me stand as he entered the room. I wasn't the submissive type.

"Good day, Ms. Harris. I hope all is well with you."

Talbert's manicured hand was soft and warm when I shook

it. Obviously he was a stranger to manual labor. "I'm well, thank you. Yourself?"

Talbert's face clouded in a well-rehearsed expression of grief. "We're still broken up over Ron's death. May I offer you coffee or tea?"

"Coffee would be great, thanks."

Talbert fingered a button on the speaker in front of him and asked someone named Gail to bring us refreshments. Moments later, the slender woman who'd brought me to the conference room returned balancing a silver coffee service on one arm. Gail set the tray in the center of the table and proceeded to serve us.

Talbert waved off Gail's offer to pour a cup for him and dismissed her with a short nod. I wasn't sure if I really saw a sneer on Gail's face when she swept the door shut behind her or if I was just projecting. I was probably projecting.

"Mr. Talbert, I wish we were meeting again under more pleasant conditions. I'm sorry about Dr. Phillips. I understand you and he were close?"

"Oh yes, Ron and I were very close. We were brothers. Once you've pledged loyalty to the brotherhood of Phi Mu Delta, it is forever. He will be greatly missed." Talbert let his eyes go soft and misty, but I wasn't buying it. Having worked with Talbert before, I knew him to be cold, calculated, and out for blood when he thought someone was betraying him. I'd met mobsters with more heart than Talbert. "What is it exactly about Ron's death that interests you?"

"Pam hired me to look into a few loose ends." I was being purposefully vague.

Talbert adjusted the way he was sitting and crossed one knee over the other. "What sort of loose ends?"

"There seem to be several inconsistencies in Dr. Phillips's behavior in the days leading up to his death."

"Such as?"

"Dr. Phillips seemed paranoid, sullen. I didn't personally know Dr. Phillips, but apparently that wasn't the norm for him."

Talbert raised his brows and exhaled through puffed cheeks. "Ron was my friend and a good man. If you think his death wasn't an accident, I'll help you in any way that I can to bring his murderer to justice."

"I appreciate that. Did Dr. Phillips ever mention that he was concerned about his safety?"

Talbert answered my question with a question of his own. "Who would want to harm Ron? I mean, what would they hope to gain?"

"Maybe an extracurricular activity or a side venture gone bad?"

"Oh no, no," Talbert said emphatically. "Ron was an extremely straight and narrow guy. He'd never do anything that wasn't aboveboard."

"When was the last time you saw Dr. Phillips?"

Talbert blew another exhale through his cheeks as he thought back. "Must have been close to a year ago?" he offered. "I should have stayed in better touch." Talbert sighed despondently. "Why didn't he tell someone he was in trouble?"

"He might not have known it himself until those last days."

"All of this is a damn shame," Talbert said, mostly to himself. His eyes grew misty and distant. Had I not done my time with the FBI's Behavioral Science Unit, I would have totally missed the micro-expression of contempt in the way the right side of Talbert's mouth tightened and raised involuntarily. The son of a bitch wasn't all that sorry his friend was dead. Interesting.

"I'm sorry I couldn't be more helpful." Talbert pushed his chair back and stood. "Now if you'll excuse me, I have much work to do. If there is anything else I can do or any way I can help with your investigation, don't hesitate to phone me. Good day, Ms. Harris."

I stood and snapped a business card onto the conference table. "If you think of anything, please do the same."

All the way across the parking lot, I felt eyes on my back from the upper windows of Talbert's office. He'd played the part of grieving friend well, but not well enough to shuttle suspicion away from him. There was no mistaking he held a certain level of disdain for his former fraternity brother. Regardless, I still had no real leads and certainly nothing on which to build a case. My tally was still lopsided; I had far more questions than I had answers.

As I was leaving Beaverton, I decided to pay the White Horse an impromptu visit and chat up a few of the midday regulars. Somebody down there knew something—who hired Tompkins, what he was into, maybe even who he went up to Portland to meet.

It was shortly after three o'clock when I arrived in Sawtell, just after shift change at the local lumber mill. The White Horse was packed with workers who had obviously just gotten off work. The same bartender was behind the bar wiping glasses with a yellowed towel.

I half expected the scene to play out like one of those old Westerns, where the stranger saunters into a bar and the music pauses mid-key, causing everyone to turn and stare. Fortunately I entered relatively unnoticed except for the barkeep. I caught his eye the moment I walked in. He motioned my way with his rag, and two heads turned in unison. Blondie and Shorty.

Blondie's nose was a swollen, red mash covered by three thin white strips of bandage, and he sported matching purple-black eyes. Shorty visibly paled when he saw me and averted his gaze to floor. As I moved toward the bar, they slid off their stools, took their beers, and stepped out of my way.

I took one of the newly vacated barstools but said nothing, only watched the bartender raptly. He felt the intention of my gaze but stubbornly refused to look at me. As I watched, I kept my ears and the eyes in the back of my head tuned for any signs of sudden bravado from Blondie or Shorty—or any other fool in the room.

Unable to ignore the weight of my stare any longer, the bartender finally stopped in front of me. "What the hell is it this time?" he asked through a clenched jaw. He talked tough, but the raised furrow between his brows gave away his fear. Then it dawned on me: the bartender wondered if I'd greased Tompkins. "I've got nothing to say to you. I think you should leave here while you can still walk."

I rolled my eyes and moved my jacket aside just a bit to flash the gun holstered under my arm. Pictures may say a thousand words, but a gun says so much more. "Tell me what Tompkins was into."

"Fuck you," the barkeep snarled.

That was the wrong answer. I leaned forward across the bar, reached out, and slapped the bartender across the face with an audible whack before he knew what had happened. The part of the room that was within earshot fell silent, while the rest of the bar partied on.

I kept an eye on the guys at the pool tables, but so far they'd remained oblivious to the action at the bar. In what was probably the smartest decision either of them had made all day, Blondie and Shorty continued to sit this one out.

"There's two ways we can do this," I explained. "Yada yada—you know where I'm going with this. But let me remind you that, as far as the police are concerned, you're the last person to have seen Russell alive, as evidenced by my card in his pocket, the card I gave you to pass on. I'm quite sure they'd be interested in having a chat with you. Now, here's the choice you need to make: either answer my questions, or I call the police. My phone is in my pocket." The bartender made no move to do anything other than glare at me. "The phone is now out of my pocket." He still didn't make a move other than to call me that four-letter *C* word that makes most people cringe. I laid it on the bar.

My hand whipped out and struck the bartender again, adding another red print to the one already glowing on his cheek. Still nobody made a move. "Come on—you're a bartender, you guys hear everything! Try again." I touched the screen of my phone and began to dial.

"Okay!" The bartender threw his towel down on the bar. "Russell came in here one night a few weeks ago. He got liquored up and started yammering about how he was going to make a quick fortune. Russell liked to talk a lot when he was drunk, and nobody really paid him any mind. Nobody asked him any questions because you never knew what was going to set him off, and when Russell got mad, people got hurt. We all thought Russell was full of shit until a week later when he showed up driving that big new rig of his."

"He didn't give a name or any indication about who he was doing work for?"

"It wasn't like we was friends."

"So who were Tompkins's friends?"

"Russell didn't have friends. Not a real people person, you know. Russell was a special kind of crazy."

"See, that wasn't so bad, was it?" I dug into my pocket and slapped a twenty on the bar for his time. When I turned to leave, Blondie found his balls and stepped up to block my path. The tables nearest us fell silent, which created a ripple effect across the bar until we had everyone's attention. I had to give Blondie credit for his burst of bravery. He was standing between me and the exit, obviously willing to put his body on the line for his ego. I closed the gap between us so that that only an inch of air separated us. His breath reeked of beer and cigarettes, but the slight quiver in his bruised and bloodshot eyes told me he hadn't yet drank enough liquid courage to make him completely invincible.

"Stand down," I said clear and concisely, "before I put you down." We continued our standoff for another couple of counts before Blondie stepped aside and I made it out the door unscathed.

Outside on Main Street, I found my pulse beating double time. My rig was parked at the curb next to the front door. I got behind the wheel before anyone stepped out of the bar with second thoughts. I pulled around the corner and phoned Mole, who had no trouble coming up with an address for Tompkins. I then promptly plugged the information into the maps app on my phone. The directions took me east past an expanse of cattle ranch land then over the river and through the woods on narrow, twisting roads where cell reception was spotty.

Then the app had me hang a right on Green Mountain Road, which took me even farther into the hills. The skyline disappeared as the forest thickened on both sides of the road. Finally I arrived at a long dirt driveway bearing Tompkins's house number. I wouldn't have been surprised at all if I heard banjos playing in the background when I got out.

At the end of the potholed drive sat a single-wide trailer circa the far side of the '60s, a time when pink house trim was fashionable. I imagined Tompkins had inherited his trailer from an older family member. A rectangle of gravel beside the screen door, which stood ajar, was the only place to park that wasn't in mud. Who knew what to expect—rabid Saint Bernards or rednecks were both possibilities. Either way, my HK was in my hand when I got out.

"Hello?" I called. There was no answer other than the call of the wild from the highest tree branches.

I circled the trailer, peering in through dirty windows at the mess inside. That's not to say I believed someone had broken in and trashed the place; Tompkins just had poor housekeeping habits. Empty beer cans littered the floors. Through the kitchen window I spied a large bag of dog food, which brought me up short. Where there's dog food, there's usually a dog to go with it. Slowly I backed away from the window, turning my attention away from the structure to the overgrown yard.

"Is anyone here?" I called once I got closer to my vehicle, should the dog the bag of food was purchased for come loping out from one of the decaying outbuildings. No canines or rednecks—rabid or otherwise—came at me, though. I'd not drawn down on an animal before, and without my life being challenged, I wasn't sure that I ever could. Humans, on the other hand, were a different story.

Satisfied there were no attack dogs nearby, I climbed up the worn stairs to Tompkins's screened front door, which was hanging askew by a single hinge and came off altogether when I gave it a tug. Without bothering to knock on the thin aluminum door, I put my shoulder into it and gave it a shove. The rotten doorframe gave way easily to my persuasion, and I nearly tumbled inside.

There was no way to tell the original color of the floor beneath the gray-brown grime. The interior smelled like unwashed dog, cigarettes, and mold. When Tompkins had scored his high-paying gig, he certainly hadn't used the gains to improve his living conditions.

With trepidation—mostly because I didn't want to step in something—I picked my way across the living room floor to a broken-down recliner beside a chipped particleboard table. The water-stained top was loaded with precarious piles of unopened mail. I took my time riffling through the stack of unpaid bills and junk mail but discovered nothing of major importance.

Moving on to the kitchen, I saw my first real score: an ashtray overflowing with cigarette butts, each of them burned down to the filter and the same generic brand as those found beside the trail and at the Phillips's back door. But I wasn't looking for proof to put Tompkins at Dr. Phillips's. I was looking for the money trail that would lead me to who bankrolled the hit.

Leaving the kitchen, I made my way over a mountain of dirty laundry piled at the end of the hallway. A broken-down, king-sized bed took up most of the bedroom. A Pink Floyd poster hung askew on the wall over the headboard alongside a tribute band's concert playbill from a music venue in downtown Portland. This must have been the girlfriend's gig. The stained mattress sagged in the center and carried on it the stench of stale sweat and sex.

It didn't take me long to rummage through Tompkins's belongings, which consisted mostly of racing memorabilia, a vintage die-cast car collection, and porn. In the nightstand, I found a collection of sex toys. I opted not to dig any further there.

The rest of the trailer was empty. I dumped the garbage from beneath the sink in the middle of the floor and used a pair of chopsticks from the old takeout on the counter to sort through and extract bits of folded and crumpled paper. I hoped that one of them might have something on it that I could use, like a name or an address. They turned out to be legitimate bits of trash. This place was a wash. I was beginning to get tired of this pattern.

I exited the same way I came in, pulling the ruined screen door shut behind me as well as I could. Tompkins's next of kin would be coming around sooner or later. They could deal with it.

There was still no dog to be found, though I found plenty of evidence of its presence in the not-too-distant past. I doubted any mutts would be hiding silent in the outbuildings. That was where I was headed next. Dog bombs like brown land mines hid in the tall grass between the trailer house and a dilapidated barn out back. There was a shovel caked with red clay dirt just inside the barn door along with several rusted handsaws hanging from the rafters and dried leather harnesses.

Dusty boxes and moldy hay bales piled almost to the rafters took up most of the space. It was going to take me all day to paw through everything. Hopefully I would find something before I had to go moving around hay bales. I peeled back the interwoven cardboard flaps of the boxes to find them filled with old dishes, heaps of pastel plastic containers faded from age, and towels and shirts that rodents had claimed for their nests. I got the feeling someone had once prepped for a yard sale that never happened.

There was enough space for me to get between two tall stacks. I squeezed through, trying not to disturb too much dust. I pulled my shirt up over my nose to prevent inhaling mold spores and followed the path all the way to the back of the barn. There wasn't much to see other than more decaying bales. I peeked through the slats of a stall and noticed that the thick coat of dust along the top of the railing had recently been disturbed. It took a minute to move the bales that had been stacked to block the entrance into the stall, holding my breath against the cloud of dusty mold my movements stirred up. A thick layer of hay had been fluffed and scattered across the earthen floor. When I toed the straw aside, I recognized that the dirt floor had been recently dug up then repacked and smoothed.

I retrieved the shovel by the barn door and made quick work of excavating whatever Tompkins had buried. It turned out to be a black plastic garbage bag inside of which were a thick stack of banded bills and a demolished computer hard drive.

CHAPTER SIXTEEN

"You want me to do *what* with this?"

"I want you to see if you can retrieve anything off of it."

Mole turned the ruined hard drive over in his hands. "It looks like he took it out and used it for target practice then ran it over with his truck. I'm good, but…" He dropped the demolished hard drive on his workbench. "I'll let you know if I get anything." Mole waved me off before adding, "Your new security system is up and operational. I took the liberty of assigning a temporary passcode you'll need to change later. It's N-O-T-T-O-D-A-Y. You'll have thirty seconds to input the code before the alarm starts."

I forgot about the thirty-second delay the moment I opened my front door. When the alarm went off, it was an obnoxiously loud electronic screech that made me want to put a bullet in my wall. I keyed in the passcode, and the racket silenced. I wasn't sure I'd ever get used to that, but I could deal with fixing the volume later. I rang Wickowski and filled him in on my day, omitting the bit about the cash and the hard drive. If anything turned up on the ruined hardware, I'd pass it on. As for the money, with Mole's help it would find its way to Pam Phillips's bank account. It wasn't justice, but it felt right. Wickowski was just getting ready to leave the precinct for some food where he could watch the Blazers home game, so he invited me along like old times.

"I'll meet you in forty-five," I told him. I wasn't a sports fan by any stretch of the imagination, but I would never tell Wickowski that.

I grabbed a quick shower and changed into jeans and a Pearl Jam t-shirt I'd found at a thrift store some years ago. Cindy and I used to spend hours lying on her bed listening to the band. I still played the album *Ten* every year on her birthday. I slid the HK into the waistband of my jeans then pulled the t-shirt down over it. It was a rare evening for spring—clear, dry, and without a breeze—so I opted to walk the twelve blocks to the restaurant. Jake's Famous Crawfish, having been in business for over 120 years, was a historic Portland establishment that was as popular with the hipster crowd as it was with businessmen.

I found Wickowski in a booth toward the back of the restaurant with a perfect view of the big-screen television on which the Blazers pregame was already playing. A plate of fried calamari and a schooner of Bloody Mary sat in front of him. The waitress appeared the moment I took my seat across the table from Wickowski, so I ordered the nachos and a pint of porter.

"Tell me I'm not crazy, Wickowski," I said, helping myself to the pickled bean dangling from his drink.

"Nuh-uh," he answered and tossed a couple of calamari rings into his mouth.

"I can't get a break on this one, Wick."

"Come on Harris, *think!*" Wickowski rapped his head with a meaty finger. "You're a natural when it comes to putting pieces of the puzzle together. What does your gut tell you?"

"That I'm hungry," I deadpanned.

My nachos arrived right on cue, along with my beer, which I immediately slugged down and asked for a refill.

"Did you catch the Blazers game two nights ago?" Wickowski was an avid basketball fan who rooted for Oregon's home team, the Portland Trail Blazers.

"No, can't say that I did."

"Oh, you missed a good one." Wickowski launched into an animated retelling, giving me a play-by-play. My mind wandered to thoughts of Vin and how he'd gotten the short end of my attention since I took on the Dr. Phillips case. I vowed to make up for it once I had things wrapped up. Wickowski cleared his throat.

"Fascinating," I said automatically and a beat too late.

Wickowski threw his hands up. "I just don't get you, Harris. How can you not get excited over a game like that?"

"Because I get enough excitement from my daily life."

The game started on the big screen, so I ordered another round of drinks for Wickowski and me. In an effort to get me onto Team Basketball, Wickowski walked me through each play and each time-out and explained every whistle and the importance of each in the strategy of the game. At halftime, I knew more than I had ever wanted to about the sport. I finished my beer before bidding Wickowski good-night.

"But it's only the end of the third quarter," Wickowski protested. "Wait until the game is over, and I'll give you a lift."

By then I had a proper three-pint buzz, a full belly, and enough of basketball. "I'll talk to you tomorrow."

Wickowski wiped a napkin across his mouth. "At least let me call you a cab."

"I'll be fine. Me, Heckler, and Koch got it covered."

"Well then, at least ring me when you get home so I know I don't have to send out the cavalry. We still don't know who's gunning for you."

"Yes, Dad."

The sidewalks were vacant, and the sky had turned to night. I looked both ways before crossing Burnside in the middle of the block and walked up the north side of the street. There were parts of Portland that it made sense to steer clear of after nightfall, but downtown wasn't one of those. Still, when a cat jumped out from behind a dumpster, my hand instinctively flew to the gun beneath my jacket.

Somewhere along Eleventh Avenue, I became aware of a tail. If it was Wickowski, I was going to kneecap him. However, the closer I listened to the hushed footsteps falling in time with my own, the surer I became that it wasn't him.

I rounded the corner of the next apartment building and ducked into its recessed doorway. Mounted on the ceiling over my head was a single bare bulb that gave off just enough light for a tenant to find the keyhole in the metal door. It also served as a spotlight, making me an easy target. With my sleeve pulled over my hand to keep from getting burned, I unscrewed the bulb just enough for it to go out. Then I stood in the shadows and waited.

The footfalls followed me in a rush around the corner then slowed when they realized I was no longer in their sights. Logically there was only one place I could have ducked into in such a short time. I crouched down into the dark corner of the doorway and made myself as small a target as possible.

Everything slowed. *Breathe deeply...in and out...in and out...but above all else, don't think—just do!* I had no control over my body's response to threat, but I used rhythmic breathing to slow down and quiet my mind.

Slick-slick.

The mechanical sound of the bolt being slid back on a handgun to chamber a bullet was a game changer. The HK was in my hand. I flipped the safety off with my thumb. My timing had to be perfect or I was dead.

Shoes inched toward the doorway. *Five, four, three, two.* The silhouette of a handgun swept in my direction followed by the whisper of suppressed gunfire. A single bullet hit the cement wall with a chink where I'd been standing moments before, blowing a chunk out of the brickwork at heart level.

It was all autopilot from there on out. I launched my body upward and outward, taking my would-be assassin full in the gut. He doubled over me, and together we tumbled onto the sidewalk, both of our guns skittering away out of reach on impact. I struggled to be the first one standing and was successful. Then he wrapped his arms around my legs and pulled me back down. This guy was quick and agile, but he was also muscular and strong. He rolled back on his shoulders then sprang up and got his feet beneath him. I scrabbled for his ankle and caught the full force of his kick in the stomach for my effort.

Adrenaline flooded my system and overrode a wave of nausea. Only my reflexes saved me from a second field goal kick to the gut. I rolled and lashed out with a foot, calling on as much forward power as I could from my quads. I landed a perfect flat-footed kick to the lateral side of his left knee in the strategic spot where fibula, femur, and patella meet. There was a moment of resistance before his cruciate and lateral ligaments gave way with a sickening crunch. Howls of pain filled the street, surely prompting someone to call 911.

I got to my feet and braced for the next round. With a move taken straight from the professional wrestling arena, my attacker lowered his head like a bull and charged. With the building at my back, I had nowhere to go. He caught me in the torso and flung me to the cement once more, this time with deliberate force. The hit drove the air from my lungs and immobilized me momentarily.

His right knee was still in good working order, so he used it to lift himself up and straddle my torso, carefully keeping his ruined knee out of harm's way. Every alarm bell went off inside my head just before his fist smashed into the center of my face. Instantly I tasted blood, which bolstered my instinct to survive, whatever it took.

When I was able to take a breath again, I inflated my lungs with energy-giving oxygen and tried to roll out from between my attacker's legs. He caught me by my shoulder and pinned me to the ground to deliver another punch. The blow caught me just below my left eye. Sparkles danced across my eyelids. A series of fierce blows rained down. I deflected some, but took most. This guy was steroid-strong and meth-crazy—a lethal combination. For the first time, thoughts that I might not survive started to surface.

Fight or flee, fight or flee! my brain screamed to my muscles, demanding action. Struggling to stay conscious, I balled my hand into a fist and then lashed out sideways, connecting fully with the inside of his traumatized knee. Another furious howl of pain ensued.

His guttural rage was like a madman's, stealing his ability to form words. He wrapped his hands around my throat. Instinctively, I brought my cupped hands up to grasp him by the thumbs, wrenching them outward and pulling his hands down to my shoulders. A quick jab to the throat had him sputtering and gasping for breath.

I knew his knee was the part of him I needed to exploit if I were going to get out of the situation. Again I kicked out with my flat foot and caught him there. No longer able to keep himself balanced on his good knee, his body came down hard on the lower half of mine and trapped my legs beneath him. I pushed up onto my hands and tried to crabwalk backward. He overpowered me again as he climbed up my torso using handfuls of shirt and jacket, and pinned me under him once more.

I kicked with my feet, flailed with my legs—anything to free myself. My arms reached back behind me, searching for leverage—the trunk of a tree, a parking meter—anything to grab hold of and pull myself out from under him. My desperate hands found nothing.

When his hands wrapped around my throat again in earnest, I knew I wasn't long for the world. I'd exhausted all my resources, my strength was gone, and nobody was coming to my rescue. Maybe this was how I was destined to die, fighting to the end.

They say one's life flashes before their eyes when they pass from this world into the next. Vin's face swam into focus, followed by Wickowski and Mole. I knew Wickowski wouldn't give up until he found the bastard who had killed me and that when he did, the guy wouldn't make it to lockup. Vin would mourn me and probably enter a dark period in his work. Who knows how Mole would react, probably crash a credit card company or something. My only regret was that I never got to say good-bye.

Sammy, you've got to fight! I heard Cindy's voice in my head. *You promised me you'd never give up. Now just reach out for help. It's right there—just reach for it!*

I didn't understand. Had Cindy come to escort me to the other side? *Reach out, Sammy! Reach out!*

So I did. I reached out with both of my arms, waving them back and forth like I was making a snow angel on the concrete. My fingers brushed against something hard, metal, and familiar. My gun was right there, just out of reach. Like an action hero rallying in the final battle, I pushed against the darkness closing in around me and forced my arm another inch to the right until I could wrap my hand around that beloved HK. Without further thought, I shoved the barrel up and buried it in the center of my attacker's torso, just under his rib cage, and fired a single round.

A .45 caliber bullet is relatively slow, traveling at approximately 850 feet per second. Fired point-blank, the gas and energy of the bullet gets spent inside the chest wall, creating extreme internal damage and pulverizing the soft tissue there. With the sudden loss of oxygenated blood, my attacker's grip around my neck reactively tightened. However, the impact of the shot propelled his body up and away from me, pulling his rigid hands from my neck. He landed, dead, across my left shoulder. Rivulets of thick crimson began to flow from his inert body, forming a gruesome river that emptied into the street gutter.

The air was a repugnant mixture of gunpowder, singed skin, loosed bowels (not mine), and copper, but it was the sweetest air I had ever breathed. I tried gulping lungfuls of it, but my esophagus seized up and I could only get tight, shallow breaths.

Sirens were coming. A few of the apartment's curious residents had finally begun to venture out in response to all the commotion. They filled the doorway, but none noticed the bullet that was embedded in the wall behind them. The police turned off their sirens, and only the flashing of their red-and-blue disco lights announced their arrival.

I slid my shoulder out from beneath the body and put my HK back into its holster. I stripped off my bloody jacket with as little movement as possible, just barely getting my arms out of the sleeves and letting the rest lie crumpled beneath me. The first officer at the scene took one look at the body on the sidewalk, the blood on me, the gun at my shoulder, and assumed the worst. Blue uniforms surrounded me, weapons drawn, each of them screaming orders.

"On your stomach! Put your hands out from your body!"

"Now! Put your hands out from your body and roll over!"

"Now, now, move it!"

"Hands out, on your stomach!"

With all four officers barking their own set of instructions and waving their weapons, the scene quickly turned chaotic. How many people were charged with resisting arrest when really they were just confused as hell? With the heightened tension, it wasn't a good time to explain that I was one of the good guys. I didn't want to survive being attacked only to be gunned down by nervous friendly fire. As gingerly as I could, I rolled my battered body over onto my belly with my arms stretched straight out from my sides. The officer closest to me reached down and removed my gun from its holster. Lying prone did nothing good for my broken ribs, but if I tried to get up, these cops would put me back down—forcefully—and that would hurt even worse.

"My identification and permit to carry are in my jacket, inside pocket," I tried to tell them in my hoarse and hard-to-hear voice. I shut my eyes against the next wave of nausea. As the minutes ticked by, the adrenaline dissipated from my blood-stream. I began to stiffen in reaction to the soft tissue trauma, and the blood on my face began to get dry and crusty. A deep, all-encompassing agony settled into my entire body as I faded in and out of consciousness.

"Jesus, Harris, next time I offer a ride, please do us all a favor and take me up on it." Wickowski swam into view when I opened my eyes and looked up. He stood over me with his thumbs hooked on his belt buckle, a series of emotions playing across his face—worry, anger, and finally relief. He crouched beside my head. "I'd ask about the other guy, but he ain't looking so hot." Wickowski caught sight of my face in the wash of the ambulance's headlights and winced. "But then, neither are you."

I coughed and spit a glob of blood onto the sidewalk. "At least I'll live another day."

In a moment of tenderness I'd never seen before or since, Wickowski gently helped me to roll over, but he stopped me from sitting up. "Think you should be looked over by the EMTs first?"

"Give me a second." I felt like a coed after a frat party. The world took off at a spin. Bile rose to the back of my throat, and I focused my attention on not wearing regurgitated nachos and porter. I really disliked this case now. "Okay," I said with a tentative sigh. "Help me up."

Wickowski motioned to the closest cop, and they each took an arm and shoulder and helped me to my feet. The EMTs unloaded a wheeled gurney and brought it around to the front of the vehicle, where Wickowski was helping me to stay vertical. The gurney bumped up to the back of my legs so all I had to do was sit down and the ambulance team took it from there, working together to swing my legs up while guiding me to lie back.

"We're taking her to Emanuel," the driver told Wickowski. "Do we have permission to transport and treat you?" he asked me directly.

It should be known that I've never liked doctors, I've always hated hospitals, and I've never felt any love for the ER. Nothing against the medical profession. I'd had my share of stitches and broken bones, and the pain and needles that go along with them. I'd even had a couple of bullets pulled out of me, but that's another story altogether.

"She gives you permission," Wickowski said in such a way that neither the driver nor I argued with him. He gave my hand a squeeze; it was probably the only part of my body that didn't hurt. "I'll be right behind you."

{* * *}

The distance across the river to the hospital was barely three miles, but it was near the Moda Center, and they were post-Blazers-home-game-traffic miles. When we arrived, two nurses and a doctor met the ambulance at the entrance, and the EMTs gave them their report: blunt-force trauma to the head and torso, possible broken ribs, likely ruptured spleen.

Someone came in and took my vitals then left me to fight my hospital phobia on my own until the nurse came around. I tried to rub my hands up and down my arms, but any movement amped up the throbbing in my head. I closed my eyes and let my body do what it needed to do.

"Oh, you poor dear," purred a kindly nurse when she popped her head into my room. She disappeared momentarily and returned with a warmed flannel blanket draped over her sausage-like arm. "Look at what that bastard's done to you," she said as she gently laid the blanket over my quaking body. "My name is Martha, and I'm going to take good care of you. No need to worry about that son of a bitch now." Martha gave my hand a reassuring pat. "The police will see that he gets what's coming to him." What Martha didn't understand was that I'd already seen to that.

My shivering didn't subside right away, but the heat penetrated deep and made things more bearable. The atmosphere of the room changed with the arrival of the attending doctor, a trim gentleman whose hair had begun to thin and gray.

"Miss Harris?" the doctor read from the paperwork the EMTs left behind.

"Here," I muttered and raised a finger off the bed.

"I'm Dr. Gillespie." The doctor extended his hand, but I only nodded. It hurt to move. I knew he understood. "Miss Harris," Dr. Gillespie continued, "it says here that you refused pain medication."

"I'm all for drugs—bring them on—I just refused the needle."

"Why would you refuse pain medication?" he asked, clearly not getting my angle. To make his point, the good doctor walked his fingers along my abdomen, and I cried out in pain. He didn't need to look so smug.

"I want to be clearheaded when I give my statement to the police," I explained, hoping he'd back the hell off.

Dr. Gillespie had nothing to say to that. He picked up my wrist and took my pulse. With a satisfied nod, he pulled a pen light from the pocket of his white coat and flashed the beam across my pupils. "A minor concussion, but nothing serious," he said, mostly to himself. "I smell alcohol on your breath. You've been drinking?"

"I had dinner with a friend, and we had a couple of beers."

"Enough to intoxicate you?"

"Hardly," I said with a snort, then paid the price for my cheekiness with the bolt of pain that flashed across my brain.

Dr. Gillespie crossed his arms and shifted his weight back on his heels. "I don't have to be an emergency room doctor to see you're in a great deal of pain and discomfort, but we cannot give you anything until we know what you've already got on board. Do you understand that, Miss Harris?"

"Trust me, Doc, I have a high threshold."

Another woman appeared in the doorway as if answering a silent call. This one didn't give off the kindly vibe that Martha had; she was uptight and all business. She introduced herself as liaison to the district attorney's office, Dorothy Cromwell. "When you're ready, I'll take your statement and answer any questions you may have about the process of pressing charges against your attacker."

I couldn't help a small chuckle, even though it hurt. "Who would I press charges against?"

Ms. Cromwell stepped to my bedside with her clipboard and a disapproving look. "How many times has he done this to you, and how many times will you survive his attacks? The DA's office can't do anything unless you press charges. That's the only way we can stop the cycle of abuse."

I understood—and appreciated—the swift response to my suspected domestic abuse but felt the attention could be better spent on someone in real need. "You don't understand—"

"I do understand. You're not the first woman to balk at pressing charges against her abuser. If you just give me his name, we will send the police to pick him up, and I can personally guarantee he'll spend the next forty-eight hours behind bars. That should be enough time to get you out and somewhere safe. Just give us a name."

"I don't have a name, but I'm pretty sure you'll find him in the meat wagon on the way down to the city morgue."

"Wait a minute." Liaison Cromwell's voice spiked a couple of octaves. "You mean he's dead?"

"A single .45 round point-blank to the heart. He's beyond dead—more like a slushy inside a skin sack."

The truth will set you free. It will also garner you unwanted attention. Ms. Cromwell turned to Dr. Gillespie. "Is she serious?"

Dr. Gillespie could only shrug.

Nurse Martha returned, only this time she kept her charm sequestered, sensing the shift in the room. She pulled the curtain around the bed closed against Ms. Cromwell, who was already heading for the door, and handed me a thin gown. She began cutting up the length of my jeans with a pair of blunt-ended scissors all the way to the waistband. She repeated this with my other pant leg until she could separate the two halves, essentially freeing me from my pants. She helped me sit up then came at my shirt with the same scissors. I threw my hands up. "Whoa, not Pearl Jam." I worked to ease my arms from the sleeves myself. Nurse Martha helped get my arms through the proper holes of the gown. My body continued to spasm and quake. I wrapped the flannel blanket around me, but it had lost its immediate warmth—kind of like Nurse Martha.

Another orderly darkened my doorway to wheel me upstairs to x-ray. After my photo session, they wheeled me in to get a CT scan of my noggin.

Where the hell is Wickowski? I thought once they wheeled me back to the curtained room. The pain in my head had really begun to dig its heels into the backs of my eyes. The pillow was light enough to rest on my forehead and cover my eyes without touching my nose, which, by the grace of the Almighty, I hoped wasn't broken.

I had no idea how long I lay there in the curtained room. I must have dozed off; I woke when the edge of the bed sagged. I opened my eyes and peeked out from beneath the pillow. Wickowski was grinning beside me.

"Hey, Harris," he said in a voice just above a whisper. His hand was warm on the back of mine.

"Hey, Wick."

"Where does it hurt the most?"

"You see that spot on the top of my head?"

Wickowski leaned forward and clearly didn't know what I was talking about, but he nodded anyway.

"Now see that place right above the bottom of my foot?"

"Yeah..."

"I hurt in all that space in between."

"Smart-ass."

"At least that's not broken."

"You know, in a way, that guy is lucky he's already dead."

"Why's that?"

"Because when you see what he did to your face, you're going to want to kill him all over again. You've got quite a nice purple-and-green necklace of bruises, which complements your eyes." Wickowski did his best to keep the mood light. "Seriously though, how do you feel?"

"Like I just got the shit beat out of me." A thin smile crept over my lips. "But I won."

"You want to give me your statement? It can wait until tomorrow, you know."

"No, I'm ready." I tried to adjust my position but really could only bend my knees. "I picked him up right after I left you at the restaurant," I began, taking him all the way through the encounter to the point of shots fired. He listened intently, wincing at the appropriate places, but jotting nothing down on paper.

"Did you get a look at him?"

"Well, Wick, he probably looked just like he does now, but with a little more color to his cheeks."

"I meant have you ever seen him before tonight?"

"I didn't get a solid look at him. He had a hood on at first, then with the dim lighting..." My voice trailed off into a shrug.

"You've either angered someone or frightened them. Either way, they're gunning for you hard."

"It's my job to piss people off."

"Overachiever. I'm going to put a detail on you for—"

"No."

"Harris—"

"No, Wick. I don't need babysitters or bodyguards." Wickowski opened his mouth in protest, but I cut him off. "What I do need is pants."

Just then Dr. Gillespie pulled the curtain partition aside with the results of my x-rays and CT scan in his hand. Wickowski excused himself and ducked around the curtain, disappearing down the hall.

"Four cracked ribs, but no fractures. No factures of any cranial or facial bones either. Your CT shows some evidence of previous trauma. Have you ever been struck in the head, or fallen and hit it?"

It would be safe to say I'd taken a few punches in my time. "Do bar fights count?" The scowl on the good doctor's face answered my question.

"You've a mild concussion, nothing serious, but I would like to admit you overnight for observation—"

I was already shaking my head at *admit*. "I understand, Doc, but I do home better than hospital."

"With all due respect, ma'am, I highly recommend—"

Again I was shaking my head. "I appreciate it, but I've been to this rodeo before. No sports, nothing strenuous, watch for migraines and nausea."

With a sigh, Dr. Gillespie told me to wait for a nurse with my discharge papers. Wickowski returned with a pair of police-blue sweatpants rolled up under his arm. "Best I could do. It's cold in the morning, so I wear these over my shorts when I go to work out, but they're clean."

I looked suspiciously at the proffered sweatpants. "This is the closest I ever want to get to your junk, Wick."

"I said I wear them over my gym shorts!"

Nurse Martha appeared with my discharge papers, and Dr. Gillespie joined us with after-care instructions. "Your bruised ribs will heal, but in the meantime, let pain be your guide. If something hurts, don't do it." He told me to go home and rest then repeated the grocery list of watch-out-fors that I was already well versed in. Like I said, not my first rodeo. "You're extremely fortunate not to have suffered further injury, Ms. Harris. Let us hope your luck never runs out."

"Like I've always said, what doesn't kill me better run like hell."

My brand of humor missed its mark on the doctor. He had me sign on a special line admitting that I was denying overnight accommodations. Then he turned to Wickowski. "Will she have anyone to see she gets home safely?"

"Yes." Wickowski nodded. "I'll make sure she makes it home without shooting anybody else." The doctor didn't find Wickowski humorous either.

"One last thing: I'm going to write you a prescription for some pain medication. What do you normally take?"

"A couple shots of whisky and a hot bath."

Dr. Gillespie's face remained mirthless. He tore off a page from his notepad, scribbled on it, and handed it to Wickowski as they exited my curtained room.

When I finished pulling Wickowski's sweatpants on and donned my bra and t-shirt, something that took an extraordinarily long time by myself, the same wheelchair was waiting for me. Wickowski handed me a plastic evidence bag and my shoulder holster when I emerged. Inside were my bloody jacket and my HK.

"Hospital procedure says you've got to ride in the chair all the way to the curb." Wickowski smirked—he was enjoying seeing me at the whim of policy. Much to his surprise, I didn't make a stink about being wheeled out. It beat walking in my current condition. Being a cop had its privileges. Wickowski's car was parked right next to the emergency room doors in a spot marked for emergency vehicles only.

Over the Fremont Bridge and I was back home. Wickowski double-parked and helped me up to my loft. It was the wee hours, and nobody, not even Mole, was up. He made a quick walk through my place to make sure I didn't have any more surprises to contend with.

"Do you want me to stay here tonight? I could sleep on the couch."

"I'll be fine. It's late, go home to your wife." I wondered what he told Mrs. Wickowski on nights like this, or if she even bothered to ask anymore.

"They wanted to keep you in for observation. You should be observed."

"I'm going to sleep, that's it. Call me in the morning to make sure I'm alive if you're worried."

"You want me to ring Vinny?" Wickowski asked. "Let him know what happened?"

"No, he'll only worry. I'm sure I'll look better come morning."

"Don't bet on it. Call me if you need me."

"Sure." I walked Wickowski to the door and locked it behind him. My bed sounded heavenly, but I only made it as far as the couch, where I peeled off my bloody shirt and Wickowski's sweats and left them in a heap on the floor. I crawled under the throw blanket, wanting to mull over the fact I'd killed a man. Killing in self-defense isn't something I set out to do; when it came down to kill or be killed, I made my choice. *Don't think, just do.* I wasn't feeling any remorse for taking his life, however, and that bothered me.

CHAPTER SEVENTEEN

THE FOLLOWING MORNING, I WAS GREETED BY AN OVERCAST SKY and the incessant buzzing of my intercom. Whoever was at the lobby door was very persistent in wanting to come up. My thoughts were fuzzy and unclear, the typical pre-coffee morning haze. The events of the previous night didn't come to mind until I attempted to roll off the couch, which made my body scream in agony. Then it all came rushing back: the attack, the beating, the shooting, and the pain.

The buzzing from downstairs continued, so I did what I could and reached for the phone. "Mole, tell me who's at the front door."

"Looks like it's your cop friend."

"Will you let him up for me?"

"Your legs broke?"

"The hospital said nothing was broken," I said, letting Mole hang on that cryptic bit before I hung up.

Not needing Wickowski to see me appearing incapacitated or naked, I gritted through the pain and used the back of the couch to help pull myself up then carefully put my feet over the edge to the floor. The world didn't take off at a spin, nor did I feel like hurling—so far, so good. However, that all changed, at least momentarily, once I finally stood.

When the tilt-a-whirl in my head eventually stopped, I unlocked the front door and shuffled to the bedroom, where I donned one of Vin's oxford shirts over a pair of running shorts. "Come in," I hollered when Wickowski knocked.

Wickowski stepped inside dressed in one of his usual gray suits, smelling of Irish Spring and the coffee that he carried in. A bakery bag was tucked beneath his arm.

"Good morning, Sunshine. I brought you some breakfast and coffee."

"You are my favorite human right now, Wick." I took a coffee from him and managed a careful sip. My mood was instantly improved.

Wickowski opened the bakery bag and gave it a shake. "Have a bagel. I had them cut it up into tiny little pieces for you. Easier to chew that way."

"Thanks." It was out of character for him to be so thoughtful. He was more of a fend-for-yourself kind of guy.

"Full bloom." Wickowski circled a finger in front of his face in reference to my injuries.

"I'm afraid to look," I admitted, talking around a piece of bagel. It hurt my jaw to eat, but at least I still had all my teeth to chew with. The picture in my head of what I must look like wasn't pretty. I touched my face with gentle fingers and gasped at the size of my cheeks. I was going to have matching shiners for sure.

"Vinny might say your bruises are from Monet's palette—myriad hues of aubergine and indigo," Wickowski said poetically.

"Dude, stop. You're creeping me out."

"With Hollywood lips." Wickowski made a duck-faced pout. His antics made me laugh, which quickly turned to a moan.

"I also went back and dug this out of the wall." Wickowski handed me a plastic zipped baggie, which held the 9mm slug.

"You guys ID him yet?"

"Actually we did. This is where things really get interesting. We ran his prints and got a hit: Trevor Erickson, a low-level thug whose last cellmate was an old friend of Tompkins's going back to their juvey days. Erickson had his dirty fingers in all sorts of things, from running girls on MLK to a series of home invasions in the Hawthorne District."

"And I was starting to get concerned that I didn't feel bad for putting a bullet in him."

"Way I see it, you took out a major player from Team Scumbag. Regret is highly overrated. Someone out there wants you dead." Wickowski gave a humorless chortle. "Dammit if you're just stubborn enough to still be alive. Maybe you should take some vacation time and go back east for a while. Visit your family for a few weeks while I get to the bottom of things here. Might keep you alive for a little longer."

Wickowski has obviously never met my family. "I'll take my chances on this coast."

"Okay, but for the record, I think you're taking this lone renegade thing a little far." Wickowski checked his wristwatch then stood to leave. "I've got places to be and people to fry. Try not to kill anyone today, all right?"

"Can't make any promises." I walked him to the door.

Wickowski turned to me with soft eyes. "Don't get dead."

"Not in my plan, at least not today." I waved Wickowski off and placed the chain in its groove but ignored the alarm. I was beginning to second-guess my decision to have it installed. I gripped my coffee cup and leaned against the door with the dire thought that this case was about to get messy. Real messy.

Being in pain was exhausting. I reclaimed my place on the couch and snuggled under the knit throw. Sleep taunted me, lulling me into its circle and then ousting me before I could fully fall. I'd never been one for narcotic pain relief; I preferred to keep control. *Break the pain cycle and get some real rest*, my inner voice urged. I looked at the prescription lying on the coffee table. *I've always been able to tough my way through any pain. Why should this be any different?* As if to answer myself, a tickle in my throat caused an involuntarily cough, which almost had me passing out and made the decision a whole lot easier.

The trek to the drugstore was a short trip by foot made even shorter by driving. I pushed through the door into the small store filled with modern medicines and time-tested remedies. At the counter in the back of the store, I passed the prescription to a technician who eyed me with a mixture of sympathy and curiosity.

While I waited for the prescription to be filled, I took the time to stock up on bandages, sterile tape, aspirin, and antiseptic. If the past couple of days were any indication, I'd be needing them. When I got back in line to make my purchase, I noticed the lingering gazes of those around me and self-consciously pulled up the collar of my jacket to hide the bruising around my neck. Without making eye contact, I paid the woman at the counter and dropped the little bag containing the pain meds into the bigger bag with the rest of my supplies.

Returned home, I shook two Vicodin tablets into my hand and downed them with the last of the now-cold coffee that Wickowski had brought, then chased it with a shot of whisky straight from the bottle. Just as I was headed back to kick it on the couch, my cell phone began to buzz. I picked it up off the coffee table and cringed. It was Vin.

"I was wondering if you'd be interested in joining me on a visit to the Japanese Garden. Everything's in bloom, and it's going to be beautiful. Oh"—Vin's train of thought changed—"did you hear some guy got shot a couple blocks over? People are downright crazy."

"You're preaching to the choir, Vin."

"So, want to hang out today?"

Either the pain meds were kicking in or someone possessed my body and thus my mouth. Either way, I was overtaken by extreme honesty. "I'm the one who shot that guy last night. He started it, so call it self-defense if that sits better with you."

Honestly I didn't know what I expected Vin to do with that bomb. It is what it is. A long, hollow silence followed. I would have thought he'd hung up if not for the traffic I could hear in the background on his end of the call.

"Were you hurt?" Vin finally asked.

"My ego is worse for wear. Besides, pain is only temporary, and guys dig scars."

"I don't mean your body—it will heal. I mean you. How are *you*?"

Oh. To be honest, I was physically on the mend, and mentally— well, it was always chaotic up there. Remorse wasn't forthcoming because the way I saw it, I'd done Portland and the world at large a giant favor by making it short one bad guy. Of course, that wasn't what Vin needed to hear.

"I could use some company," I offered. "Someone to hold an ice bag or something."

"I'm on my way."

I hung up the phone with cautious relief. Vin took the news surprisingly well—much better than I'd expected. The Vicodin had started a pleasant, full-body buzz in my center that was working its way down my limbs and up to my head, bringing a goofy grin to my face. My eyes wanted to close, and I wished I could turn on the stereo from the couch. Instead I dialed Mole.

"Hey, Moley," I said overenthusiastically when he picked up. "Holy Moley!" I added with a laugh.

"Sammy?" Mole asked suspiciously.

"Holy Moley?"

I heard him scoff, "Sammy, are you drunk?"

"Nope, Vicodin, though I'm not sure if they've kicked in yet or not."

"Oh, Sammy," my name rode out of his mouth on a laugh, "they have."

"Really? I feel all warm and fuzzy, but my head still hurts."

Mole gave a low whistle. "Give them a few more minutes. Say good-night, Sammy."

"G'night, Sammy."

I hung up with a sigh and stared at the ceiling, having never before noticed the texturing up there that, if I gazed long enough, formed images and shapes like clouds used to when I was a kid. My drug-addled daydreams were interrupted when I heard Vin rattle my doorknob then use the key I gave him to let himself in. There was noticeably less pain when I pulled myself up as he entered. He tried several times to say something when he saw me, but either he couldn't find the right words or his mouth refused to form them. Then he stepped inside and wrapped careful arms around me in a soft hug. I was officially feeling little pain.

As gently as if picking up a wounded bird, Vin carried me in his arms to my bed. I mumbled something incoherent when he laid me down; he settled himself beside me. The last thing I was cognizant of were Vin's fingers brushing the hair away from my eyes and his soft, butterfly kiss on my cheek. Then the world went dark and silent.

{* * *}

My loft was empty when I woke up the next morning. The urge to stretch overcame me before I could stop it, and to my pleasant surprise, my pain levels had dropped from a nine to a solid six, which was tolerable. I eased the bed covers aside and warily sat up, both pleased and surprised when the room didn't take off at a spin.

Still using caution in my movements but not needing to use the wall to help myself along, I wandered into the kitchen. A note was resting against a shiny new coffee pot, beside which was a matching chrome bean grinder and a two-pound bag of Sumatran beans. I pick up the note and read it:

Sam—

I'm sorry I couldn't be here when you woke up, but frankly I don't know when that might be. You've already slept about twenty hours. I didn't want to disturb you—you looked so angelic lying there. I'll check in on you later. Call me when you wake up.

Enjoy your coffee pot!

Love, Vin

To my knowledge, nobody had ever put the word *angelic* and me into the same sentence before, though I'd been called plenty of other things. A coffee pot hadn't graced my kitchen counter previously because I wasn't overly domestic, and places like Steam existed for that reason. But it was the thought that counted, so I took the new appliance for a spin. I'd seen Seth go through the motions enough to muddle my way through the brewing process, first grinding beans then transferring the grounds to the basket and adding water.

Before a quick shower, I downed a couple of Excedrin Extra Strengths as a preemptive measure. The prescription from Dr. Gillespie was good and all, but I'd lost a day somewhere in there, and that wasn't cool.

When the coffee pot was done, I filled a pint-sized canning jar and carried it onto the balcony outside my bedroom where the early afternoon sun gently warmed the tiles beneath my feet. What a difference a day makes. It was much easier and less painful to breathe. The day was still relatively young, and I had work to do. I reached for my phone.

"Wickowski." His bark had more bite to it than usual.

"Who pissed in your cereal this morning?" I asked.

"Burnell is kissing ass with the mayor over the Phillips case. Burnell wants to take the case back under PPB control. The mayor sees that as a PR nightmare, and I'm the one stuck in the middle."

"Anything I can do?"

"This drama will blow over soon enough. Shit rolls downhill, is all. On second thought..." He paused. "Stay alive. That'll make my life much easier." Wickowski hung up without his usual good-bye.

A familiar concern worked at the back of my mind: *Had I missed something at the Phillipses' house?* That was when I decided that, despite not being in fighting condition, I would return to the Phillipses' house and not leave until I found whatever it was that I was looking for, even if it took me the rest of the day.

{* * *}

I drove around the block twice, alert for anyone suspicious. When I came to the conclusion that danger wasn't hiding in the bushes or behind tinted glass, I pulled into Pam's driveway and parked. Samuel was playing in his yard next door and came running the moment I stepped from my vehicle.

"Samantha!" he called, waving.

"Hey, Sam. Staying out of trouble today?"

"Mom says she knows when I'm up to no good because everything gets quiet. Now I try to make noise when I'm doing something I'm not supposed to. It throws her off." Sam looked over his shoulder toward the house. "Don't tell Mom I told you that."

"Hey"—I put up my hand in a sign of solidarity—"your secret's safe with me, little buddy." I decided to change the subject and squatted down to his eye level. "Have you seen anybody besides the police come by Dr. Phillips's place since I was here last?"

Sam shook his head and shrugged. "I think people avoid death whenever possible."

"I find it's a good rule to live by when you can," I said, then turned for the front door. "Take care, Sam." He gave me another wave and scampered back to his trucks and pile of gravel.

Never one to be under-cautious—a point Wickowski would surely argue—I walked the perimeter of the house and looked for signs of further visitations. Everything appeared to be as I left it, locked and pretty much intact. I used my key to open the front door and found the air inside stale and lifeless. Taking no chances, I pulled the HK and started up the stairs. If I encountered anyone, my plan was to drop them and sort it out later. Today was not a day for negotiations.

The last time I searched Dr. Phillips's office, I hadn't known what I was looking for. After the events at my office and the attack on the street, I had to also assume that whoever employed Tompkins hadn't found the goods either. Thus I made a more in-depth, methodical search of Dr. Phillips's office, reading each piece of paper and looking over every check stub, receipt, and bill with patience. The only things I discovered were Pam's shopping habits and the family's outstanding debt, which was in the hundreds of thousands and included a recently purchased vacation property in Bend plus Pam's new car, a fully loaded Volvo. When I measured their debt-to-income against old bank statements, it was clear that the family had spent well beyond their means. In my line of work, I called that a red flag.

These financials didn't necessarily mean Dr. Phillips was dirty. His favorite aunt could have passed away and left all her worldly possessions to the family, or they may have picked the lucky winning jackpot numbers or played the stock market with success. From everything I'd heard about Saint Ronny, he wasn't a candidate for deadbeat of the year. He did not seem the type to have willingly put his family into financial difficulty, so he must have felt confident in his abilities to meet his commitments.

With an exasperated huff, I put everything back into the file cabinet as neatly as I'd found it. Then I recalled seeing a report in the bathroom while I was trying not to bleed to death on my last visit. It hadn't meant anything to me at the time, and it still might not. It had something to do with vaccines, exactly what McPherson was dabbling in down in Brazil. I retraced my steps to the bathroom and found the interoffice communication I was looking for:

Outsourcing clinical trials from the United States to developing countries has grown exponentially. Pharmaceutical companies continue to struggle against rising costs and tighter regulations, making globalization of clinical trials inevitable.

"Malaria remains an underappreciated epidemic, killing 2.7 million people a year—most of them children. This disease claims nearly 4,000 young lives daily. We look forward to helping to save the lives of millions and to curb the misery caused by this dreaded disease," says Dr. Faustino Ignacio Oliveira, Senior Vice President of Novus Laboratories, São Paulo, Brazil.

I fished my cell from my pocket and rang Mole. "I need more intel on Novus, N-O-V-U-S, in São Paulo, Brazil."

"Sure, hang on."

I held on the line for several minutes, waiting for Mole to do his magic while listening to him hum the theme song from *Dragnet.*

"All right, I'm in. They've got some pretty good security, but since I'm a god...What are we looking for?"

"I want financials: investors, corporate grants, anything of that sort."

"Hold a second, por favor." More whistling as he typed, a lively Latin tune this time.

"Okay, got it. Umm, Sammy, there's not a whole lot of stuff here. A few personal investors—"

"Is there anyone by the name of Talbert or Phillips listed?"

"Nope."

"All right," I said, disappointed. "Print off the page of personal investors for me. I'll stop by for them later."

"Sure. How about these corporate grants?"

"How many are there?"

"Only two listed that are corporate, but there's a lot of government ones."

"I'm only interested in corporate right now."

"There is a Mentor Waterhouse LTD and a Promega Solutions Trust."

"Can you look into both of those and see if you find a connection with Talbert or Phillips?"

"Sure, but it will take a minute."

"Just call me back when you have it." I slipped the cell back into my pocket and returned to Dr. Phillips's office to continue pawing through the paperwork in his desk. It didn't take but a few minutes before Mole rang me back.

"That was quick," I marveled.

"I've got both boxes crunching, and I got a hit right off. Promega Solutions Trust gave Novus $500 million back in '99, which, by the way—whoa—is a lot of cash. Anyway, I hacked into Promega's shareholder page, and—score!—found Talbert's name. You owe me."

"Steven Talbert, of S.T. Finance?"

"One and the same."

"Mole, you're a prince among men. I don't care what the others say."

"Wait—what? Which others? What are they saying about me?"

I rolled my eyes even though Mole couldn't see me through the phone. "It's a figure of speech, Mole. Relax. I'll bring you something this evening."

"Okay," Mole said skeptically. "If it isn't a blonde or a six-pack, don't bother."

When I was a kid, I had loved to do connect-the-dot pages. My sister, Frankie, and I always tried to guess what the picture was before we finished the page. I had dots to connect here, but I couldn't make out the picture yet. I was getting close, though.

Novus Labs seemed to be the axis of this triumvirate. If Talbert and Dr. Phillips were involved with McPherson and his vaccine trials, all three stood to become very rich men upon the vaccine's successful release. That would explain the Phillipses' inflated lifestyle. Money has always been the oldest motive for murder. Well, that and love.

I now had motivation and opportunity, but what I really needed was evidence so I could wrap it all up into a neat, tidy package to hand over to the DA. Yeah right. And for Christmas I wanted a pony.

Having exhausted my search of Dr. Phillips's office, I ventured back downstairs to the living room and sat on the uncomfortable antique couch to change my perspective and think. The clock on the mantel kept time while life marched on. The refrigerator down the hall cycled on with a loud hum, ruffling the blanket of silence that had descended over the home.

Statistically speaking—though human nature is also a factor—there are a handful of places an individual will hide something in their home. There's the freezer and the toilet tank, like we've all seen in the movies. If the item being hidden is small, taping it to the underside of a drawer is a popular choice. I'd seen diversion safes sold at gun stores that were made to look like typical household items. I took Dr. Phillips as an intelligent man but not all that street-smart. It took me four hours to exhaust all those possibilities, in addition to unscrewing all the electrical plates, another popular hiding place. I knocked around for false walls and loose floorboards in the office. Nothing.

Once again, I sat down—this time at the kitchen table—to regroup and listen to my stomach rumble. My head was beginning to throb. Sure that Pam wouldn't care, I raided her refrigerator and relieved it of two slices of bread with a smear of grape jelly, plus a couple of Oreos from the cookie jar to satisfy my hunger. As I chewed my jelly sandwich and crunched my cookies, I broke down my thoughts. With the theft of the electronics, it made sense to believe Tompkins was looking for digital information, so I was pretty sure I was searching for a thumb drive or the like. If the house was the wife's domain, the garage was the man's. With determination in my step, I exited the front door and followed the walk around to the single-car detached garage that had been a carriage house back in the day. Luckily the front door key also fit the garage side door.

A length of string dangled from the ceiling. When I pulled it, a row of fluorescent tubes spurted and hummed to life. When the pallid light revealed a cement pad swept clean and oil-free, I felt I should have taken off my shoes lest I track something in. In lieu of typical garage odors like motor oil, paint, or lingering exhaust, all I could smell was the green tree air freshener hanging just inside the door.

The repurposed garage was only big enough for one vehicle, and Dr. Phillips's BMW was parked in the middle. Metal shelves lined both of the long walls with a wooden workbench at the far end, which didn't show any signs of heavy use. The family's bicycles hung from J-shaped hooks screwed into the wide ceiling beams.

I ran a finger across the hood of Dr. Phillips's BMW, on which a fine layer of dust had settled. The metal shelves along the side walls were stacked with plastic-lidded boxes color coded by holiday and marked with a permanent marker. Unfinished craft projects sat forgotten in a woven laundry basket.

An upright toolbox like you might see in a mechanic's bay stood beside the workbench. Six-inch casters mounted along the bottom of the heavy toolbox made it easy to roll away from the wall. I got down on my hands and knees and ran my hand along the underside. A spider trying to escape my reach skittered out of the way.

I pulled my hand back and gasped, my heart pounding inside my chest. *Seriously?!* I'd happened upon bodies in various stages of decomposition, and it's a spider that made me go all girly?

The toolbox was locked, but it was nothing a screwdriver and some leverage couldn't remedy. Ironically, those were locked inside. A tire iron among the larger tools on the wall helped me with that. The screech of resisting metal had me gritting my teeth as I gave the tire iron one last torque and the lock mechanism fell apart. Feeling that I was getting warmer, I ran my hand along the underside of the drawer, but found nothing. I repeated this with each subsequent drawer, working my way down, only to come up empty-handed.

Frustration was beginning to raise its impatient head. I leaned against the Bimmer with an exasperated sigh, nails tapping double time on the hood. *Think!* A thumb drive is a tiny thing and easy enough to stash anywhere. A decade ago I'd be looking for something disc-sized—*Oh!* A hunch kicked me hard in my own spidey sense. Quickly I rounded the car to the driver's side, hoping it wasn't locked, and I let out a whoop when I found it wasn't. Truth be told, I would have smashed the window with the tire iron had it not been unlocked.

The scent of leather, tinged with a vestige of the doctor's cologne that still lingered, enveloped me when I slid in behind the wheel. I pulled down the sun visor, and a set of keys fell into my lap. The police had stashed them there knowing they were leaving the victim's car inside a locked garage. I slipped the key into the ignition and turned it so that the electrical came on.

The dashboard lit up like a cockpit. I reached over and touched the stereo's eject button. With a whir and a click, out popped a silver CD-R. Two simple words were printed across the middle of the disc in Ronald Phillips's blocky handwriting, and in that moment, I knew I'd found exactly what I had come looking for:

Free Bird.

CHAPTER EIGHTEEN

"What's this?" Mole asked when I shoved the "Free Bird" disc into his hand.

"Let's find out, shall we?" I asked anxiously. Leaving the Phillipses' house, I'd doubled back and taken side streets. I was pretty sure I hadn't picked up a tail, but sometimes *pretty sure* can equate to *pretty dead.*

"Can it wait for an hour or so? I have a hot conversation going with this techno chick in New York—"

"No!" I cut Mole off with my eagerness. "This is it. This is what everyone, including me, has been searching for."

"You were looking for Lynyrd Skynyrd's lost recordings?" Mole mused, pondering the disc in his hand.

"Something like that."

Mole gave me his perturbed expression and blew a sigh through his cheeks. "All right," he said as he typed a message, "but this is gonna cost you." He sent off his text and looked at me like a dog that had been denied the neighbor's bitch. "Lexi may not have been Ms. Right, but she was definitely Ms. Right-at-the-Moment."

"I apologize, Mole. I'll make it up to you, I promise."

Mole batted his lashes at me. "Oh, Sammy, you tease. Don't make promises you have no intention of keeping."

I slapped him on the shoulder good-heartedly. "Grow up. I was thinking more along the lines of a six-pack."

"Are you kidding me? You want me to interrupt my chat session with this wickedly beautiful specimen of the female form, and all you bring to the table is the offer of beer? I can get beer delivered *and* satisfy my carnal desires." He turned away with a humph, like I'd genuinely insulted him.

I put my hands up and gagged. "Dude—TMI! Fine." I sighed. "Name your price."

"Ten grand."

"Name another one," I rebutted.

"Seventy-five hundred."

"Five, and I'll tell you the truth about why I left the FBI."

Mole suddenly grew somber. "Seriously? Like an actual personal detail about yourself?"

"Hey." I shrugged. "A girl's got to have her secrets."

"So, you didn't just rebel out of the bureau?"

I smirked. "We have a deal?"

"Five grand and a Samantha secret? Absolutely." Mole held his hand out, and we sealed our deal with a shake. "But I'm still gonna want those beers, though," he said as he turned me toward the door and shooed me away.

Walking back to my loft, I thought of Vin and knew I should have phoned him hours ago. My cell had been blowing up with texts from him all day, and another rolled in as I made my way into the kitchen and grabbed the bottle of whisky on the counter. It wasn't that I was avoiding him, I was just afraid he was going to be the overattentive boyfriend. I preferred to lick my wounds in private. I knew I wouldn't be able to stay away long, though. I'd sort of gotten addicted to the man. Dammit.

"So what dire secrets worth killing for did you find?" I asked after I'd returned to Mole's loft and put the whisky in his outstretched and expectant hand. "I'm out of beer right now."

"It's encrypted," he said, disappointed. "I wish they'd used 40-bit key instead of PGP, which for me isn't impossible but may take a while."

"40-bit versus PGP?"

"The longer the key, the stronger the encryption."

"Okay, I understand that."

"Forty bits is actually a very small key," Mole explained, "unlike PGP, which uses the same encryption method but with a 1,024-bit key."

That was significant. "What does PGP stand for?"

Mole flashed me a grin. "Pretty good privacy. With PGP encryption, only the recipient of the information can read it. That way, nobody who might be eavesdropping on the network can intercept and decode it."

"But pretty good still doesn't mean impossible, does it?"

"Never underestimate the powers of a hacker god."

"How much time are we really looking at?"

"I have no way of knowing. Tomorrow morning, if I stay up all night."

"No earlier?"

"I can call you if it happens."

"I can live with that. Thanks, Mole."

Mole gave me a wave over his shoulder and set to work. I left him to it and set out in search of something that would make my aches and pains go away.

{* * *}

The light beaming through the window was all wrong, muted and coming in at the incorrect angle. I raised myself up on an elbow and blinked away the sleep from my eyes. I smelled acrylic paint and sandalwood. Then it all came back to me: I'd spent the night with Vin in his studio. I rolled out of the tangled sheets and picked one of Vin's button-down shirts from the antique wardrobe in the corner of the room to throw on over my nakedness, buttoning the middle two buttons.

A handwoven tapestry from Budapest that Vin got in his travels hung in the doorway and served as a break between rooms. I moved it aside and stepped out into a loft that overlooked a sea of canvases and paint pots below. The ceiling was glass, delivering optimal natural light. Over the loft hung a wide canvas sail that offered shade from sunny days and gave a semblance of privacy from the multistoried buildings that surrounded him.

Miles Davis played on the stereo as I walked to the kitchen and slipped my arms around Vin's waist from behind. His clothes were permeated with the smell of paint, though the steady infusion of incense helped as a cover-up. Vin was busy preparing a feast of eggs with chopped vegetables smothered in grated cheese.

"Morning," I purred, feathering his neck with kisses.

"Good morning." Vin turned and enveloped me in a gentle bear hug, staying conscious of my bruised ribs. "Drink this." He pulled away and handed me a steaming mug of—*What's this...green tea?* I'd hoped for something a little darker, something with a little more kick, but I took the proffered mug nonetheless.

"How did you sleep?" Vin asked.

"We slept?" I asked, testing the tea only to find it too nuclear-hot to drink.

Vin took the mug away from me and set it on the counter so that he could pull me in closer and kiss me like he meant it. His hands found their way beneath the shirt I was wearing. What was quickly turning into a continuation of the previous night was abruptly interrupted by the buzzing of the downstairs door.

"Ignore it," Vin said, his voice muffled against my neck. "I'm not home."

"Could be Ed McMahon," I teased, not really wanting him to stop. "You might be a lucky winner."

"I have all the prize I need right here."

The buzzer sounded again, this time with much more urgency and backed up by a burst of knocks. "I'll get rid of them," I said, breaking away from our embrace. "Plus I can unlock the door for the fire department." I pointed to the stove, where the pan was beginning to do more than steam.

"Oh shit!" Vin grabbed a lid and threw it on the pan.

I bounded down the stairs with my shirttails flapping. I had no idea who or what to expect, so I had the rest of the shirt buttoned by the time I reached the door and eased the blinds aside. Ed McMahon would have been a pleasant surprise; instead, it was Trisha Blackwell.

At eight o'clock in the morning, Trisha was perfectly coiffed and dressed to the nines, whereas I was naked under a paint-stained shirt two sizes too big for me. My hair was wild from a night of passion, and my mouth tasted like Vin. In addition I was still plenty puffy and purple from my most recent brawl. This was going to be loads of fun.

Trisha was digging through an oversized designer handbag when I pulled the door open. "Good morning, darling!" she said in a general singsong voice without looking up.

"Back at you, sugar booger," I answered. It was still too early in the morning for maturity.

When she realized I wasn't who she was expecting, Trisha snapped her head up in surprise. "Oh," she sneered, "it's you."

"In the flesh," I retorted. "What can I do for you?"

Trish stood on her toes as if to scan the room. "I'm here to speak with Vinardo."

She did *not* just call him *Vinardo*. Personally I hated that name, for no reason other than it sounded counterfeit. Of course, Trish didn't know how I felt about the moniker, but still—strike one.

"Aren't you going to invite me in?" Trish asked expectantly.

"Sure, just let me go grab a wooden stake first."

"Oh puh-lease," Trisha scorned as she pushed the door aside and called out, "Are you home? Hello, Vinardo?" There it was again. Strike two.

"I'm sorry, Trisha, but now isn't the best time." I picked up the hem of Vin's shirt, trying to convey the state of my undress, which implied that Vin and I were otherwise occupied.

In a foolishly brave move, Trisha took two steps forward to stand in my face. I couldn't breathe without getting a lungful of her perfume. She spoke low so that her words were only for my ears. "Here is one of those moments when the powerful ply their power. Look at me. I'm rich, I'm known, and I've got friends in high places. Who are you, Samantha, but a two-bit gumshoe who pays more attention to criminals than she does her own lover? I can put Vinardo on the cover of the *New Yorker* and have him in every major gallery between here and London. I will make him a very rich man. That's what I can do for him." Then Trisha made a dire mistake: she stepped closer to whisper in my ear, "You don't deserve him."

Strike three. Before I had the chance to defuse the signal from my brain, my arm was cocked. Then it wasn't. A solid sock to the jaw spun Trisha's head on her shoulders, and she crumpled to the floor like a rag doll. Her mouth opened and closed like a guppy, her eyes stuck open in surprise. I regretted my impulsiveness the second my knuckles connected with the sculpted side of her jaw. I was sure I'd just undone some pricy work.

Tousled and in shock, Trisha picked herself up from the cement floor. She pulled her suit jacket down and straightened her hair. "You'll be hearing from my attorney," she threatened through clenched teeth.

"Can I help you to the door?" I offered.

"No!" Trisha screamed. "Go to hell, Samantha Harris!"

Hearing the commotion, Vin peered over the loft railing just in time to see Trisha storm out the door and slam it shut behind her.

"What was all that about?" Vin asked as I came back up the stairs.

I shrugged my shoulders. "Who knows? She's high-strung."

Vin nodded in agreement as he came down the stairs. He was distracted by something on the floor near the door that I'd passed without noticing. He picked up a large tan envelope held shut by a loop of elastic. "This yours?"

"Not mine." I stood beside him as he unwound the string and slid a short stack of eight-by-ten photographs into his hand. They were surveillance photos of Vin and me that were taken at his gallery opening, him getting coffee at Steam, and me walking to my office. The photo on the bottom had been snapped the previous night—Vin and me in a private moment, taken from the vantage point of an office window overlooking Vin's loft. By the photos, I could tell that the stalking had begun the day that Pam hired me to find her husband's killer.

"I don't understand," Vin said, holding the fanned photos like a losing hand. I couldn't help but think he sounded like a little boy.

"Someone's been following us, both of us—together and separately."

"But why?" Vin asked, his voice full of question.

"Because of the case I'm working on. They want to shake me, get me to stop digging. These"—I tapped the photos in his hand—"are a warning."

"Seems like sending a warning would be antithetical."

I stared at Vin wide-eyed. "What did you just say?" I whispered.

Vin raised his eyes to mine. "Well, it just seems like this is something that would only egg you on, not discourage you," he said, slipping the photos back into the envelope.

I couldn't suppress the smile that spread wide across my face because in that moment, I realized that Vin understood me. He got my drive and my aggressive tenacity, and he hadn't run screaming. Still, I greatly disliked that I'd brought him into my tumultuous world.

Vin locked the door and slid the chain before we walked back up the stairs. Our appetites gone, I got dressed and finished my tea, which had cooled to a manageable temperature. Neither of us spoke much. A car backfired on the street, and Vin flinched away from the window.

"Vin, I don't know how long this case is going to take to wrap up, but you need to find somewhere to stay, preferably out of the city."

"Why can't I stay here? I live here."

"They're watching you here. Get out of town, maybe visit that illustrator friend down in Springfield, the one with the corny sense of humor and the Flintstones collectibles you were telling me about—what's his name?"

"Mark?"

"Yeah, him. Go down and hang with Mark for a couple of days until things here cool off."

"I suppose I could give him a call. But you know I can also pull the drapes, lock myself inside, and paint uninterrupted for as long as it takes."

"I'd feel better if you weren't here."

Vin stared at the floor, refusing to meet my gaze. "This is really dangerous, isn't it?"

"Two men are dead, and whoever is behind this sent a hit after me. So yes, it's getting treacherous. I need to know you're safe so I can go out and do my job."

"What about you?" Vin raised his green eyes. "Where will you be?"

I would have told him not to worry about me, but why waste my breath? "I'll be out there making our world safe again." I felt like I'd just quoted a superhero. I adjusted the straps of my shoulder holster and pulled on my jacket. "I'll call Wickowski and get a detail put on you until you're out of the city." Vin held my hand and walked me downstairs. He promised to lock up and stay away from the windows before closing the door behind me. I heard the dead bolt slide home before I walked away.

My cell phone beeped with a 911 message from Mole. He'd finally cracked the disc. I texted him that I'd be right there. Then I phoned Wickowski, briefed him on the latest development, and arranged a security detail to sit on Vin until he left town. I sprinted all the way home, arriving out of breath and anxious.

"I stayed up all night with this thing," Mole gushed when he let me in the door, "but once the sequences started falling into place, it was only a matter of time until I had them all. I reformatted the information onto this thumb drive. There's a lot of stuff here, but I didn't read it. I don't want to know. Plausible deniability."

I took a second to catch my breath. "Mole, could I ask you one more tiny favor?"

"Depends."

"I need to know if McPherson is still in Brazil."

He smiled widely. "Already took care of that. McPherson cleared customs in Dallas/Fort Worth yesterday afternoon." Proud of himself on both counts, Mole pulled out his computer chair and formally offered me a seat, which I took. He punched a button and brought up what someone had deemed to be worth killing for: photographs.

Frame after frame of disfigured babies—some alive, many stillborn with their umbilical cords attached to their purple torsos. There were dozens of such photos, each as heartrending as the next. Then there was a series of photographs of one small, malformed baby girl who was alive and bawling into the camera. A letter written in what I suspected was a broken form of Portuguese was included. Fortunately the translated version was also attached:

Dear Sirs,

I work with Tribal Survival, an organization without profit from São Paulo, Brazil. We are a small group. I write you seeking immediate and urgent aid. It is in regard to recent vaccinations given our local Amazonian tribes by your company. There have been many births of late of very ill children among the Waiapi people. Most of the mothers have received your vaccine. I have enclosed many photos of the children from one tribe alone. There are many children born this way, and those few who survive birth die soon after from complications.

We at Tribal Survival are very concerned and anxiously await your response.

Sincerely, Miguel Tomas Pérez
cc: Alejandro Garcia

"Once again, it's profit over people," Mole fumed, shaking his head. "Only when the last tree is cut down, the last fish eaten, and the last stream poisoned will we realize that money cannot be eaten," Mole said morosely.

It was a despicable predicament. With so many clinical trials being conducted in the United States, outsourcing to developing countries by pharmaceutical companies had grown exponentially. Problematic legalities and lenient regulations had allowed for the exploitation of the native peoples, who were often uninformed of the risks inherent to clinical trials. Novus was exploiting a vulnerable population for its own gain.

"I knew you were going to ask me to track down this Alejandro dude." Mole closed the program and ejected the original disc before bringing up another screen. "He teaches at a university in Rio."

"Keeping a lid on the company's activities and protecting their investment is certainly a motive for murder."

"You think?" Mole said sarcastically as he took me by the elbow and guided me to the front door. "I'll be keeping my door barred until you wrap this one up, Sammy. If you need me, be sure to phone ahead." He pressed the original disc and the thumb drive into my hand then shut the door on me without any mention of payment. He *was* spooked. And I had to admit, I was glad to be packing heat.

Following the link Mole set up, I located Garcia through the Instituto de Medicina Social in Rio de Janeiro, where he was a professor of microbiology. The page also gave me Garcia's extension. His phone picked up on the second ring; it turned out to be an answering machine. There was no prompt to hit one plus the star key for English, so I listened to the long-winded message in Portuguese—a language I was in no way familiar with—before it was relayed in English. The recording stated that it was the institute's regret to inform the caller of Dr. Alejandro Garcia's sudden and unfortunate passing. All school-related calls could be forwarded to the institute switchboard by pressing one.

I opted out of transferring to the switchboard and hung up more than a little disappointed. *Great.* Someone was being extremely thorough in covering both their tracks and their asses. Not one to give up, I looked up and called the head offices of Tribal Survival, but the live person I got didn't speak a syllable of English.

If the mountain won't come to me, then I must go to the mountain.

CHAPTER NINETEEN

THERE WAS NO SUCH THING AS A DIRECT FLIGHT OUT OF PORTLAND to São Paulo. I ended up booking a flight later that same day that routed me through both Los Angeles and Miami. My return ticket was open-ended; no way would I leave Brazil without the information I had come for. I left my rig in short-term parking and made my flight with minutes to spare.

Twenty hours later, my fellow travelers and I disembarked into heavy humidity that had me feeling like I was back home on a DC summer afternoon. We crossed the tarmac on foot to the airport doors as a slow herd. Most of us were dressed in tropical-print shirts and were appropriately giddy with holiday excitement, regardless of the long flight or the sultry air. I, however, was overdressed in jeans and a cotton blouse with the sleeves rolled to my elbows. I wasn't there to play tourist.

At the door, we were instructed to have our passports ready. Broad-leafed plants in oversized earthen pots flanked both sides of the entrance. After the wilting heat outside, the air inside the airport was downright frigid, raising goose bumps along my bare arms. We all followed the signs to a series of kiosks, each occupied by a customs agent and an armed guard. They eyed me suspiciously when I declared no luggage, only the backpack slung over my shoulder.

"I don't plan on staying long," I explained.

"What is your business in São Paulo?" the agent inquired, tapping the keys of her keyboard and looking at the screen through bifocals.

"I'm here looking for somebody."

"And who are you seeking?" she asked flatly, as if she asked that question all day long.

I'd once tried to look up a high school friend of mine in Chicago. Her name was Jill Smith. See where I was going with that?

"Miguel Tomas Pérez."

The agent raised her eyes and considered me with a bored expression. "That is a very common name here. There must be hundreds of Miguel Pérezes."

"Lucky for me, I only need to find one of them." I softened my smart-aleck response with a smile. There was no need to end up in cuffs before I even got out of the airport.

With a heavy hand, the agent stamped my passport and slid it back beneath the thick, bulletproof glass. The guard, who'd watched all of this with an interest that made me uncomfortable, dismissed me with a flick of his hand and turned his sights to the next person in line. I shouldered my bag, in which I had the necessary toiletries, a clean shirt, and underwear, and set out to find the nearest machine to exchange currency. Banco do Brasil had an automatic teller mounted on the wall beside the airport's main entrance. The exchange rate was in my favor: just under $130 in US dollars gave me $500 in Brazilian reals. That was enough to get me started.

Leaving the air-conditioned comfort of the airport lobby was like walking head-on into a wave of hot, wet air. A long line of taxis sat waiting for fares along the curb, their tailpipes burbling patiently. I walked straight to the nearest ride and climbed into the back seat.

"Aonde?" the cab driver asked in an accent as thick as the air.

Assuming he'd just asked me where I wanted to go, I handed the driver a piece of paper on which I'd jotted an address. Tribal Survival's headquarters lay in the hills outside of town.

"Uma hora, uma hora e meia, huh?" the driver said, seesawing his hand back and forth. I had no idea what he said, and it must have shown on my face. He raised a finger and pointed to his wristwatch, then drew a full circle and a half in the air. Oh, I got it—*an hour, maybe an hour and a half.* Communication! Hot diggity-damn and bring on the charades! I smiled, nodded, and threw him a double thumbs-up, which turned out to be a universal sign for all that was good. We pulled away from the curb and got underway.

Neither of us spoke again, charades or otherwise. I sat back and watched as neighborhoods of low buildings with clay-tiled roofs inched past the window. Gridlock traffic was worse as we neared the center of town. The scene outside the window slowly went from small dwellings to taller, larger buildings built closer together. São Paulo was founded long before there were cars to occupy the narrow streets.

Once we finally made it to the other side of town, we began to wind our way up into the older part of the city. We finally arrived at a squat red brick building. A flock of pigeons perched along the crumbling roofline.

"Tribal Sobrevivência, huh?" the driver asked, bobbing his head and pointing to the meter. "Me aguarde para você, huh?" he asked, pointing to the office's front door and then to his wristwatch.

I was getting good at this. "No." I shook my head. "No need to wait." I peeled several notes from my wad of reals and handed them to him over the seat before stepping from the cab.

"Obrigado," he thanked me and pulled away with a cough of exhaust.

There were no signs to validate that I was indeed standing in front of the offices of Tribal Survival. I peered through the iron bars that protected the window from vandals and saw a woman sitting at a desk inside. Her head snapped up in surprise when I pulled open the door. Recovering quickly, the woman pushed her wireframe glasses up her nose and flipped a strand of black hair behind her ear. Her cotton, floral-print dress reminded me of curtains my mother once had.

"Posso ajudá-lo?" she asked in Portuguese.

"Habla inglés?" I asked in Spanish.

"Yes, I speak perfect English." She really did.

"Good, because my Portuguese sucks."

That earned me a small laugh. "How might I help you?"

"Is this the office of Tribal Survival?"

"It is."

My smile of relief was genuine. "I'm looking for Miguel Tomas Pérez."

A look I hadn't expected clouded the woman's face as she diverted her eyes momentarily. "Miguel is no longer with us," she said with great effort.

"Do you know where I can find him?" I asked, already knowing the answer.

The woman's eyes became twin pools of unshed tears. "Miguel passed away three weeks ago." She could no longer hold back. Tears streamed down her cheeks. "Excuse me. I don't mean to become emotional, it's just that Miguel and I were—close. There is so much tragedy and sadness for his family. First Miguel, then his uncle. I don't—"

"Cecilia!"

Both Cecilia and I snapped our heads up at the sharp calling of her name. Filling the doorway across the room stood a woman dressed in a crisp linen suit, matching taupe heels, and a triple string of pearls. Her black hair was pulled back into a severe bun, and the black glasses dangling against her chest gave her the air of an overbearing schoolmarm. From her ears dangled tear-shaped diamonds earrings—brave accessories for that part of town.

"Hello and good afternoon. I am Christiana Romano, head of

this organization." Christiana stepped from her office and approached with her hand extended. "You will have to excuse my assistant, Cecilia. She is a silly girl prone to outbursts of emotion."

"I understand. It's always difficult to lose a friend. How did Miguel die?" I asked Cecilia directly.

Cecilia began to answer, but Christiana cut her off with a withering look. "There was a most unfortunate accident," Christiana explained. "Miguel and his crew were returning from the mountains when a terrible rainstorm struck. They were caught in a flash flood that swept their bus from the road and plunged them down a ravine into the river below. There were no survivors."

Another lead bit the dust. Ironic, though—death by ravine.

"Are either of you familiar with Alejandro Garcia?" I asked, still fishing for something to go on.

Another muffled wail erupted from Cecilia's desk. "It's so terrible," she hiccuped into a tissue. "Professor Garcia and his wife and their new baby girl—"

"Cecilia!" Christiana barked once more. "My apologies again, miss. Please, come into my office where we can have a conversation without these disruptions." Christiana turned on her heel, and I followed her into her office, where I took a seat in a straight-backed chair not meant for comfort. My backpack went on the floor between my feet.

Christiana swung the door shut and took her seat behind the desk. "So sorry. She is such an absurd girl."

"What happened to Alejandro Garcia?" I asked, not giving her opinion of Cecilia any attention.

"Another tragic accident." Christiana sighed. "There are reports of a gas leak explosion in the apartment next door to his home early one morning. They could not escape the fire. Alejandro, his wife, and their three-month-old daughter perished."

"Did Miguel ever mention any concerns he had about some upper Amazon villagers?"

"I am brand new to this position, Ms.—"

"Harris." I extended my hand. "Samantha Harris."

"As I was saying, I am brand new to this position, Ms. Harris. I began only days after the organization lost Miguel and his crew."

Of course you did.

"This is a nonprofit, volunteer-based organization. We operate strictly off of donations and private funding. We recently received a substantial donation, and I was brought in to help manage it in Miguel's unfortunate absence."

I sat back in my seat and crossed my leg over my knee. "Do you draw a salary of any kind, or are you also a volunteer?"

"I am employed by the corporation that gifted the money," Christiana said with a sniff.

"Isn't that a conflict of interest? I mean, you could appropriate the funds wherever they want you to."

"It is Tribal Survival's mission to help the indigenous tribes of our country survive in this ever-changing world with their culture and dignity intact," Christiana spouted like an infomercial. "It is our mission to help our indigenous people keep their way of life from being destroyed. There is little that I or my employer could, or would, do to exploit such a noble cause."

Spoken like a true politician. She could have a career back in the States. She had her stonewalling skills down pat. Wonder what would happen if I threw a hornet into the mix?

"Do you believe in coincidence, Christiana?"

"I don't understand your question."

"Miguel, the team he worked with, and his uncle all met with unfortunate accidents right about the same time. As did someone back in the States who's somehow connected to this office. At the very least, don't you find those odds staggering?"

"I do not pretend to understand how God works."

"No, neither do I, but I bet he had nothing to do with this."

I stood to leave. "Oh"—I snapped my fingers as if just remembering something—"could I get Miguel's address?"

"I'm afraid I cannot. For privacy reasons—you understand." The joy Christiana got from denying me was evident in her eyes. I didn't like being rebuffed.

I smiled coyly. "I'm sure Miguel won't mind. The dead don't care."

Christiana seemed to consider that for a moment, or maybe she just wanted me out of her offices before I got nosy. "No, I guess they don't, do they?" She opened the Rolodex on her desk, a relic from past, and riffled through the alphabetized cards until she found Miguel's address, which she copied onto a piece of stationery and handed to me. "I don't know what you hope to find, Ms. Harris."

"How far is this from here?"

"Several blocks."

"Thanks."

Christiana held her office door open for me. I swung my backpack over my shoulder and stepped around her.

Cecilia met me halfway across the room with a small gold cylinder in her hand. "Oh, miss! You dropped your lip balm when you walked in earlier."

Lip balm? I didn't really do lip stuff, but I knew a handoff when I saw one. I made a show of patting down the pockets of my jeans and blouse to go along with the ruse. "Oh yep, it's mine. So glad you found it too. I'm going to need it in this weather." I slipped the tube into my pocket. Christiana bid me farewell from the doorway of her office before disappearing back inside and closing the door.

Back out into the oppressive air, I was fortunate enough to flag down a cab that just happened to be passing. I gave the driver the address to Miguel's home, and we lumbered off with no sense of urgency whatsoever. I had to learn to be on São Paulo time. You get there when you get there.

My only regret at that point in my journey was not sticking around the office long enough to see Christiana pick up her phone and make the call I was sure she was making.

{* * *}

I fished the tube of lip balm from my pocket and pulled off the cap. Where the balm had been was a scrolled slip of paper on which was scrawled a phone number and a message that Cecilia needed to talk. I'd have to call her later.

After several minutes of weaving our slow way through the narrow streets—maneuvering around market stalls selling fresh produce, meats, and various handmade wares—the taxi pulled to a stop just outside a two-story brick-and-stucco structure.

"Stay, por favor?" I asked the grizzled old man behind the wheel.

"O que?" His thin voice sounded like dry leaves on parchment.

I pantomimed with my fingers climbing stairs, knocking on a door, then pointed at my watch and put my hand out in a *stay* command like I would a dog. That seemed to get my point across. He nodded and put the car into park, then fished a pack of smokes from his shirt pocket.

Miguel lived in unit 212. I took a set of wooden stairs up to the second floor and counted down the whitewashed doors until I found Miguel's. I wasn't sure if he lived there alone or if he had a roommate, so for formality's sake, I knocked and waited the requisite thirty seconds before picking my way through the lock using a tool from my key ring. I looked both ways down the long porch before I let myself in.

At first glance, Miguel came off as a slob, but then I realized someone had beat me to the punch. The floor was littered with broken glass, upholstered chairs were split open with their stuffing spilled everywhere, and anything that could be smashed had been. The place looked like an axe-wielding psychopath had stopped in and worked it over. Holes were hacked in the walls; even a couple of floorboards had been pried up.

A surprised gasp sounded behind me. I spun and came face-to-face with a squat older woman who stood in the doorway carrying a pile of empty cardboard boxes. "O que o inferno tem-no feito!" She stubbed a finger into my chest with each word.

I put up my hands in the universal sign of surrender. "Habla inglés?" I rushed. English was my best bet; charades wasn't going to cut it.

"What have you done!"

"No, no," I protested, shaking my head. "This happened before I got here."

The woman looked at me suspiciously. "Why are you here?"

"I was looking for Miguel."

"Miguel died," the woman stated matter-of-factly and crossed herself in the Catholic gesture.

"Yes, I know. I'm very sorry for your loss," I added, thinking she might be apt to cooperate if I were more sympathetic.

"Then why do you come here?"

"I came looking for information."

The woman surveyed the room with her dark eyes. "I hope you found what you look for. Now I call the polícia; you come to steal from my son." The woman dropped her boxes and turned for the door.

I had only taken one step toward her when she spun around with a knife in her hand. Where the hell had she pulled that from? I put my hands up again, not only in surrender but also as a first line of defense. "I'm with the police," I lied. "The bus accident—I don't think it was an accident at all. I think someone wanted Miguel dead. I'm here to find that someone."

The woman's eyes softened, but she held fast to her knife. "Miguel was a smart boy. He could have been someone important."

"If it's any consolation, Miguel died trying to make the world a better place. He *was* someone important."

This brought a small smile to the woman's mouth. Pride and pain filled her eyes.

"Did Miguel seem at all different the last time you spoke to him?"

"Different?"

"Was he nervous or frightened?"

The woman shook her head. "No. Miguel was excited. He'd found a new girlfriend, and his work was going well."

"Did Miguel and Alejandro collaborate in their work?"

"Miguel was Alejandro's charge. Miguel attended the institute to study social medicine like his uncle Alejandro, who paid for Miguel's education, but Miguel decided to leave school and go into the jungle and minister to the tribes."

Of course. It made total sense. "I need to go," I said, stepping over the broken glass.

"Where are you going? What about Miguel's murderer?"

"I can't do anything from here. I need to get back to the States."

Miguel's mother dropped her knife into one of the empty boxes and reached up to remove a necklace, which she coiled into my palm and folded my fingers over. I opened my hand and saw a small medallion bearing the figure of Saint Michael the Protector. "For my son," she said. I gave Miguel's mother a reassuring smile, promised to find whoever was responsible for her son's death, then walked out before I made any more promises I wasn't sure I could keep.

I took the stairs back down two at a time and climbed into the back of the cab. I slipped the necklace over my head and let it dangle between my breasts inside my blouse. I needed to reach out to Cecilia, and doing it from Miguel's hadn't crossed my mind once Mom showed up.

"Excuse me—pay phone?" I mimicked dropping coins into a slot and holding a phone to my ear.

"No problemo," answered a deeper voice than I'd expected.

"Wait a minute—what happened to the other driver?"

"His workday end," the cabbie explained in broken English, "now I come." My new driver pulled from the curb with no more urgency than the last. At a stop sign, we waited for a herd of women on bicycles laden with laundry to cross. The dashboard radio played a tinny rumba punctuated intermittently by the static of poor reception.

Outside, waves of solar heat rose from the asphalt, which made me grateful for the air-conditioning inside the cab. We passed a small café occupied by folks seeking shade beneath wide umbrella canopies and sipping iced drinks.

A dilapidated truck loaded down with cages of unhappy chickens screeched to a stop in front of us, forcing us to do the same. The driver of the truck swung down from his cab and walked away without a glance backward. I watched and wondered what was going on when my driver put the cab into park, opened his door, and sauntered off too.

What the hell?

Having never visited São Paulo, I was unsure of any weird midday customs—like abandoning cars in the middle of the city during afternoon traffic. I figured at any moment the drivers would return to their vehicles, maybe with a round of ice-cold refreshments, and then we'd all continue on our way. That hopeful scenario diminished when my driver began to run. Someone behind me goosed their horn, and people on the sidewalk turned and stared. I was getting a really bad feeling.

My attempt to open the door was an exercise in futility. I jiggled the lock, pushing it up and down, but it was useless. The electric mechanism had been tampered with. I frantically tried the other doors with the same results. I was trapped.

The previously crowded sidewalks had cleared as the locals faded into the background. Doors closed and windows shuttered like they knew something I didn't, but I was a quick learner. With both feet and all my might, I kicked the window as hard as I could. The impact sent a shockwave through my body that reminded me of the beating I had taken days before, but the glass didn't give. What I needed was something small and preferably pointed. I would have sold my soul for a screwdriver right about then. A quick mental inventory of my pack and pockets gave me a couple of options.

Every cell in my body screamed that time was running out.

With surprisingly steady hands, I unzipped my pack and got my keys. My mailbox key was the biggest of them all, so I wrapped my hand around it and held it in my fist so that the metal bit stuck out just below my pinkie finger. My system was laced with adrenaline, which I knew could work to my advantage. I slammed my fist and key into the center of the window with force.

Nothing happened.

Not one to give up, especially when my life and well-being were at stake, I struck out at the window again and again until a tiny spiderweb of cracks spread out from the point of impact. The seconds that ticked by felt like hours. With each hit, the web of cracks widened until I knew I could lean back once more and break the window with my foot. Tempered glass exploded outward onto the cobblestone street. Without hesitation, I grabbed my pack and threw it out the window, shimmied out on my stomach, and landed on my hands on the cobblestones. I didn't even bother to yell a warning. I just ran.

CHAPTER TWENTY

THE EXPLOSION WAS DEAFENING. THE CONCUSSION SENT ME FLYING forward, sprawling on my hands and knees. Instinctively, I covered my head with my arms as pieces of hot shrapnel rained down. When the threat of falling debris had passed, I rolled over and looked back. A column of black smoke rose from the inferno that had been the taxi, which looked like a tin can that had been torn open by a giant's hand.

I should have experienced a certain level of fear, but I felt nothing except outrage. If someone had this big of a hard-on for my death, they should step forward and take me on head-to-head, not attack from the shadows like a terrorist. I was in a foreign country, unarmed and with nobody to trust. My cell didn't have an international plan, so it was nothing more than a hunk of inert plastic and metal at the bottom of my pack. It would be safe for me to assume whoever wanted to take me out was going to come around to check out their handiwork and gloat. The joke would be on them when they didn't find a charred body in the ruins. Of course, they were bound to come looking for me, so I needed to regroup and make a plan. First, though, I needed to get the hell off the street.

Evade and survive—I wasn't sure if it was Doc's or Cindy's voice issuing the advice. It sort of sounded like my own but with an edge of uncharacteristic anxiety. I picked myself up off the ground. Except for a couple of minor cuts and scrapes on top of my already existing injuries from the beatdown I'd taken, I'd managed to escape unscathed. Evade and survive. Right.

You've managed to stay alive this long, kid. What's another couple of hours? Now move your ass! That one was unmistakably Doc. Not one to ignore sound advice, I got my butt out of there.

With no destination in mind, I crisscrossed streets and doubled back on myself, ducking into alleys and pausing only in doorways, all the while staying alert for a tail or any other sign of ambush.

At about hour three post-explosion, I started to settle down. Don't get me wrong—my guard was running on high, but I felt secure enough to stop into a bodega to buy a bottle of water and a sandwich. I had the clerk make change and used the pay phone at the back of the store to dial the number from the lipstick tube.

"Olá!" Cecilia answered.

"Cecilia?"

"Yes," answered a hushed voice. "Is this the American?"

"Yes."

"We must meet. I must speak with you." She fought to keep her voice at a whisper through her eagerness.

"Meeting isn't really a possibility right now. Can you talk now?"

"Where are you?"

I don't think so, sweetheart. "I'm using a pay phone in town. I'll call you back in five minutes?"

"Yes, I will excuse myself for a cigarette."

I hung up and used the washroom, where I dampened a handful of paper towels and tried to wash the sweat and dirt from my face. I changed into the shirt from my backpack then returned to the pay phone to ring Cecilia again.

"Three days before Miguel died, some men came to the office. Two were in suits, and they were escorted by two men in uniform."

"Police?"

"No, like military uniforms, with guns."

"What did they want?"

"They asked to speak with Miguel. Then one of the uniformed men took me by my arm, shoved me outside, and locked me out. Their voices grew fierce, but I couldn't make out what they were saying. Then they left."

"Did Miguel say anything to you?"

"No, but he was scared. He tried to contact his uncle, but he couldn't get ahold of him."

"Have you seen any of those men since that day?"

"No, but after Miguel died, things went missing from the office."

"What sorts of things?"

"Our digital cameras, videotapes, and most of Miguel's files were taken. And I think somebody broke into my home."

"Did they steal anything?"

"No, but things weren't exactly where I'd left them, like somebody went through looking for something."

"Cecilia, by talking to me, you could be putting yourself in danger. You understand that, right?"

"But I don't know anything!"

"That doesn't mean a thing. Just be careful, and don't tell anybody we spoke."

"Okay."

"Especially Christiana. If I were you, I'd stay guarded around her."

"I will try to be safe and stay strong for Miguel's sake." She got the last of her sentence out with a sob. Cecilia had alluded to her and Miguel being close, but they were clearly a lot closer than coworkers.

I hung up the phone and leaned against the cool brick wall. My next call was to book a flight back to the States. My faith in a power bigger than myself was bolstered when I was told there'd been a cancellation for the next flight out that afternoon. I hung up with higher hopes for survival than I'd had when I made the call.

There were still a few more hours until my flight back home, but getting on it might prove more difficult than expected. Having used my credit card, anyone who'd flagged it would know where to find me and when. It was a chance I had to take. I placed another call, this one to the United States.

"Wickowski." His gruff voice sounded hollow, like he was speaking from inside a chamber, but it had never sounded so good to me.

"Wick, it's me."

"Holy shit, Harris! Where the green goddamn are you? Vin's been calling me nonstop. The poor guy is having a nervous breakdown, says you gave him orders to get out of town for a while because you thought he might be in danger. I put a detail on him like you asked. Without pressing you for a lot of details, I might add."

"I told you to trust me," I interjected.

Wickowski lowered his voice. "Do you know how many people have told me to trust them? Do you know how many of them I actually do?"

That stung. I got it—trust for people like us was a rare commodity given to extremely few people. I trusted Wickowski explicitly, and I knew I was on his short list, but his implication was still like a tiny dagger.

"I think I deserve some sort of explanation, Harris. What the hell is going on?"

"I'm in Brazil," I stated straightforwardly, "and things got complicated."

The line went silent for a long time. I feared our connection had been disrupted.

"You're *where*?" Wickowski finally hollered, making me pull the receiver from my ear.

"Look, I can't go into it completely, so do me a favor, will you?"

"You're in fucking *Brazil*?" Wickowski was having a hard time with that.

"Yelling isn't going to change my location. Look, I need you to sit on Talbert until I get home."

"And when will that be?" Wickowski's attitude softened but still carried an edge of sarcasm.

"My flight takes off in a few hours."

Wickowski sighed heavily. If I had been there, I would've seen him grimace as he pinched the bridge of his nose. "Answer me this: Do you have enough on the guy for me to make an arrest?"

"Yes and no."

I actually heard Wickowski roll his eyes. "I hate that answer."

"I have enough to haul him in, but wait until I get there."

"And...what's the no part?"

"It's all circumstantial at this point, but there is enough to connect him to Phillips's murder. I'll get the rest when I return."

"Circumstantial isn't going to cut it with a good lawyer, and the DA won't dance with that either."

"I have people on my ass down here, and I still have to get to the airport and make my flight. Just have some uniforms sit on Talbert for now, and don't lose him. Meet me at PDX tomorrow afternoon, flight number 2293 coming in from Dallas/Fort Worth."

"What do I tell Vin?"

"Tell him to sit tight. I'm coming home."

"Harris?"

"Yeah?"

"Don't get dead."

"That's my goal." Hanging up, I realized how far away from home—and how alone—I really was.

{∗ ∗ ∗}

After hanging up with Wickowski, I found a quiet alley in which to eat my sandwich and formulate a game plan. Making it on foot to the airport didn't seem like the best approach. Aside from the distance, the streets offered too much visibility, and I had no idea who was hunting me. I meandered in that direction, still alert for a tail. A military jeep full of soldiers came by. I ducked into the shadow of an alley and watched the jeep pull to the curb at a café and flash a picture to those sitting around the tables. If my picture had turned up on an APB, I was screwed. No cabbie was going to pick up a fugitive. I had to believe they were just getting their search organized and underway and hadn't put my face on the airwaves. I doubled back out of the alley and made my way to a busy intersection, positioning myself so I could see all approaching traffic. I made my move when a cabbie dropped off his fare at the curb and jumped into the back seat. The driver was surprised but showed no agitation or signs he was aware of the manhunt.

We arrived at the airport without incident. I paid the driver and took refuge in the shadows of a double-decker parking garage directly across from the airport's main entrance. From my vantage point on the second floor, I counted four possible thugs: two of them dressed in suits who appeared to be waiting for a ride, one in a janitor's uniform who had been continuously cleaning the same stretch of sidewalk for the last twenty minutes, and another loitering just outside the front doors dressed as a tourist in the tropical shirt and straw hat with a newspaper tucked under his arm.

I could also see the service entrance. Security was tight worldwide post-9/11, and the Guarulhos International Airport was no different. I watched the comings and goings of various delivery trucks, each being stopped by an armed guard and searched with electronic devices. Mirrors were used to scope the trucks' undercarriages. Some of the drivers were fingerprinted and probably added to a database before being allowed through the electric gates onto the airport's grounds.

All I needed to do was get to and through the front doors. I checked my watch again—still an hour before takeoff. Piece of cake, right?

I checked the cars parked in short-term. It didn't take me long to find a cell phone left inside a vehicle. I used the key-in-fist method to break the passenger's side window and leaned across the shattered glass to take the phone plugged into the dashboard. I also grabbed the orange-and-blue Tigres de Quintana Roo ball cap from the back seat. I peeled off several reals from my wad, enough to replace the window at least, and left them on the driver's seat out of immediate sight of passersby.

I dialed airport security and posed as a concerned and vigilant citizen: "There is a man outside the airport wearing a tourist shirt and a straw hat. I think I saw a handgun wrapped in his newspaper."

In today's climate of fear and panic, airport security worldwide took such calls with potent seriousness. Within minutes, five armed guards had the unsuspecting man surrounded with weapons drawn. I couldn't hear their commands over the din of planes taking off overhead, but their body language said they were ready to shoot first and ask for specifics later. The man in the gaudy shirt obeyed immediately. He dropped his newspaper, and I saw a flash of gunmetal. All five guards took the guy down and subdued him with a hail of blunt rifle-butt blows. I almost felt bad for the guy. Almost.

One down, three to go.

My next call went to information, and after a long while on hold suffering through a Latin version of "Hotel California," I was connected with the airport's janitorial service.

"Habla inglés?" I asked the dispatcher.

"Sí, how can I help you?"

"I was just in the ladies' room near the gift shop, and the place is an absolute disaster. There's trash all over the floor, and the toilets are overflowing." I did my best to sound like an impatient, angry American. "If this is how you treat visitors to your country, then my company can take its business elsewhere!"

"Oh no!" exclaimed the obviously distressed woman. "My greatest apologies, ma'am. This is an unusual circumstance. I will try to locate a member of our custodial staff to address this immediately."

"One of your men is sweeping the sidewalk just outside the front door," I offered. "He's leaning on his broom and smoking a cigarette as we speak."

"That isn't possible. We have no shift rotations on sidewalk duty."

"Are you calling me a liar?" My words dripped with stereotypical American entitlement. "If he isn't in the employ of this facility, then who is he and what is he doing outside the airport?" I hung up with that cliff-hanger and waited. People are so easily duped when they're afraid the big bad wolf is outside the door. I plied that fear to get what I needed and wasn't going to let it ruin my day. A second wave of armed guards appeared to surround the faux janitor. The scene played out pretty much the way it had with the fake tourist, but security was going to get even tighter.

Two down, two to go. The playing field was leveling.

I checked my watch again. I still had time. I didn't see the other two in suits, but that didn't mean they weren't around. The thought of going inside blind didn't appeal to me. Opportunity presented itself when a shuttle bus full of German tourists from one of the big hotels stopped at the curb and began to unload its passengers and their luggage. It was an instant mass of confusion, and I took full advantage. With my backpack slung over my shoulder and the ball cap lowered over my eyes, I worked myself into the middle of a cluster, which created the perfect cover. We walked together as a group through the wide doors. I needed to make my way down terminal one to gate B, but the crowd turned left and started in the opposite direction, leaving me stranded and solo in the middle of the foyer.

"Flight 2293 to Dallas/Fort Worth is now boarding. Please make your way to gate B," instructed an announcement from the loudspeaker.

Movement in the corner of my eye caught my attention. It was one half of the suited duo. Our eyes locked, and I held his stare for a moment. By the look on his face, I was never meant to make it inside, and he wasn't sure what to do—it wasn't like he could tackle me right there. I smiled. He sneered. We were in a standoff and playing chicken. Which of us would make the first move?

That would be me. An airport security officer—not an armed guard, but I wasn't going to complain—entered the area through a door marked Sem Entrada—No Entrance. I shot the suit another cheeky smile and then called out to the guard.

"Excuse me, sir," I called out in full flustered character toward the young security officer. "They're calling my flight, I don't know where the gate is, I'm not sure I'm going to make it." I squeezed my eyes and mustered a few tears. "This can't be happening." I let emotion enter my voice as I began to ramble. "I have to get home tomorrow, I have to go to pick up my kids from their grandparents, I have to be to work..." My words trailed off, replaced by fat crocodile tears. *I'd like to thank the Academy.*

"Let me call for a steward," the security officer replied, rattled, but in perfect English.

I broke out into more controlled sobs, keeping a hand over my mouth as if trying to compose myself. I took a sideways glance at Mr. Suited Thug, who nervously eyed our interaction.

"No, no, no, please, ma'am, don't cry. Please, come, I will take you to your gate." He offered me his elbow like a gentleman, and I took it, wiping the croc tears from my cheeks with the back of my other hand. The security officer looked back to make sure no supervisor or coworker was watching and then steered us toward security screening, where a female security officer performed a gentle pat down. He then helped me print out my boarding pass. Once through security, I was home free.

I glanced over my shoulder and saw both suits standing on the other side of security screening. Without a boarding pass or official airport identification, it was the end of the trail for them. They looked far more frustrated than menacing at that point.

"Here is your gate, ma'am," the security guard offered.

"Thank you very much, Officer." I smiled sweetly with a sniffle and a swipe at my cheek.

I fished out my boarding pass and handed it to the steward. Being the antagonizing smart-ass that I was, I turned and gave the dynamic duo a wink and a wave before descending the ramp to the plane. I found my seat beside the window and settled in with a sigh of relief. We began to taxi down the runway, and for a brief moment my window was parallel to the terminal windows, from which glared two sets of eyes from my black-suited friends. I shot them a final smile and, in a moment of heightened immaturity, put both hands up against the window and flipped them twin birds. *Adios, assholes.*

CHAPTER TWENTY-ONE

WICKOWSKI MET ME AT THE GATE THE MOMENT WE ARRIVED. HE sported his badge on the outside of his jacket as if he were on official departmental business. He didn't give me a hug, but I knew he was relieved to see me.

"I can't believe you went all the way to South America without keeping me in the loop, Harris. I hope you found what you were looking for."

Wickowski's department-issued car was double-parked outside the front doors with the light on the dashboard swirling red and blue. "We need to call a meeting of the forces," I said, pulling closed the passenger door.

Wickowski turned off his safety flashers and stowed the red light under the front seat. He didn't speak until we'd entered the flow of traffic. "So you're ready to bring this case to a close?"

"Yes. We can even get it done tonight. Where's Talbert?"

"I've got two unis sitting on him as we speak. He arrived at his office early this morning and hasn't left."

"Great. Leave your uniforms on him, and put out an APB for McPherson."

Wickowski merged onto I-205 southbound. "Is McPherson in the country?"

"He arrived a couple of days ago."

"How do you know that?"

"I just do."

Wickowski knew I'd never divulge my source, so he didn't push it. "You need to call your boy Vinny before he does something drastic. It's kind of sweet, in a highly annoying sort of way. I've never seen somebody so twisted up and inside out over a chick."

Going over my love life with Wickowski was the last thing I wanted to do, so I steered him away from the topic by giving him the short version of what Mole had discovered on the disc and what I'd learned in São Paulo.

"Phillips's death goes all the way down to South America?"

"Yeah, imagine that. You guys never saw that coming, did you?" I turned to face the window. "Accidental death, my ass," I mumbled under my breath. "More like death by association."

"Whoa now, just you wait a goddamned minute!" Wickowski was more than a little irritated with my attitude. "Not all of us have the funds to jaunt down to Brazil—"

"I know, I'm sorry. It's the jet lag speaking." I was tired, dirty, and in the middle of the worst caffeine withdrawal headache known to man, even though I must have downed a whole pot of coffee onboard the Boeing. I suspected it had been decaf. "Drive through the next coffee shop you see, and then drop me at my place. I need to grab a quick shower, the disc, and the thumb drive copy. I'll meet you downtown at the precinct. That should give you enough time to gather your people and get Burnell briefed."

"All right, but don't plan on making any friends with the captain today. We all know he made a wrong call, and he's taking quite a beating for it from the mayor. Everyone is watching closely to see how this plays out. They're all afraid the Widow Phillips is going to hire herself an attorney and sue the city. Promise me you won't rub this in Burnell's face, because remember: shit rolls downhill."

I wasn't out to piss anybody off—at least not intentionally. It just happened to be an unfortunate by-product of...being me. And I couldn't be held accountable for what I might say or do where Burnell was involved. If he wasn't such a jackass, I would play a whole lot nicer.

Wickowski left me at my front door and zoomed off. I didn't need to hit play on my voicemail to know it was full of frantic messages from Vin. I was going to have to make some serious decisions about my personal life. I cared for Vin, to a depth that both surprised and frightened me, but I couldn't subject him to any more emotional roller coasters like the past few days had panned out to be. I knew what my life could be like, and it wasn't fair to anybody who happened to be in close proximity. Trisha was right when she said people like me tended not to let anybody get too close. I'd never believed in fairy-tale endings; my life ran more like film noir.

With a heavy sigh, I stripped down, leaving my clothes on the floor in a heap, and jumped in the shower. The hot water had never felt so good as it coursed across my skin, stinging every nick and cut I'd experienced in Brazil as it went. I pulled on clean jeans and a black t-shirt with the words mean people suck written in small red letters across the chest.

I picked up my HK and made sure the magazine was full, then put it in my shoulder holster. It only took me a second to remove the lint screen from the clothes dryer and pull off the packet I had taped to it. The disc and thumb drive were protected by a thick plastic bag that I put into the inside pocket of my leather jacket, right beside my gun. I was going to need a goddamned good vacation after tonight.

{∗ ∗ ∗}

The parking garage beneath the central precinct was all but deserted when I got there, all office personnel having already left for the day. I went through the ritual of signing in with the officer on duty at the front desk, clipped my visitor's badge to the lapel of my leather jacket, and took the elevator upstairs. Wickowski met me when I stepped out. Even with our earlier exchange in the car, he seemed more tense than usual. His flushed face told me he'd taken a verbal beating from Burnell. I didn't envy his position one bit.

I was ushered into the same conference room Wickowski and I had used a few days earlier when they'd found Tompkins's body. Burnell sat at the head of the table like a patriarch, his mouth set in a grim, thin line. Flanking him on either side were two officers; one I recognized, but the other I did not. All three looked up in unison as I came through the door.

The officer on Burnell's left was small and mousy in his uniform. I recognized his pasty complexion as that of someone who spent more time behind the desk than on the beat. His shock of red hair and the freckles across his pale nose and cheeks made him a true ginger. In front of him was an open laptop. It didn't take profiler skills to sum up that this guy was on the information systems team, a glorified geek with a badge. *My geek can kick your geek's ass.* I kept my thoughts to myself and tried not to smirk. The officers in charge of information systems were the equivalent to those guys in high school who handled audiovisual equipment during assemblies. Wickowski turned to him and made the introduction.

"Officer Peates." I shook his hand. "Good to meet you."

On Burnell's right was Lieutenant Joe Weber. Weber and I had never met in an official capacity, but I was familiar with his exploits. Weber was Burnell's golden child, because they shared the same philosophy that there are three kinds of people in the world—cops, cops' families, and assholes. Weber also hailed from the same southern good ol' boy perspective that believed women had a place, and it wasn't in law enforcement. I knew Weber held himself in high regard as a ladies' man, but I believed it was a one-way opinion.

Weber wasn't as tall as Wickowski; at five-six, Weber was on the shorter side of average for a man. His jet-black hair showed nary a gray strand and was slicked back, mafia style. His moustache was outdated and belonged in a porno. His plain clothes were freshly laundered and immaculately pressed, a stark contrast to Wickowski's perpetual appearance of having slept in his car.

I took a seat at the opposite end of the table from Burnell. I liked to think it symbolically made us equals. I'd perfected my cop look long ago, what some call resting bitch face—a blank stare devoid of emotion, my eyes turning to cold pools. Burnell's gaze burned, and I refused to meet it. This went on until Peates grew uncomfortable with the invisible daggers and coughed to break the silence.

"Harris," Wickowski started, "I've caught the captain and Detective Weber up on the Phillips investi—"

"Harris," Burnell bellowed, "how the hell did you end up with this disc?"

Knowing I wouldn't be doing anyone any favors by getting into a pissing match with Burnell right out of the gate, I took a couple of seconds before answering. Didn't mean I couldn't be honest, though. "Some might say through good detective work. I acquired the disc by doing the job I was hired to do."

Burnell put his elbows on the table and leaned into them. "What are you implying? That my department, my men, didn't do their job?"

I put my hands up. "Hey, your words, not mine."

So much for trying to avoid confrontation. Burnell's eyes became angry slits. He put both hands firmly on the table and thrust his body forward like he was going to leap over it. "Need I remind you, *former* Agent Harris, that it was a unanimous decision—supported by the district attorney—that Dr. Phillips's death be ruled accidental. We didn't have the intel that seems to have led you to this." Burnell wasn't even trying to keep his cool at this point; a scowl crossed his face like a freight train.

Bring it.

"Oh, come on, you two. We're all on the same team here!" Wickowski sat forward in his chair to interject. "Captain, how about we take a look at that file. Peates, is the system up?"

I handed Peates the thumb drive, which he took without looking at me and inserted into his laptop. Burnell, Weber, and Wickowski all got out of their seats to read over Peates's shoulder.

I decided to give them time to digest the new evidence. "I'm going for some coffee." I pushed back from the table and headed for the door.

"Make mine black," Burnell instructed, never taking his eyes from the screen.

"Two sugars and two creamers for me," Weber added.

Wickowski held his tongue, and Peates seemed to sink down in his seat a little further. I left them gawking at the monitor and made my way to the empty break room. Visitor's pass or not, cops don't like civvies invading their space, and I was in no mood to explain to some pencil-pushing uni why I was raiding their coffee pot. I filled a white foam cup with dark, acidy sludge. This was cop coffee made from canned grounds and tepid tap water. I took a sip and decided that, crap or not, it was still coffee, and I appreciated that.

Wickowski appeared shortly. "We need you to come back in here."

I followed Wickowski to the conference room, where Burnell and Weber looked up at me expectantly. "You didn't seriously expect me to come back with anything," I said.

"Sam, we all agree this gives motive—" Wickowski began before being cut off by Burnell once again.

"All of this is circumstantial, Harris. You've given us no triggerman, nothing that's admissible in court. We're as good as standing on square one!" Burnell shouted. "All you're giving me is a letter of complaint and some pictures of messed-up kids!"

"The letter is from a man who worked with the indigenous tribes. This creates a direct link between Novus and these deformities. He sent a copy to Novus and a copy to his uncle. Now both he and his uncle are dead. I don't pretend to know your thought process, Burnell, but at the very least this information is enough to issue some search warrants." Now I was the angry one. "What's your real issue here, Captain?"

"My issue is that I have nothing that a good lawyer won't decimate in court—if it even gets that far!" Burnell stood to leave.

"We may not have enough to hold Talbert, but we could haul him in anyway," Weber offered.

"Hold him for what?" Burnell demanded, still standing at the head of the table.

"Burnell's right," I said. "If we pick up Talbert now, he'll be back on the streets before the ink on the paperwork is dry."

"What are you working at, Sam?" Wickowski asked. It wasn't often I agreed with the captain.

I put my hands on the table and leaned forward. "We get him to tell us the truth."

"You think he's just going to confess to murder?" Weber scoffed.

"At the very least, he'll confess to accessory." I turned to Wickowski. "You still got a uniform sitting on Talbert?"

"Yes. Last he checked in, Talbert hadn't left his office."

I took out my cell phone and dialed Talbert's office. "Hello, this is Samantha Harris calling for Mr. Talbert, please."

I waited while my call was transferred. But instead of getting Talbert, the receptionist's perky voice came back to inform me that her boss was busy on a conference call and couldn't be disturbed.

"Please let him know that I found his missing 'Free Bird' disc and that I think it's extremely informative." His receptionist assured me she would pass on my cryptic message and bid me a good day.

"What was that?" Wickowski asked.

I sat back with a typical shit-eating grin and held up my finger. *Wait for it...* I finished my coffee and looked at my watch, all the while being stared at by Wickowski, Burnell, Weber, and Peates. I started counting down from twenty; when I got to eight, my cell phone rang. With a quick raise of my brows, I answered.

"This is Samantha Harris."

"Ms. Harris." Talbert's voice sounded weary.

"Mr. Talbert," I said, more to the room than to the person on the other end of the line. "You almost sound disappointed to hear from me."

"I received a message just now that you wished to speak." Talbert managed to keep his voice light and friendly, like he was calling for lunch reservations, but he couldn't hide the edge of anxiety.

"I thought we should get together for a little chat, you and I."

"Oh? And may I ask to what I owe the pleasure?"

"Come now, Steven, coy doesn't become you."

"I must admit I don't know what you're talking about."

"You don't?" I scoffed. "Oh, well, forgive me. I'll just save us both time by turning this disc over to the FBI. I have contacts there, you know. I have one hell of an adventure tale to tell them, which I think they'll find riveting. But I understand your hesitancy. Wouldn't want to miss our tee time on the green, now would we, Steven?"

There was a long silence on the line, but I knew by his breathing that Talbert was still there. "I am listening."

"I want to call a truce. I'm tired of looking over my shoulder and deflecting your hit men."

"Let's say I understand what you're talking about. What kind of deal are you willing to make?"

"I give you the disc in exchange for calling off your hit squads. Then I walk away."

"That's it?"

"I'd ask for the truth and an apology, but I know a long shot when I see it."

Talbert's laugh made my skin crawl. "Why, Ms. Harris, how very noble of you. But you and I know the truth is rarely what you expect it to be. Such a pliable thing, truth is—one of life's greatest ironies. You say you found something that belonged to Ronald; what of it? Ronald was quite a chameleon, a very secretive man. I'm sure that whatever you've stumbled upon is completely immaterial. I don't see the point of this discussion."

"Well, why don't you humor me anyway and meet me tonight."

"Fine. Come to my offices this evening. Everyone will be gone by six o'clock."

"I don't think I want to meet the lion in his den. Meet me on the east side dry docks tonight at midnight."

"A clandestine meeting on the dock at midnight. You do have a flair for the dramatic. And supposing we do this, you will have the disc with you?"

"I thought you said you didn't care what was on the disc. I think your exact word was *immaterial.*"

"And as you suggested earlier, let's just humor each other, shall we?"

"Fine. Then I'll see you at midnight, slip seventeen, just down-river from the grain elevators. Come alone."

"I expect the same courtesy."

I disconnected the call. "We're set."

"Set?" Burnell asked as he screwed his face up into a look of disgust and let out an exasperated rush of air from his lungs.

"Sam, what did you just do?" Wickowski asked.

"I'm meeting with Talbert to get the truth and an apology tonight at midnight," I replied pragmatically. "Duh."

"I'm a little fuzzy on this whole confessional thing, Harris." Wickowski's brows were furrowed, a sign of latent duress.

"Never underestimate the powers of my persuasion."

"You'll go in wired."

"Nope."

"And you'll wear a vest," Wickowski added, ignoring my protest.

"No way." I shook my head.

"You're still a civilian, Harris," Burnell reminded me, lest I had forgotten. "You don't have a choice. Besides, this is my department, and in this department, vests are policy."

"However, as a civilian, I'm exempt from departmental policy. If I show up in tactical gear, I no longer look like someone who just wants to make a deal and get out. No vest."

Wickowski bit back his retort when Officer Peates spoke up for the first time. "I think it's a good idea." Everyone in the room, including me, looked at him in surprise. I for one had forgotten he was there. "The wire, I mean. It's a good idea. I've been working on a new setup. It has a longer range and is interference resistant."

I was so shocked by Peates's dissertation, I acquiesced—on the wire.

"Everyone meet here by nine o'clock," Burnell instructed the room. "We'll get Harris fitted with her wire and down to the docks by eleven." He pointed fingers at Wickowski and Weber. "You two will get into position and wait. I want to get SWAT on scene as well."

"SWAT?" I asked.

"I don't want there to be any mistakes. I barely have enough ass left as it is. The brass upstairs have been feasting on it a lot lately." I almost felt bad until he added, "I'm putting this in your hands, Harris. Don't fuck it up and make me look bad for letting you take charge."

With that, we were all dismissed. Wickowski went back to his desk, and I trailed behind him. He sat down heavily in his chair, and I took a seat on the corner of his desk.

"Are you sure you're up for this?" Wickowski asked as he leaned back in his chair, his hands folded behind his head.

"Hell yeah."

"Seriously, Harris, I think you're taking a big risk going in there without a vest."

I gave Wickowski a kind smile and turned toward the window. I knew he cared about me, and I suspected some of those feelings extended beyond camaraderie. He was genuinely concerned for my safety, even if I wasn't.

"Well then, I guess this is it. I'm going home to get ready. Call me if there are any changes on this end." I stood up and started for the elevator then turned back with one last bit of counsel. "Don't take too much shit from Burnell."

"Don't worry about me." Wickowski waved me off. "I'm used to it."

Down in the lobby, I signed out and returned my visitor's badge, and the officer on duty handed me back my gun. I took the elevator down to the basement garage. The lighting was dim, and I'd be lying if I said I wasn't hypervigilant, peering into the shadows and around every car. Nobody jumped out to tackle me, but I popped the hood of the Geländewagen anyway to examine my electrical system for any hidden surprises. Thankfully I didn't find any. Paranoid much?

CHAPTER TWENTY-TWO

I SPENT THE REST OF THAT EVENING TRYING NOT TO THINK ABOUT the coming hours. I attempted to reach Vin on the phone, but my calls only rolled to voicemail. I didn't think too much of it—he was most likely down in Springfield throwing back beers and spinning old Police albums with his artist buddy, Mark.

At a quarter to nine, my phone rang. It was Wickowski. "It's about that time."

I didn't reply. I didn't need to. After I hung up, I went directly to my bedroom closet and my gun safe and was immediately welcomed by the scent of the ozone dehumidifier, CLP—cleaner, lubricant, and protectant—and leather. When people told me to find my happy place, this was where I came.

Wickowski's words of caution came back as I fingered the rough Kevlar of my tactical vest. I'd only worn it a couple of times since I left the FBI, and tonight wasn't going on that short list. I turned away from the vest and moved on to deciding what gear I was going to bring. From habit, I put a couple pairs of zip ties into my pocket and hung a miniature version of my T-handled knife strung on a black cord around my neck. If Talbert didn't come alone and I got frisked, the blade would be mistaken for a necklace. A knife needs only one and a half inches of penetration to be fatal. Contrary to popular belief, smaller can be better.

I gave home one last look before pulling the door closed and locking it behind me. Mole's loft was dead silent. I put my ear to the door, heard the telltale sound of busy fingers clacking on a keyboard, and decided not to disturb him.

Wickowski stood beside the parking garage entrance when I arrived. I stopped and let him in.

"Don't get me wrong, Harris, and I don't mean to freak you out, but I got a real bad feeling about tonight."

"Thanks for the reassuring pep talk, Wick."

"I'm serious. I know you've got experience in this kind of thing, and I know you've got even more history that you've never shared, but something about tonight just doesn't feel right."

"It's a covert operation. It's only natural to try and anticipate the unexpected. I'm not cocky, but I'm not anxious either." *Liar.* "Besides, I'll be covered by Portland's finest and wired for sound."

I drove belowground and picked a parking spot close to the entrance beside a black pickup truck with a lift kit and oversized tires. With Wickowski in the lead, we bypassed the guard's station completely and entered the precinct through a separate door that led to a private elevator.

"We bring high-profile perps in and out through this door to avoid the press," Wickowski informed me.

"How come you always make me go through the front door?"

"This elevator is for special circumstances."

"Well, golly," I joked, "do I get to learn the secret handshake when we get to the top?" My attempt to lighten the mood with humor was lost on Wickowski. He was having none of it.

Burnell came out of his office and headed our way the moment Wickowski and I stepped off the elevator. "You ready for this, Harris?" he bellowed down the hall. The precinct was a hive of activity, but everyone stopped what they were doing and turned their attention to me.

"I am," I said confidently. Everybody within visual range was staring at me expectantly.

"All right, everyone, gather around," Burnell ordered. He stood in the center of the room, his thumbs hooked over his waistband. He rocked back on his heels and puffed out his chest, reminding everyone that he was in charge. Someone had sketched the layout of slip seventeen and the surrounding docks on the dry-erase board. Burnell began marking up the sketch with a red pen, then fired off orders like a coach at halftime.

Officer Peates tapped me on the shoulder and waved me away from the gathering. "We need to get you wired, Ms. Harris. If you'll please follow me."

Wickowski stepped in front of me and lowered his voice so that only I could hear him. "You won't do a vest, but you'll do a wire?"

A wink was my only answer. Without a word, I stepped around Wickowski to follow Peates to the elevator. When the elevator doors opened onto the eighth floor, it looked like we were about to step onto the deck of a spaceship. The windows were covered with a darkly tinted film that sunlight wouldn't penetrate, even on the brightest summer day. The atmospheric controls maintained the room's temperature at a steady sixty-five degrees to keep the banks of computer towers cooled. An overwhelming electric hum filled the room, making it sound like an apiary.

"This way." Peates motioned as he navigated through a maze of computer stations and electronic gadgets. This place was Mole's wet dream. If he ever decided to go legit, maybe I could pull some strings and help him get his foot in the door. It would be a smart decision to have Mole working with the law rather than against it.

Peates led me to the desk of a young woman gazing at a computer screen. We stood beside her for several moments, until I cleared my throat and sat on the edge of her desk. She finally tore her attention away from the monitor and acknowledged us.

Peates made the introductions. "Officer Gregg is in charge of audio prep." Officer Gregg was a thin, wiry woman with black-framed glasses and a uniform one size too big. Her hair was a mass of dark curls controlled in a bun at the nape of her neck. I'd pin Gregg as having a military background, probably in missile guidance systems.

"Ms. Harris." Gregg held her hand out for me to shake. Her grasp was cold but firm, though she gave me one of those girly handshakes, barely holding the tips of my fingers. Niceties out of the way, Gregg rolled her chair back and rummaged through a cabinet before coming up with a small black plastic box. She set the box on her desk and lifted the hinged lid.

"This is my favorite little device. I call it 'The Know-It-All.'" Gregg tittered at her own cleverness as she lifted the device from its box. The Know-It-All consisted of a black plastic-wrapped wire with a tiny microphone on one end and a small transmitting device at the other about the size of a watch battery. "This is a true NBFM receiver, which is compatible with VHF FM communications in the 138 to 240 MHz band." She paused in her admiration to look at me expectantly, as if I'd understood anything of the past five seconds.

A look of disappointment crossed Gregg's face. I was just another technologically illiterate civilian. With a heavy sigh, she asked me to lift my shirt. Instead of holding my shirt up to my armpits, I pulled it off over my head. Modesty and I were never bedfellows. My purple bra was something I had bought on a feminine whim at one of those specialty shops in the mall and could hardly be considered underwear, more like a cute bikini top. Officer Gregg was unaffected by my unabashed behavior. She began taping the wire in place.

Officer Peates, on the other hand, didn't handle my exhibition so gracefully. His initial reaction was a wide-eyed stare followed by a creeping crimson that spread across his face. He didn't walk away, but instead sat down heavily in a seat as most of the blood rushed away from his brain. If I were a betting gal, I'd say Officer Peates still lived with Momma and was as pure as the driven snow.

"Nice six-pack, Harris. Will you take it all off if I stuff a buck in your waistband?" asked someone arriving behind us.

"You couldn't afford this, Weber," I countered.

Weber put an elbow out and leaned against a support post. "You're such a tease. You know I could show you a good time."

I rolled my eyes. "I'm not your type. I don't come with an air-release valve."

That seemed to punch his bravado in the feels, and he sniped, "You're needed upstairs."

"Hey, Weber," I called to his retreating back, "is that your jacked-up black Ford in the parking garage?"

He spun on his heel. "What of it?"

"Nothing." I shrugged. "Just—sorry about your penis, man."

Weber flipped me off and walked away. Yeah, I still trusted him to have my back. He might be a douchebag, but he was a cop first and foremost, and I was part of the brotherhood by proxy.

"Okay," Gregg announced, "this should about do it. Don't forget this." She opened a drawer and brought out another piece of hardware. "You'll need this wireless earpiece." She fit the small, hard plastic device inside my ear like a hearing aid. It took a moment of fiddling to get it comfortable. "This will enable the team to speak to you if they need to."

I thanked Gregg for her time and returned to the tenth floor alone. I left Peates downstairs, stunned and bewildered.

"Hey, I hear I missed a little skin show downstairs," Wickowski said when he caught up with me. "Rod Stewart was right: some guys have all the luck."

I rolled my eyes and rejoined the group now packed together in the conference room. Aside from Wickowski, Weber—who refused to make eye contact—and Burnell, everyone was now sporting Kevlar vests with SWAT emblazoned across their fronts and backs in gold lettering.

"Okay, people." Burnell clapped his hands and got the group's attention. "Let's go over this one more time. Hildegaard, Michaels, and Torres: you'll be covering the south and southwest. Williams, Smyth, and Ingram, you'll be covering the north and northwest. The rest of you will stay in the van and move on my command. Harris, you'll be in the central location here." Burnell pointed to a spot marked with an X on the dry-erase board. "The surveillance van will be parked just east of your location, out of sight. Nobody will move in until I give the command. We only get one chance at this, ladies and gentlemen, so we get it right the first time."

I held my tongue on that one.

We broke the huddle and moved toward the back-entrance elevator, the same one I'd arrived in. Wickowski caught up with me, carrying a Kevlar vest. "Here, put this on."

"I can't," I said and kept walking.

"What the hell do you mean *you can't*?"

"Like I tried to explain to you earlier, I can't. First off, it'll muffle the wire. Second, like I said, if I show up tonight wearing that and looking like I just went shopping at Cops "R" Us, he's going to be suspicious. I can't wear it."

"Do you know how many lives each day are saved by people wearing their vests? The statistics are—"

I spun on my heel with my hand up to cut him off. "Wickowski, let it go! I don't want to take a bullet any more than you want me to. If you think he's going to take me out, then I'll depend on you to shoot him first. Fair? Good." I hastened my pace and squeezed onto the jammed elevator before the doors closed, leaving Wickowski holding his vest.

In the parking garage, our clutch broke off into two groups. I went to my vehicle, and the others piled into a big black panel van. Peates was suddenly in my ear.

"Test, test, test. Ms. Harris, can you hear me?"

"Loud and clear."

"All righty then, from here on out there's no more secrets."

The SWAT van pulled out before me, followed by the surveillance van. Wickowski came jogging across the lot and climbed into my passenger seat.

"One more word about the vest and I'll toss your ass out on the corner," I warned when he pulled his door shut. "Don't think I don't appreciate your concern, but I can't be second-guessing myself here."

"Hey, it's your skin."

"Have you heard from your boy sitting on Talbert?" I asked.

"Talbert left his office around eight o'clock this evening and drove directly home."

I hung a left out of the parking garage and made my way to Front Street and over the Fremont Bridge. I took another left off the bridge and continued to Swan Island and the docks. Slip seventeen wasn't hard to find. I stopped at the entrance and let Wickowski out. He gave me a thumbs-up before slamming the door and disappearing into the darkness.

The dock was deserted, just as expected. SWAT and the surveillance van were nowhere to be seen, which was the point.

"The team is in place, Ms. Harris. They have on their night-vision goggles, and all eyes are on you." Officer Peates's voice carried with it a high level of confidence that he hadn't displayed earlier in the meeting. Sitting in his van, surrounded by computer and electronic gadgets, he was the reigning nerd king.

I drove into place where I had a clear view of both ends of the lot and cut my engine, leaving the running lights on. I got out and walked around, getting a good sense of the surroundings. Just north of me were stacks of containers waiting to be loaded onto outbound ships. Running parallel to the docks were warehouses and storage units, all buttoned up for the night. Rows of packing plants lined the opposite bank of the Willamette River, their empty, dark windows staring across like blank eyes. Farther upriver, toward downtown, tall grain elevators loomed like sentinels keeping guard over who passed.

"Harris," Wickowski's voice came through my ear, "a car just came around and picked up Talbert from his home."

"I told him to come alone."

"Did you really expect he would?"

"No. I didn't."

My earpiece went silent. I looked at the glowing face of my wristwatch. I figured I had less than twenty minutes before Talbert arrived. "Game change," I said to those listening and removed my HK and shoulder holster.

"What the hell are you doing?" Burnell's voice crackled in my ear a little too loudly.

"I'm losing my gun."

"Harris," Wickowski scolded, "that is a very bad idea."

I walked around to the rear of the Geländewagen and opened the back door. I found what I was looking for tucked into the cubby near the wheel well—a fresh roll of duct tape. I tossed my holster into the back and shut the door.

"Before anyone else decides to throw in their opinion, let me tell you what I'm doing. Talbert isn't coming alone; he's coming with backup. I'm going to assume a pat down. If I'm going to have to lose the gun anyway, I might as well buy myself a little insurance." I stretched out two long strips of tape and bent down to affix the gun to the Geländewagen's undercarriage.

"Cover your ears," I warned before I reached inside my shirt and ripped out the microphone Officer Gregg had so meticulously camouflaged as part of my bra. "I hope this is as powerful as you claim it is, Peates." The spaces in the grille of my rig, around the large Mercedes emblem, were the perfect place to position the mike. It would still pick up conversation.

I climbed back inside the cab and waited. I didn't notice my raised heart rate until I took a deep breath. Vin's face suddenly came to mind, but I pushed it away. *Focus.* This would all be over soon enough. Precisely at midnight, Peates's voice carried through my earpiece. "Heads up, people. We have incoming."

A set of headlights pierced the darkness as the vehicle approached, rolling to a stop nose to nose with mine. I didn't make a move until the driver's side door opened, but it wasn't Talbert who stepped out. I didn't recognize the man, but he stood at least six-foot-four, with a shoulder span about the size of Rhode Island. The cut of his suit and bulge beneath his left arm screamed hired security.

The man crossed around the back of the car to the opposite side and opened the passenger door. Talbert stepped out, smoothing the front of his suit with his hands. I opened my door and stood beside it. It was showtime.

"Ms. Harris, prompt as usual. Let's make this quick, shall we? You have something I want, and I have something you want."

"Tell me, Steven, at what point did you figure Dr. Phillips was a liability?"

"It wasn't Ronald directly that was the liability."

"So why did you have him killed?"

"You said you wanted the truth. And I told you the truth is rarely what you expect it to be. To my knowledge, Ronald's death was in all honesty an accident."

"Then explain Tompkins."

"I have no idea who you are talking about." Talbert's body language didn't flinch, and his voice didn't waver. In fact, he was giving off none of the physical or verbal signs of lying. He was telling the truth. I was beginning to share in Wickowski's uneasiness.

"I don't believe Novus anticipated the indigenous population would experience such an adverse reaction to their testing," I stated in an attempt to get Talbert to think I sympathized with his position. "Their heart might have been in the right place—until it wasn't."

"Every warning label you see on any product," Talbert countered, "is there because someone subjected themselves to testing. Every one of them suffered a side effect of some sort. And these people were well compensated for their participation."

"Don't you find the practice of testing your drugs on people who are struggling just to provide the basic human needs for their families ethically questionable at best?" I was hit by a sudden revelation. "Dr. Phillips was blackmailing both you and McPherson, wasn't he?"

Talbert arched his eyebrows. "Well done, Ms. Harris. But that is only a half-truth. You see, I wasn't in a position to be threatened. William, however, was another story."

"But why did so many have to die?"

"Let me tell you a little something about how the world works. Companies like Novus work hard to make the world a better place, but sometimes you have to sacrifice a few for the good of the many."

"Spoken like a politician. If your current gig doesn't pan out, you might consider switching careers."

Talbert laughed heartily. "You still don't understand, do you? I had nothing to do with the deaths of any of those unfortunate souls. I've meticulously kept myself separate from everything."

"You just fed funds and were set to reap the benefits."

"We are here to make a medical difference and improve the lives of entire populations. Profit is just a result of all that."

"But you forgot one important detail."

"And what would that be?"

"The disc that Miguel sent you. How is it that it ended up in Dr. Phillips's hands?"

"The disc was sent to William originally, who forwarded a copy to both Ronald and me. I don't know if he sent it to us out of concern or out of self-preservation. You understand that if all three of us knew what was happening deep in the jungle, we all three had to make the decision to keep silent."

"To sacrifice a few for the good of the many."

"Precisely." Talbert clapped his hands together as if he were about to address a room of toddlers. "Now you understand. And speaking of that disc"—he turned to his driver—"Mr. Olaf, why don't you show Ms. Harris what we have for her. Maybe that will hasten our transaction."

My gut instinctually clenched. Something was amiss. Olaf pulled open the passenger door and leaned inside to grasp something heavy.

"Heads up, Sam," Wickowski sounded a warning in my ear. "We can't get a visual of what's in that car."

Olaf came out with something large and awkward. He dropped his burden on the tarmac in the wash of headlights. Vin stared up at me with large, frightened eyes. Both his feet and hands had been bound together behind his back like a pig ready for the spit. A strip of duct tape covered his mouth. His face was bloodied and swollen; he'd put up a good fight. My blood ran cold and deadly.

Burnell's voice brought me out of my reverie. "Everybody, hold your positions. We have a civilian on the scene."

"Keep your cool," Wickowski coached. "We're going to get Vin out of there. He's going to be fine."

Something inside me slid sideways to allow room for calm rage. Of course we were going to get Vin out. Of course he was going to be fine. It was Talbert and Olaf about whom I had doubts. By abducting Vin, they'd made a very poor life choice.

"Now that the playing field has been leveled—you've got something I want, and I have something you want—we can get down to business. The disc, if you please."

"I'll make you a deal," I said coolly. "I'll give you my personal guarantee the DA will look upon it favorably if you cooperate." Of course I was blowing smoke. I'd put a bullet in both their heads as soon as Mirandize them. The edge? Oh, I had gone over it the moment Olaf opened the passenger door.

A succession of voices flooded my earpiece at the same time so that I couldn't make out a single command or comment. Talbert's Cheshire cat grin told me he didn't take me seriously. Olaf, however, panicked at the mention of the district attorney and produced a gun from beneath his jacket.

"Gun!" Burnell's voice squelched in my ear. "Everyone move in, move in! Go, go, go!"

The SWAT van squealed in, lights flashing wildly. Both Talbert and Olaf spun in quick circles, searching for immediate escape. I ducked and pulled the HK from the undercarriage. Olaf spun toward the river. I raised my gun and fired a warning shot that threw up splinters of wood decking in his path. The SWAT van's back doors swung open, spilling out the combat-clad squad with guns drawn. They quickly surrounded Talbert and took down Olaf, who resisted arrest.

I slid the HK into my jeans, pulled the knife from around my neck, and dropped to my knees beside Vin. The sharp blade made easy work of the plastic zip ties that bound his ankles to his wrists. "Give them a minute for the blood to recirculate," I told him as I gently rubbed the areas of his ankles.

Vin flexed his hands open and shut to get the circulation going again. I helped him stand and let him lean on my shoulders to balance on his deadened feet. Gingerly he worked at the duct tape across his mouth until he got a corner up, then he ripped it off in one swift motion. Ouch.

"You all right?" I asked, giving him a visual scan for signs of injury. They'd roughed him up. Dried blood crusted the corner of his mouth, and his right eye was swelling shut. His knuckles were bloodied and swelling, which meant he got in a few good licks himself. I had no idea where a Renaissance man would learn to fight, but I was glad he had.

"I'm all right," Vin said. "Can we get out of here?"

"Yes, we can." I motioned to my vehicle. "Go ahead and get in. I'll be right there."

"Good work, Harris," Wickowski said as he slapped the cuffs around Talbert's wrists.

"This isn't done yet. We need to locate McPherson."

"We'll find him."

A patrol car rolled in to take Olaf and Talbert downtown. The Feds and Interpol would take it from there. Wickowski walked Talbert by the elbow to the back of the patrol car.

Suddenly a small, puffy sound came from out of nowhere. The noise registered in my brain at the same time Talbert's head exploded in a bloom of crimson and tissue.

"Sniper!" someone screamed.

Talbert's body hit the ground with a wet thud. The smell of released bowels and copper filled the air. Everyone dove for cover.

"Vin!" I cried out in warning. I'd never reach him in time to get him out of harm's way.

Time slowed dramatically. Vin's eyes locked onto mine. In that instant, I knew one of us wasn't going to make it. I shouted at him to get down, but even as the words escaped my mouth, it was too late.

Then everything changed.

I could no longer hear the shouts of those around me. I was being swallowed by a deep black silence. A burning began in my chest, a hot searing sensation that penetrated every synapse of my being. It was as if a hot poker had speared into my body, through my chest, and I felt bones shatter within. Everyone stared at me with alarm. I followed their gaze to my chest, where two spots of crimson grew outward across my shirt.

I dropped to my knees like someone pulled the earth out from beneath me. I balanced there as if sheer will could keep me alive. I knew it couldn't. I felt myself begin to fall backward, but

Wickowski, and then Vin, were suddenly there to catch me. Both of their faces were consumed by frantic knowing. Wickowski screamed for a medic. Vin cradled me in his arms, his mouth working desperately. All I could hear was the rush of blood in my ears. Vin pressed a hand to my chest, trying to stanch the flow that ran between his fingers and stained his skin. Tears brimmed in his beautiful green eyes.

The searing pain was fading away. I begin to shiver. It was suddenly so cold. *Don't worry, Vin*, I tried to say. *I'll be all right. It doesn't even hurt anymore.* All that came from my mouth were blood-tinged bubbles.

The pulsing strobes atop the police vehicles began to fade around the edges of my vision. I was suddenly so tired. *I'll just close my eyes, just for a moment.* Wickowski shook my shoulders until I opened them again, but I couldn't keep them open for long. A peacefulness I'd never experienced before or even known was possible overtook me. I let it. My vision faded into a velvety darkness.

CHAPTER TWENTY-THREE

THE VOID ENVELOPED ME. I WAS ALONE AND STANDING AT THE PRO-
verbial crossroads, not knowing which fork to take. One beckoned
with things left undone and words left unsaid; the other held the
promise of peaceful oblivion and eternal silence.

The darkness was pierced by the sudden sound of children's
laughter as a scene from my childhood began to materialize around
me. It was as if I'd stepped into a moment of my life as an invisible
spectator. I watched as my sister, Frankie, and I, both twenty-plus
years younger, played in the sprinkler on a hot July afternoon in my
grandma Bubbie's Vermont backyard. My sister and I wore matching pink-and-orange-striped bathing suits that Mother had made for
us. We were laughing and running, playing tag, and getting soaked. I
could feel the parched grass beneath my feet and each shock of cold
water from the sprinkler as it pummeled our sun-kissed skin. The
humid air carried the familiar scent of sunblock and the occasional
waft of flowers from Grandma's roses. My inner child could still
recall the perfection of that afternoon: sun, sprinkler, and family.

Then the scene jumped ahead in time. We were sitting on the
front porch at night and watching the fireflies dance about
the lawn. Frankie and I were eating frozen ice pops, the taste
sweet and cold on my tongue.

"The grape ones were always your favorite, weren't they,
Samantha?"

Still having the fly-on-the-wall perspective, I turned toward
the familiar voice that had long been lost to me. Even in my limbo
state, I knew what I was experiencing was impossible.

"Bubbie?" I whispered unbelievingly.

Warm arms encircled me in a hug and buried me in my grandmother's ample bosom. "Yes, darling, did you expect someone else?"

"How is this possible? You passed away when I was still in high school."

Bubbie laughed her deep-chested chortle. "My darling Samantha, don't be so silly. My body may have died, but I never left you. As long as you remember me, I will always be here." She laid a hand over my heart, and I was surprised by the weight and warmth of it.

"Am I dead?" I asked.

"No." Bubbie shook her headful of gray curls. "You aren't dead, Samantha. But you aren't fully alive either. Your body lies in a hospital bed, but you are here."

"Like a coma?"

"Precisely that."

"How do I get back?"

"That, my dear, is entirely up to you."

"But I don't know how."

"Dig deep, my darling girl, dig deep..."

Bubbie's voice trailed off. Darkness pushed around her until she began to fade and became part of the void.

Dig deep, I heard echoing inside my head, repeating like a mantra. *Dig deep. Dig deep.*

Then another voice sliced through the darkness, this one closer and more immediate.

"Sam." It was Vin. I could sense him bending over my body and whispering in my ear. "I'm here, Sam. You need to fight your way back here. Come back to me."

Vin! I screamed. *I'm here!* Wherever I was, I was desperate, but my body was unresponsive.

I held on to the sound of his voice, hoping it would guide

me back, but it faded and was replaced by another long-lost, familiar voice.

"Sammy, what are you doing here?" I turned to see a young girl emerge from the darkness that surrounded me. It was Cindy, still twelve and looking exactly as she had on that fateful day. She smelled of sour-apple candy and bubble gum.

"Cindy?" I asked in a trembling voice as a single tear slid down my cheek.

"Don't cry, Sammy. Everything is fine now."

My heart clinched with the guilt and culpability that I'd been trying to absolve myself of since that night. I'd gotten scared when I realized what was happening to Cindy in the back of that van, but it was cowardice that had me run away when I knew she was about to die. It wasn't that I should have tried harder; I should have *tried*. I should have jumped on him, bit him, kicked—but instead, I ran.

"If you hadn't have gotten away, you would be dead too," Cindy whispered as if reading my mind.

Silent tears streamed down my face. I closed my eyes against the scene that replayed around me.

"Don't blame yourself. When he grabbed us and threw us in the back of his van, he hit you so hard, I was afraid you wouldn't wake up ever again. He was a bad, bad man, Sammy. He wanted to kill us both, but not before he hurt us and made us scream. He really wanted to hear us scream." Cindy gave an etheric shiver. "I didn't feel the knife go across my throat. It didn't hurt much to die. And then I came home, to here."

At last I found my voice. "I never stopped thinking about you, Cindy."

"I know that, silly head!" Cindy's giggle was like the tinkling of wind chimes. "I've always been watching over you. Man, you get into a lot of trouble now that you're all grown up!"

That made me smile. "Are you okay? Where you are?"

"Inside the All is the most wonderful place! And it's nothing like they taught us in Sunday school. But you can't come here yet, Sammy. You're not done."

"What do you mean, I'm not done?"

"With your life. You've too much unfinished business."

"Didn't you when you left?" I countered.

"No," she said as if stating a fact, "it was my time to leave. Besides, you made me a promise."

Yes, I had, and it was that promise that had propelled me through most of my adult life. "But my body's broken, Cindy. I don't know the way out of here."

"You never give up, Sammy. It isn't who you are." Cindy's parting words faded like exhaust on a cold morning. I was left alone in the silence once more.

There was no telling of time, no way to know if it was day or night or how many hours or even days had passed. My consciousness returned to my body occasionally, but nobody knew how close to the surface I really was. I heard occasional voices and felt the touch of those that sat at my bedside. I also felt my wounds.

"There's nothing more we can do," I heard someone say from beside my bed.

The blare of an alarm interrupted their discussion with an electronic voice calling, "Code blue! Code blue!" I felt myself slipping away and was suddenly at the top of the ceiling looking down on my own body lying feebly in the hospital bed. I watched with detached fascination the activity that erupted around the inert shell of my former self. I was fascinated by the tubes and wires leading from my body to the bank of machines that tried to keep me alive. A sudden, powerful electrical jolt sent me back into my body.

Things felt different. The bed felt more solid beneath me, the air on my skin from the vent overhead was overly cool on my face. I tried to take a deep breath and felt the tube in my throat. The glow from the bank of ceiling lights illuminated my inner lids. My eyelids fluttered as I tried to adjust to the brilliance of the room.

{* * *}

It was several hours before the doctors removed the breathing tube from my throat and let me eat anything other than ice chips, which Vin spooned into my mouth. I was fidgety, which added to my discomfort. A morphine drip was mainlined into my vein, a dose available at my discretion.

Observing my squirminess, Vin offered to fluff my pillows yet again. "No." My throat was still raw from the breathing tube and my voice raspy. "I don't think it'll do any good. These things are worthless, but they're better than the other pillows I have." Vin looked perplexed. "I don't have any other pillows," I pointed out.

"I could run to your place and bring you your pillow from your bed," he offered.

"Nah," I protested.

"You sure? It wouldn't be a problem." He leaned in closer. "And it'll smell like me."

He had a point, though the heavily bleached pillowcase over the flattened plastic-encased pillow had either burned my olfactory, rendering it useless, or I'd gotten used to the stringent smell. The thought of my own down-filled pillow had me agreeing with Vin. "If it's not too much trouble?"

Vin placed a kiss on the top of my head and stood to leave. Just then, Mole appeared in the doorway with a cup holder from Steam and a newspaper under his arm. A Blazers ball cap rode low over his eyes, and the lenses of his glasses were darkened.

"Vin," Mole said cordially, touching a finger to the bill of his cap.

"Neighbor," Vin replied with a casual smile, then he excused himself.

Mole stepped inside and took up the seat Vin had occupied. The shock at seeing him outside of his lair must have been all over my face.

"What?" he asked innocently.

"You're outside. In public. Where other people are."

"I'm not a total shut-in. I venture out when there's a need."

My eyes grew bigger. "I've been running errands for you since I've known you!"

"And I greatly appreciate your continued willingness to do so. Do you know the roundabout way I had to take to avoid security cameras? I had to stay away from intersections, ATMs, mini-marts. Did you know the DEA and ICE are putting surveillance cameras in streetlights?" He shook his head vehemently. "Privacy and freedom in America are fairy tales."

"Well, I'm glad to see you."

"Truth is, Sammy, you're the only family I have."

Before things got sappy, Mole straightened the copy of the *Oregonian* he'd brought with him and laid it on my lap. He'd circled the story of McPherson's arrest in red. "You told me if I cracked into that disc, you'd tell me why you really left the FBI. Spill it, sister."

I considered the offer I'd made out of desperation, the one that in hindsight I'd totally planned to renege on. Desperate times and all. But after what I'd just survived, I had a whole new appreciation for both life and Mole. A deal was a deal.

"Shut the door."

ACKNOWLEDGMENTS

SPECIAL THANKS GO OUT TO EVERYONE WHO HAD A HAND IN THIS
novel: Todd, for obvious reasons; my ballistics consultant, retired
Lance Cpl. Robert Virostek, USMC, for our time on the range and
illustrating for me just how a bullet "wounds on one end, and
kills on the other"; Heather Frazier, for helping me push my work
out into the world; Lee Shaw for your continued guidance and
encouragement, and to Nat Sobel of Sobel Weber Associates, New
York, for challenging me and sculpting me into a better writer.